Gidesha City

Evie Series, Book 2

Patty
Be an Evie! Keep
blessings! Happy reading!

A novel by

Anne Calvert

Jackson, Tennessee

Blessings,
Anne Calvert
2 Cor. 5:17

Biblical References from:
Holy Bible, New Living Translation (NLT)
New King James Version (NKJV)

Published in the United States by
Zoe Grace Publishing, LLC
Jackson, Tennessee
www.zoegracepublishing.com

ISBN: 978-1-7364079-4-3

Printed in the United States of America.

To Wesley Calvert

Thank you for believing in me and encouraging me to follow

my dream. I love you.

In Memory of my dear friend

Alesha Giddens Hodge

1969-2004

My Sincerest Thank You

To Father God for Your faithfulness. All glory and honor are Yours. Working with You has been the best education.

To Kim Wahl for taking the time to read my story and provide detailed feedback and double-check that everything lined up with the Word of God. For encouraging me with your kind words. Time is valuable but you always manage to make time for me.

To Denise Centola for answering countless questions and educating me about Italian foods, people, and traditions.

To Adam Brown for answering my law enforcement questions.

To Shayne Plunk for helping get my writing journey rolling.

To everyone who bought Banderidge, read it, shared how the story touched you, and asked when Book 2 would be out. Your kind words and encouragement are priceless and keep me going!

To Tammy Yosich at Zoe Grace Publishing, LLC for going round 2 with me.

To Shelley Mascia at Shelley's Editing Services for continuing this journey with me.

One

The quiet rumble of the bus slows and the airbrakes hiss, announcing Evie's destination. As she gathers her bags and waits to get off the bus, she glances out the window at the rundown terminal full of spray-painted artwork. Colorful bubble words cover old bus schedules and advertisements. Stepping off the bus, she spots that the bottom of a wall is painted with little blue creatures that appear to be in line for tickets.

Evie wonders how the artists were able to graffiti the awning in front of the terminal without being seen when a taxi stops in front of her. She leans against the passenger door.

"Need a ride?" He opens the van door before she can speak.

"Yes, please."

"Hop in. Where are you going?"

Evie starts to tell him but stops as a siren loudly rushes past them. Then another patrol car, sirens blaring, rushes by them. Before she speaks, she looks out the back window to see if anything else is coming.

"Is it safe now?" Evie laughs.

"Yes, but you better hurry. Sirens are not foreign around here."

"Oh goodness. Okay. Four, four, seven, seven East High Street."

"Really? Are you sure?"

"Yes. That's what it says."

He turns and drives towards East High Street. Working streetlights are spotty, but where the lights do work, Evie sees store after store with graffiti and bars on the doors and windows. Plywood covers the windows of dilapidated houses. People of all ages are on the corners collecting change. Stopping for a traffic light, Evie watches a child, no older than five, with no shirt or shoes, go into the corner store alone.

Oh, Father, this is going to be tough, isn't it? It's dark and that small child went into the store alone. I see a lot of vacant buildings, rundown homes, and children with no supervision. Make Your light shine through me to lead others to You. Let my words be from You and give me the boldness I need to help the ones I am here to help. Search my heart Father, keep me from being offensive, and give me discernment. Shelter me with Your protective wings. You are my Father and my trust is in You.

"I understand your question now." Evie says.

"This area is rough, but East High is a couple of blocks over and not as bad."

"I appreciate the heads-up. I travel often and have seen some good and some bad people, places, and things."

"You're here on business?"

"Yes. I'll be here until the job is finished, whenever that is."

"What do you do?"

"I help people find their way."

"Okay, like a traveling life coach."

"Yeah. I like that!"

The van pulls up in front of a row of houses.

"Here you are."

"Thank you. How much do I owe you?"

"I forgot to start my meter."

Evie gasps. "Will you get in trouble?"

"No, not at all. Sometimes, something inside of me tells me not to turn it on. It happens."

Sweet Evie, I told him to stop for you and not turn it on. He is safe and will be a friend. Don't be afraid.

"Well, thank you. I'm Evie."

"Nice to meet you, Evie, I'm Toby." When he comes around to her side of the van, something crunches under his feet. He removes her bags and points up at the blinking streetlight. "This is about as common as sirens around here. It's easier for evil in the dark. Take this card. That's my number. Do me a favor and call me when you need a ride. If I'm available, I'll come and if not, I'll send a buddy."

"Thank you. That's very kind."

"Stay safe Evie. I'll see you again."

She picks up her bags, goes up three steps, and stops, thinking she hears a voice. She turns around. Toby, back inside the van, is waiting for her to go inside. Shaking her head, she continues up the steps. Toby watches until a short, plump woman answers the door, hugs Evie, kisses her on each cheek, then leads her inside. Once inside, Evie looks around the poorly lit living room. The wallpaper is peeling and dark drapes cover the window. Although she can see beautiful, old decorations and furniture, she struggles to make out the details.

"Evie, nice to see you."

"Nice to see you, you must be Ms. Rose."

"Honey, just Rose."

Rose takes one of her bags and leads her down the hall. Unable to stand it any longer, Evie asks Rose what the alluring smell is.

"It's gravy," Rose replies.

"Brown or white?"

Rose places her hand over her mouth and stops short. "Honey, have you never tasted red gravy? Macaroni?

"Macaroni and gravy? I've had spaghetti and meat sauce if that's what you mean."

"Oh, oh, you're in for a treat! Honey, my grandparents came over on the boat from Southern Italy in the late 1800s. I have been using their original recipe since I was a child!" She leads Evie to a little room off the hall. "I'm sorry it's not much to look at, but it has a bed, a mirror, and a place to put your clothes."

"It's perfect. I'll get settled in and be out shortly for some gravy. Where's the bathroom?" Rose opens the door to the bathroom between Evie's room and her room.

Gracious Father, bless this sweet woman. She doesn't have much, but she so kindly invited me into her home. Please bless her financially and keep her safe and healthy. Let me know what I can do for her while I'm here.

Evie comes out of the bedroom to the savory smell of garlic. Comforted by the aroma, she follows the scent to a well-lit, vibrant kitchen, where Rose is checking a pan of bread in the oven.

"Is there anything I can do?"

"Not at all. Try the antipasto. It's delicious. We're just waiting on the bread."

Pulling out the chair, Evie guesses the antipasto must be the tray with a variety of items on it. Wishing she would have had at least one authentic Italian experience before today she puts a piece of thinly shaved meat, a ball of white cheese, a familiar-looking round speckled slice of meat, a green and a black olive, and one small baguette on her plate. Feeling adventurous, she picks up something resembling a dark green olive with a stem.

She examines it. "I hope you didn't go to all this trouble for me. It's quite a bit of food."

"Honey, I'm just so excited to have someone to eat with. Cooking this meal brought me extra joy. I love to cook, but when I have someone to cook for it's an absolute blessing." She sets a bowl of spaghetti noodles with a pool of sauce in the middle, red sauce in a gravy bowl, a plate of meatballs and sausage, and bread on the table. "Oh, do you like Sicilian caper berries too?"

Evie laughs. "I'm going to be honest. I have no idea what half of these are. My Italian experience is spaghetti with meat sauce and lasagna."

Laughing, Rose pats her hand. "By the time you leave here, Italian will be your second language."

"Um. I thought you mentioned macaroni."

Gently mixing the noodles with the red sauce, Rose smiles. "When I was growing up, the kitchen was the heart of everything. Oh, the conversations we had in this kitchen." Rose sighs and gestures around her. "Traditionally if I call someone for gravy, what you see here is what they get. The noodles are not spaghetti noodles, it's macaroni. All pasta is macaroni. The meat is meatballs or sausage, sweet or hot."

"Interesting."

"Go ahead, help yourself. There's extra gravy in that bowl if you want more."

"Oh my! This is delicious!" Evie reaches for another piece of bread.

After dinner, Evie brings the dishes to Rose at the sink. "Do you have children?"

Before Rose answers, wailing sirens come from the street behind them. "You may need to prepare yourself. That's an ongoing thing around here. Yes, I have three children. Two girls and a boy. I married late, so I had my children one after another. They are twenty-four, twenty-two, and twenty. My daughter, the baby, surprised us. A beautiful surprise."

"I'm sure it was. Are they here in town?"

"No. Our city started going downhill not long after the children were born. It's gradually gotten worse. People left because of crime and lack of jobs. When my children were old enough, they left too. They beg me to leave, but I won't. I have a great church and friends, and although I'm sure every city has one, I volunteer for our community kitchen. I would hate to leave."

Rose places two pieces of tiramisu on the table. During coffee and dessert, Rose talks for over an hour about her children and the sudden death of her husband after twelve years of marriage. Despite the failing economy and being a single parent, she raised her children in her childhood home that she and her husband bought from her parents when they got married.

"I know you must be tired, so I will stop talking and let you get some sleep. I guess you figured it out, but I like having someone in the house to talk to."

"I am sleepy, but I enjoyed hearing some of your story. I hope you'll share more. I'll probably look around town tomorrow. Maybe you can give me some pointers on where to go."

"I'll be glad to. Good night."

"Good night, Rose. Thank you for having me."

Two

In her windowless and dark room, Evie is glad she set an alarm last night. She sits up and stretches, coffee immediately on her mind.

Sorry, Father. You are always my first thought when I wake, but this morning that full-flavored aroma of coffee sneaking into my room caught my attention. I love You, Father, and my attention is on You. Thank You for getting me here safely, although that seems to be the easy part. You are my refuge. Thank You for ordering Your angels to protect me wherever I go. I ask for wisdom as I leave the house today. Prepare the hearts of the people I encounter and especially my special people. I wait expectantly to meet them and see what wonderful things You have for me here. Father, You are faithful and true and I'll praise You forever.

Flipping on the light, she reaches for her Bible. She reads several scriptures and thinks about how it applies to her and how they can help her today.

Hide Your Word in my heart so I will always be ready.

Evie goes in search of coffee. Rose is sitting at the table, a steaming cup in front of her as she reads her Bible. She looks up.

"Come, sit. Cappuccino?"

"Yes please!"

"Did you sleep okay? The room isn't much to look at, but the mattress is in good shape."

"I slept very well. Honestly, I wanted to stay in bed longer."

Rose hands her the mug and a plate with a pastry. "We have an Italian market here which has been around since before I was born. I'm grateful for it because I can enjoy my heritage and the things I ate growing up. I don't know what I would do if I couldn't have these from time to time. Try it."

"Yum! I see why you would be sad. It's very good. Almost croissant-like."

"Yes. You are going out today. Do you have a plan?"

"Not a clue. I enjoy wandering. I saw a few stores so I may stay close by and wait about going downtown. Do you have suggestions?"

"Frankie's is always good. It's a restaurant just up the street. Just in case you need me, I'll be at the community kitchen from ten until about two-thirty this afternoon."

"Can I help?"

"Of course. But it's a bit of a walk to the church. St. Francis, on the corner of Howard and Center Streets."

Placing her plate in the sink, Evie pops the last of the pastry in her mouth followed by the last of her cappuccino.

"I'll see you then."

Evie reaches for the doorknob as Rose comes down the hall. "Be aware of your surroundings and be careful."

"I will."

Father, I am not afraid because You go before me and set Your angels around me. Thank You.

The morning sun greets her as she walks down the steps. At the bottom, wondering which way to go, she hears a faint voice.

She takes a few steps to her left and hears it again. "Hey!"

"Hello?" She responds to the air around her.

"Yeah. Can you help me?"

“I would be glad to, but where are you?”

“Under here. My house fell in on me.”

“Oh my!” Evie looks around and sees nothing out of the ordinary. “Sir, all the homes around here look fine. I’m sorry, I don’t understand.” She follows the voice. “I see a large pile of trash and cardboard next to the house.”

“Do you see me now?” The pile shakes.

“What? Okay, I’m going to help you.”

“Thanks.”

As she walks into the shadow of the houses, she realizes why she didn’t see him. It looked like any normal pile of trash sitting out on the sidewalk. She removes a blue tarp with a hole in it. Large pieces of cardboard lean into each other like a house of cards. Evie removes one piece of cardboard, and the others fall. As she lifts the last piece of cardboard, she spots a shopping cart and a large, black garbage bag.

“Sir?”

“I’m here.”

As he speaks, the bag moves slightly. She drags the heavy bag off the pallets, and he looks up at her.

“Are you hurt?”

“I’m not sure. I was trying to get my cart onto the pallets and the wheel got stuck. As I was trying to steady it, it fell on my legs and pinned my right arm. When I fell, everything came crashing down. I can’t feel or move my arm or legs.”

“Hang on. I’ll have you free in a minute.” It takes Evie some time to free him since he has a lot of stuff. The cart is still full of bulky, metal pieces. Emptying the contents, she stands the cart upright, then turns to help him.

A thin man with broad shoulders and a solemn face groans as he maneuvers to sit up.

“I’m Evie.”

“Alfred.” He averts his eyes. “I couldn’t get help.”

“Have you been there since I arrived last night?”

“Yeah. People went by last night, but they were laughing and being so loud they didn’t hear me. A lady and her dog walked by earlier.” His voice is gruff and scratchy.

“I’m so sorry. I didn’t know.”

“You rescued me today.”

"It sounds like the story of The Good Samaritan in the book of Luke." Evie pulls an unopened bottle of water from her bag and hands it to him. "The guy was attacked and left for dead. They stole everything from him. People walked by and even crossed the road not to help him. Sounds a little like what happened to you."

He nods and crushes the water bottle.

At that moment, Holy Spirit tells her Alfred is one of her people.

"Before you put your house back together, can I buy you breakfast? Are you able to walk?"

"Yes. I'm stiff, but I can walk. Frankie's?"

While they wait at the hostess stand, he makes off hand comments about the weather and traffic. A flushed man with teeth bared comes toward them pointing at Alfred.

"Alfred, I've told you before, you can't come in here! You keep leaving without paying for your meal. I can't let you in here!"

"What if he's with me?"

"And who are you?"

"I'm Evie. It's nice to meet you." Evie smiles and puts out her hand.

The flushed man squints, hesitant.

"Can I leave my debit card with the cashier?"

"How do I know it's good?"

"Okay. Fair enough. How about I leave this one-hundred-dollar bill with the cashier?"

"That will work. No funny stuff Alfred." Alfred nods.

Evie guesses Alfred is younger than he looks. His dirty gray hair is shaggy, just like his beard. A small scar sits under the corner of his left eye. The hands holding the menu are calloused, cracked, peeling, and his untrimmed fingernails are packed with dirt. He looks up.

"What are you eating?"

His eyes are filled with pain.

Smiling, she picks up the menu. "It all looks good, but I ate just before I met you. However, I'll enjoy a cup of coffee with you."

"Did Ms. Rose give you a pastry?"

"She sure did."

"They're good." He looks back down.

When the server comes to the table, she introduces herself and quietly apologizes for the manager's outburst. People leave without paying for their meals all the time. Evie realizes that the server is one of her assigned people.

"Brenda, you don't need to be concerned. We understand. Thank you for your kindness." Evie turns to Alfred. "Anything you want."

He orders a modest breakfast and Evie encourages him to order more. He hesitates then adds a couple more eggs and orange juice to his order. Not another word is said until Brenda returns with their drinks. Evie is not sure how to proceed.

Loving Father, I need help. I'm not sure how to reach him and I'm not sure why. I haven't found common ground with Alfred. I know very little about being homeless and don't want to scare him away with questions. Would you tell me what to say?

Sweet Daughter, tell him about your earthly father.

Talking about her father is not easy. She knows if God wants her to share something so difficult, she needs to be obedient. People go through trials in life and are reminded of God's goodness and faithfulness. Those trials are not wasted because God uses the experience to help someone else. This is one of those times.

"The coffee is very good. Nice and fresh too."

"That's why I like it here." He looks out the window while she gives herself a quick pep talk.

"You being trapped under your house and telling me I rescued you reminds me of my dad. I usually listen more and talk less, but would it be okay for me to tell you about him?"

"Sure."

"In 1995, I was eight. At the time we were living in Washington state because my dad was in the Navy."

"Submariner?"

"Yes. By 1995, my parents had three children and my dad decided to put in for a transfer. He spent most of our lives at sea and realized we were growing up fast. The Navy granted his transfer but asked if he would take the place of a sick seaman on the assignment set to leave the next day. My dad would then be relieved by the person as soon as he was well. He was glad to do it. He knew this was it and then he would be home with us. The transfer never happened. There was a problem while the submarine was at sea and my dad never came home."

She wonders if she will ever be able to share the story without tears. Motionless, with the food now in front of him, he stares into her eyes.

Uncomfortable, she points at his meal. "I'm sorry. I was talking and keeping you from your food." He looks down at the plate.

"It's okay." He eats quickly.

Brenda slides the check onto the table as Alfred finishes his orange juice. Evie takes the check. "Give me a minute then we can get your house back together."

"No. I'll do it. Thanks for the food." He turns to leave.

"Alfred," Evie touches his arm. "Are you okay?"

He looks down, grunts, and goes out the door.

Well, Father, You know what is happening. Please protect him and comfort him. I think he was a military man because he knew about submariners and that is not just something everyone knows. Let him find peace today as he rebuilds his home. Soften his heart so as I share with him it falls on good soil and he is receptive. Thank You, Father, for trusting me to take care of Your children.

Three

Outside of Frankie's, putting the change in her purse, Evie hears screaming and looks up as a young boy sprints past her. He disappears in a doorway just before a group of boys come around the corner and run past her. Shouting curses, they run past the doorway and down the block.

She walks to the doorway and looks in, then up. Eyes wide, the boy is clinging to the poles of the awning.

"Hi." She offers a hand.

"Don't let'em find me."

"They're gone. They turned a couple of blocks from here."

"It doesn't matter. They're going to get me someday."

"Can I help you down? You can't stay up there forever."

"I can get down." He casually swings and lands cat-like on his feet.

"You make that look easy."

"Yeah. I play at the park a lot. I climb and jump all the time." He cautiously pokes his head out of the doorway and looks down the street for the boys.

"Those boys are angry. Can I walk you somewhere safe?"

He turns to leave. "I'm not safe anywhere. I'm hungry." He crosses his arms across his stomach, his bottom lip slides out.

"Where would you like to eat?" He points behind her.

"Frankie's?" He nods rapidly. "Frankie's it is."

At the hostess stand, Evie says, "Table for two please." The girl shakes her head and leads them to a booth in the back dining room.

"So, what's your name?" Evie looks at the menu.

"James Theodore. People call me Teddy."

"Okay. What's your last name, Teddy?"

"Bayer."

"Ah. Teddy Bayer is it?"

"Yup."

"Jimmy! What are you doing?" Brenda, the server who waited on her and Alfred, asks furiously as she approaches the table.

Evie gasps. "Do you know Teddy?"

Both Jimmy and Brenda start talking. Brenda eyes him and he stops. "Teddy? This is my son, Jimmy. He knows he's not supposed to be out of the house, let alone this far away, while I'm at work."

"But Mom, those boys chased me up here. I had to hide till they were gone."

Brenda sighs heavily. "Why were they chasing you?"

"They were talking gross about Sissy. They said they want to kiss her and fought over who was going to marry her."

"Jimmy, you can't let what others say bother you."

"She's my sister and I don't like it." Crossing his arms, he looks away from Brenda.

Brenda's sad, brown eyes look around the restaurant. She leans over and hugs her son. "It's good you want to protect your sister. We'll talk about this when I get home." She turns her attention to Evie. "How did you end up with Jimmy? Did he trick you into feeding him?"

Evie grins. "He happened to run by as I was leaving the first time. I found him hanging onto the poles of someone's awning hiding from the boys. He said he was hungry."

"Did he give you the sad eyes and quivering bottom lip?"

"Was I taken?"

Brenda covers her mouth and shrugs. "You don't need to feed him. He'll be fine. I do feed him. It's why I continue to work."

"It's no problem if it's okay with you. He's had a rough day." Brenda nods. "What are you going to have Jimmy?"

"I want The Works with three extra pancakes and whipped cream on them and chocolate milk." Brenda writes on her notepad and turns to Evie.

"May I have a blueberry muffin and coffee, please."

Brenda side-eyes Jimmy as she slides her pen into her apron. "Be good."

Jimmy looks out the window. "There's them mean boys. They're just looking for trouble."

The boys are running in and out of the stores across the street, obviously causing a disturbance as more than one storekeeper chases them out, fists in the air.

"You know," Evie waits until Jimmy looks at her. "If you care so much about your sister, you wouldn't take the chance of those boys hurting you. You wouldn't be able to help your sister if she needed it."

"But I'm the man of the house now and I need to defend her." Brenda brings their drinks and rubs the back of her hand across Jimmy's cheek.

"Mom! Ugh!"

Evie laughs. "Jimmy was just telling me he's the man of the house."

"He thinks he needs to be, but I remind him he needs to be the boy who helps his mom around the house." Jimmy rolls his eyes as Brenda goes to another table, then to the kitchen.

She returns and places the muffin in front of Evie and two eggs, bacon, a hashbrown patty, and two pancakes in front of Jimmy. Scowling, he snatches his fork and stabs his eggs.

Brenda places her hand on his shoulder, "Sweetie one day you'll be able to eat The Works, but I've seen grown men that can't even finish it. We don't want to take advantage of Evie's kindness, do we?"

Glancing at Evie he pops the forkful of egg in his mouth and shakes his head. Brenda winks at Evie and goes back to the kitchen.

As Jimmy slows his pace, he finally puts his fork down. The second pancake is untouched.

"One day Jimmy," Evie pats his hand.

"I want her to know I can do man things."

"One day." She tilts her head. "I have to be somewhere. Are you gonna to be okay going home?"

"If I see'em, I'll run. It won't be the first time."

Brenda walks up as he is looking out the window for the boys. Evie excuses herself and makes a call.

"My friend Toby will be here in six minutes to give you a ride home," she says as she slides back onto her chair. "He drives a van and I have taken care of the cost. Go home and stay home. Your mom can't do her best work if she's worried about you."

Brenda thanks her as Evie hands her the bill and tells her to keep the change. She looks in the window as she passes and watches Brenda count out the cost of the bill in amazement at the generous tip left for her.

Good Father, You are merciful and gracious and full of unfailing love. Thank You for Your unconditional love. Bless Brenda and her family. Please order Your angels to protect them wherever they go. Come to think of it, can You maybe give Jimmy two? He seems to be strong-willed and independent, but loving and protective of his family. I will find out her story Father, but in the meantime, help me to reach them and build a good, trusting relationship with them. I love You.

Four

Evie checks her watch and quickens her pace. Looking down Howard Street, she spots a modest, gray brick church on the corner about two blocks away. As she approaches, she looks up at a large, circular, stained-glass window with a solid white cross which covers the space above the front doors. A yard sign with "This way" and a bright red arrow direct her to the Center Street side door.

She shimmies through the crowd excusing herself as she bumps into a young dark-haired boy with a slight gap in his teeth. He turns away quickly. Evie hears the petite woman with stringy hair and a gold and purple bruise under her eye ask who he is hiding from as she goes by.

"They're not ready for us yet." A muscular man, arms folded across his chest and a long braid down his back, bellows as he blocks the door. "You know you can't just go in there or you won't be allowed back for a week."

"Oh. I'm sorry. I'm a volunteer and it's my first time here."

His brows relax. “Then I guess you wouldn’t know there’s a volunteer entrance. Come through, but next time, you go through the back door marked volunteers.” He pats the back of her shoulder as she passes.

“I will. Thanks.”

Rose sees her almost immediately. “Evie! Honey, I’m so sorry. I should have told you about the volunteer entrance. I guess you met Steven.”

Evie nods. “Pretty scary guy until he realized we are on the same team.”

Rose laughs and takes her by the hand. “We are about to serve. Father MacKay will open the door, bless the food, and welcome everyone in.”

Father MacKay raps on the back of the door five times to which Steven raps back twice and then opens the door.

“There’s no need for the rapping, except that Father MacKay and Steven like to do it,” Rose whispers.

Father MacKay nudges Steven as he goes through the door. “Hello, friends! I hope you are well, if not come see me and we will take it to the Lord. Let’s pray. Lord, this is the day

You made, and we rejoice. Thank You for the food You provided and the volunteers You brought here today. Bless this meal and all who eat. May it strengthen our physical bodies, nurture us, and be tasty. Amen."

Admiring the creamy, yellow-tinged potatoes with flecks of pepper, Evie spoons out a healthy portion and watches as a young father with two small children lead the crowd. Shirt torn and paint stains on his khakis, the man carries the smallest girl who clings to him. The other girl follows close behind. Averting his eyes, the man thanks Evie as he holds out the plate of the smallest girl.

"It's my pleasure." Evie looks at the girl in his arms. "Hi there, sunshine." She buries her face in his reddened neck.

The other girl holds out two plates. "My mommy called us her sunshine, but she's gone now."

"I'm sorry, sweetie. I can see why she called you sunshine." The girl smiles and then catches up with her dad.

Father, my heart. Please shine Your face on this sweet little family. Heal their hurts and help them live again. Not only live but thrive. Thank You.

One by one, people file through. Although serving in a community kitchen is one of Evie's favorite ministries, it has never been easy on her heart. These people and their deteriorating circumstances make today tougher than usual.

As a volunteer replenishes her pan, she hears someone say the line is getting shorter. When Evie looks at the doors, she spots Alfred and one small, white-haired man standing behind him. She glances at her watch. It is hard to believe, but they have been serving steadily for almost two hours. Since Alfred and the man are the last two in line, Father MacKay looks out the door. Seeing no one, he locks it.

"Hi again." Evie smiles as she plops the potatoes on Alfred's plate.

He nods.

Shuffling up, the older man with white hair stands in front of Evie. She is surprised by his gentle, soft blue, smiling eyes. There's joy in them and they sparkle with life.

"Well hello, young lady. I believe this is the first time you have volunteered here."

"Hello! Yes. I'm in town for a while on business." This man wears a suit, which is easily a size, maybe two, too big for him, and is clean and looks expensive.

"Very good! Thank you for serving today. I look forward to seeing you again."

"Yes sir. Have a beautiful day."

Father, what a sweet man. I have a feeling I have not seen the last of him. Bless him, Lord.

Evie takes the mostly empty pan to the kitchen where a volunteer takes it and offers Evie a cloth to clean the dining area. By the time she gets out there, clean-up is almost done. A few men are pulling bags from the trash cans to take to the dumpster, but other than that, volunteers are giving them time to eat.

"May I sit with you, Alfred?"

He points to the chair. "But I'm almost done."

"Okay. How are the house renovations going?"

Alfred stops chewing and snorts. "That's a nice way of saying it Evie. Haven't been back yet. I went looking for something."

"Did you find what you were looking for?"

"Yup." Alfred stood up.

"Okay then. See ya."

Evie wipes the table and sees the man with the big suit still eating. He catches her looking at him. "Ms. Evie? Is that what I heard Alfred say?"

"Yes. My name is Evie and yours?"

"They call me Bud. Would you join me for my last few bites? I think I saw Alfred laugh when you were talking to him. I have never seen him laugh. Did you tell him a joke? I would love to hear it."

"Oh, just an inside joke. Nothing worth repeating."

"Well, okay. I do not want to pry. I am holding you all up."

Evie picks up his plate and wipes the table. "No worries at all Mr. Bud. You stay safe."

"Will do. Thank you and it is just Bud." He waves as he walks toward the door.

Five

On the walk back to the house, Rose talks excitedly about how loving, kind, and different Father MacKay is. She exclaims that he can make even the saddest person laugh. Evie wonders if Rose has a crush on him.

"What is different about him?" Evie asks as she bends to pick up a discarded soda bottle.

"Honey, you can't pick up every piece of trash you come across. You don't have enough arms to carry it all. At one time this was a beautiful, thriving city. Oh anyway, Father MacKay. He loves everyone. It's not just because he is a man of the cloth, but because his heart is so big."

"He sounds wonderful. I see why you adore him. How about Bud? Do you know him?"

"Bud is mysterious. Friendly, but won't talk about himself. Father MacKay offered to get him clothes that fit, but he declined. He showed up for lunch one day about a month or so ago. He looks familiar, but no one can place him."

A few steps from the house, they hear Alfred muttering a few choice words. Rose shakes her head.

"Alfred!"

"Uh. Sorry, Ms. Rose."

"What's the matter?"

"Nothing I can't handle."

"Okay, then. So we shouldn't hear that language coming from you again."

"Right."

When Rose opens the door, a pleasant burst of garlic and herbs greets them.

"Oh my!" Evie puts her purse away. "What do you have cooking today?"

"After you left this morning, I put a little roast in the cooker. It does smell delicious, doesn't it?"

Evie follows her into the kitchen and reaches for a glass. "I'm going to bring Alfred some water if that's okay?"

"Of course, honey. Do whatever you want. My house is your house while you are here."

She drops a few ice cubes in the cup and goes outside.

"Alfred." He jumps and places his hand on his chest. "Sorry. I didn't mean to startle you. I brought you some water."

He takes the glass of water and sits on the step. "I was thinking how to fix something."

Sirens can be heard to the east and west. An old, banged-up silver car with a bungee cord holding the passenger door on, blows by them followed by three patrol cars. A minute later, the crushing of metal is heard. A few minutes later an ambulance, sirens howling, disappears down the hill.

"I hope everyone is okay." Evie stretches her neck as if that would help her see down the hill.

"It's bad here. Sirens have replaced the sound of birds." Alfred sounds unexpectedly sensitive, but Evie fights the temptation to look at him.

Thank You Father for the glimpse of Alfred's tender heart. I imagine he has been through some things in his life. Show me how to help him.

"Have you lived here long?"

"Born and raised. Went to the military out of high school."

"How long have you been back?" she asks as she sits on the steps.

"Long enough to watch a beautiful, thriving city lose its life and dignity." He winces as he stands and starts back to his house.

Evie picks up his cup. "That thing you're trying to fix, can I help?"

He studies her. "Maybe, but not today. Thanks for the drink."

"You're welcome." Before she turns the doorknob, she watches Alfred place the blue tarp, the side with the holes against Rose's house, over the cardboard.

Evie goes to her room and closes the door behind her. Her heart hurts for Alfred.

Oh, gracious Father, my heart is heavy. Alfred is one of your precious children and he lives in a cardboard box. What kind of life is that for a human being? I'm trying to reach him. I don't know if he knows about You or not. Either way, I know his situation touches Your heart or You would not have brought me here to help him. I am asking You, Father, please let him be receptive. Let him see Your heart in me. Military training makes a person tough and independent. Soften his heart so he will trust me. I love You Father! Thank You for loving us.

Dearest Evie. Keep doing what you are doing. Your pure heart and gentle spirit are what he needs to see My heart. I love you.

Kneeling beside the bed, she weeps. Affirmation from her Father humbles her. Clinging to His words, she opens her Bible. When she hears dishes clanging, she washes her face and goes to the kitchen.

"There you are. Are you okay?"

"I am, thank you." Evie reaches for the plates and silverware. She puts a napkin on each plate and tells Rose about the car chase. The conversation turns to the decay of the city as they eat.

"It started slowly," Rose reaches for another piece of roast. "When my youngest was born, I noticed subtle signs. By the time my son was starting high school, the officials in this city were as corrupt as they come. Once tainted, there is no way to go but down. And that is where we found ourselves, on a downward spiral with no end in sight. My oldest daughter went off to college, my son left for the military as soon as he graduated, and my baby girl followed her sister to the same college. None of them came back here. As a mother, I am glad they didn't because there's not much here but heartache."

"I'm sorry. I know it's difficult not having your babies close by."

"Yes, but it's my choice," she laughs. "They begged me to move closer to them. Told me they would help me with everything but, I just can't leave. This was my parents' house and my grandparents before them. It's the house I grew up in. I can't let them run me out."

"Oh, Rose. That's sad."

Rose stands. "Come, follow me." She leads Evie to the dark living room, stops in front of the stairs, and flips the switch for the light, showcasing photos of her family. "This is my oldest and her twins, my son, and his dog, and my baby with her baby. I would like nothing more than to be closer to them, but they won't move here and I'm too stubborn to leave." Rose stares fondly at the pictures.

"They are beautiful." Evie puts her arm around Rose. "May I clean the kitchen for you tonight?"

"Oh honey, no. You're my guest."

"Please? You'll have plenty of other nights to clean up after me." Evie raises her eyebrows.

"Okay. You can clean up, just let me fix a plate real quick."

Evie clears the table while Rose fills a plate full of roast, carrots and potatoes, and bread. Filling the sink with hot, sudsy water, she watches Rose go out the back door. Rose hands Alfred the plate as she sits with him on the back steps under the dim porch light. Drying the last dish, Evie looks out again and sees Rose with a Bible open on her lap and Alfred still eating.

Oh, Father. Bless them both. They need each other right now. You know that better than anyone. Thank You for always looking out for those who love You and those You love. Your mercies are never ending.

Not wanting to intrude, Evie goes to the living room and turns on the reading lamp by the sofa. She looks towards the stairs at Rose's beautiful family.

Father, will You make a way?

The back door closes and Evie hears water running. A few minutes later Rose comes and sits in the chair across from Evie. "Thank you for cleaning the kitchen."

Evie nods. "Thank you, Rose, for being an obedient follower of Jesus."

Six

Coffee wafts through the door as Evie slides into her slippers, grabs her Bible, and goes into the empty kitchen. Rose had set out a cup and spoon for Evie before she left for early Mass. Reading Mark chapter four she stops and prays.

Loving Father, as I go out today, let my words be Your words and let them fall on good, fertile soil. Let them produce a crop above and beyond what I can imagine. Have the people I encounter today be willing to hear. Help them listen and understand. Allow what I say to stir a deep hunger and desire for more of You. Thank You, Father, for the opportunity to serve. You don't want any to die without knowing You, so thank You for trusting me and equipping me to help build Your Kingdom. Please keep me safe and help me be a blessing.

My precious child, thank you for your obedience and faithfulness. I am proud.

Evie loves making her Heavenly Father proud. She rinses her cup and gets ready for a full day in the city.

Alfred is not there when she opens the door. She hoped to buy him breakfast and decides to go to Frankie's anyway. An out of place eighteen-wheeler rumbles past her and gives two short blasts of his horn. She waves.

"Welcome to Frankie's. How many?"

"Good morning. Just me. May I please sit in Brenda's section if she's working?"

"Right this way." Evie follows her to a booth. As she slides in, a man outside the restaurant picks up a mostly smoked cigarette and lights it.

Brenda raises her eyebrows. "Things are tough. I didn't realize how bad it was when we moved here. I hope to be here only long enough to save some money. Then I'll take my babies somewhere they'll have a chance."

"How long have you lived here?"

"Not long." She tugs at the arm of her long sleeve shirt. "Can I start you with a coffee?"

"That would be great. Thanks."

Evie realizes Brenda is the only one wearing long sleeves. Brenda comes right back with her drink.

"May I have a parfait and two scrambled eggs?"

"You got it."

While she waits, Evie looks on her phone for public transportation. Wishing it was more user-friendly, she finds the closest bus stop and a schedule. Oh, the joys of the city.

Father, help! This place is huge! Where do I begin?

Don't worry My child, I have it worked out. You will know.

She trusts that when her Father tells her that, His plan is already set in motion. He never leaves her on her own.

Evie jumps as Brenda slides the plate in front of her.

"Sorry." Brenda refills her cup. "Thank you again for what you did with Jimmy yesterday. My three girls, I can relate to, but a young boy trying to turn man, ugh." Shaking her head, they laugh.

"I can only imagine. I'm sure you are doing a great job."

She shrugs. "I sure hope so. Keeping them educated and entertained keeps me busy. Today is my short day. You're my last table. When I finish, I'll go get my babies and go downtown."

"Sounds fun. Well, I promise not to keep you then."

"No problem. Take your time. I have some things to do before I leave."

I see what You did there, Father. I'll invite myself.

Evie sets her empty plate and parfait cup to the side. As she finishes the last of her coffee, Brenda comes back with a full pot.

"More?"

"Goodness no!" Evie covers the cup with her hand and laughs.

"Do you need anything else?" Brenda places the check on the table.

"Well, actually, I'm in town on business, and not familiar with the area at all. I was going to go downtown myself today. Would you like company?" Brenda hesitates briefly.

"Of course! Then it will be two against four instead of one." Evie laughs nervously.

"That bad?"

"No, not at all. My children are pretty good. We would love the company. By the time you pay, I should be finished cleaning your table. I'll meet you at the door."

"Wonderful."

They walk past Rose's house going to Brenda's.

Brenda talks about her children and Evie tries to keep straight which child is which. She is thankful there is at least one boy. He is easy to keep straight. Although Evie doesn't learn much about Brenda or her story, she is patient, knowing it will be revealed when it is time.

Brenda opens her door into a spacious living area. A beige sheet barely hanging onto the sofa cover the holes in the cushions. The sofa sits out in the open, back toward the front door, and facing a small television showing cartoons is sitting on an oversize table. A worn dining room table with something stuck under one of the legs, two bench seats, and a couple of mismatched chairs on either end sit under a hanging light fixture. No pictures or décor anywhere. The children are alone.

"Is Nova next door?" Brenda asks the oldest girl.

The girl shuts off the television. "Yes, when I woke up, she left, but she checked on us a few times."

"Good. Hey guys, I want you to meet my friend, Evie. This is Jill, Jess, and Janie. And you already know Jimmy."

"Hello everyone." Evie waves but they seem hesitant. The youngest, if Evie remembers correctly, is four and peeking from behind her mother's legs.

Father, bless these babies. I know something terrible has happened to this family. Brenda can hide it, but I can see it in the children's body language and in their eyes.

Brenda gives each child a chore to do while she packs a bag for the trip. They race to see who can finish first. Janie, the youngest, grabs a basket and runs through the living room picking up the few scattered toys. She takes the basket to Jimmy's room and runs back first.

"I win!" She tags her mom's leg.

"Great job Janie Lou!" Brenda scoops her up and showers her with kisses as Janie keeps her eyes on Evie. "How about everyone else?"

Running up behind her, the next oldest taps her mom on the lower back. "Finished!" Jimmy and the biggest girl tie.

"I tapped Mom first."

"No way. I did."

"Enough. Great job guys. Teamwork for the win! Are we ready?"

"Yes!"

"Then let's go!" Outside, Brenda opens the stroller. Janie straps the bag into the seat and starts pushing it. As they approach the corner, not far from the bus stop, Janie stops.

"Come on Janie, you can do it." Brenda encourages. Janie puts her hands on her hips and cocks her head. Brenda chuckles. "Okay but push a little bit further."

"Yeah," Jimmy walks in front of her and says, "Come this far Janie. You can do it!"

She pushes and passes Jimmy. Her siblings congratulate her. When they are through celebrating, Janie runs back to Brenda.

"I did it, Mommy! I did! I pushed!"

"Yes sweetie, you did. I am so proud of you! Remember, if you feel you can't go on, push just a little more. We always have that little more in us."

Evie feels the excitement but has no idea what happened until Brenda explains. This is the ritual each time they come to the bus stop. Janie pushes the stroller until she gets tired. Each time she goes a bit further. Once those hands go on the hips, they know it's time to encourage her to push herself.

Oh, Father! How sweet is this little family? I love them already.

On the bus ride downtown, Evie looks at the graffitied buildings. Windows are either boarded or have bars on them. Even at this time of day, women with short skirts, low-cut shirts, and heels, are hollering out to cars passing by. At one corner, a woman is leaning inside the car through the open passenger window as a man waves money at her.

Father, this town is a mess. My heart breaks for these people. I don't see how this was a nice city. They are in desperate need of restoration, renovation, and most importantly of You!

My sweet child, your heart is tender for the people in this town and as of now, you only know a handful. Watch and see My precious child. Be encouraged, you will make a difference.

Thank You, Father. All for Your glory.

The bus slows as they pass a small park. The equipment is shiny, new, and probably the nicest thing in the city. Across the street is a towering library with four large, white columns leading to the entrance. When the doors open, the children hop off the bus.

"Library or playground first?" Brenda asks and the children look at each other.

"We want to start at the playground," Jimmy says. The girls nod.

"Playground it is."

They run for the swings. Jill, the oldest girl, lifts Janie onto a swing and gives her a push. When they tire of the swings, they run to other areas. Brenda and Evie make small talk as they follow the children around the park.

They sit by the monkey bars, in the shade of a young oak tree.

"So what's the story with this park? It's out of place compared to the rest of the city."

"Yes, it's new. Not long ago, there was what they called a Gentlemen's Club here. Right across from the library. Someone bought it, closed it, tore it down, and donated the land to the library along with funding for a park. The donor is anonymous. Between the fence and the police, it's a safe place and the donor keeps it maintained. I'm grateful because my children have a clean, safe place to play."

Evie looks at the tall fence topped with barbed wire surrounding the park. "That's a blessing."

"Yes. The generous donor told the Library Director that the children in this city need a chance and told him to keep up the good work."

The midday sun beats down. When the children start to slow down, Evie suggests lunch, her treat. Brenda thanks her and asks the children to agree on a place. Janie points to the purple square peeking out from the other side of the library and everyone agrees. Janie hops in the stroller which Jill grabs and leads the way to the restaurant.

After they eat, the children go to the play area until Brenda calls them over.

"They will sleep good tonight." Brenda waits by the slide for Jimmy.

Janie slides her hand in Evie's and motions for her to bend. "I like you."

Evie chokes up. "You know what? I like you too."

Seven

Jimmy pushes Janie from the restaurant to the library. Brenda explains that the park and library are part of a small handful of places she takes the children. Misty-eyed, she shares that she thought there would be plenty of opportunities to start new, but is not moving forward very fast. In a town where the majority is struggling to make it, tipping is not much of a concern.

Inside the library, the children go straight to the Children's Corner where everything is for them. The words "explore", "search", "question", and "learn" are in large, neon-colored bubble letters hanging from an invisible string. Brenda stops by the desk as Janie gets a stack of books and carries them to the pink and green beanbag in the center of the room.

A young lady with a flawless smile comes out of the Children's Corner. Brenda introduces her as the Childrens Department Manager and tells her that Evie is in the city on business. After introductions, the woman tells Brenda about an upcoming story hour, from 2-3 on Tuesdays and Thursdays, that introduces children to marine life.

Evie shakes her head. "This is a great library and the staff is exceptional. They seem to enjoy what they do."

"Oh yes, very kind. Not long ago, the people coming through here were destructive and disruptive. They brought in a security guard," she nods toward the door as he walks in, "but this is quite a bit of territory for just him."

"Has it helped?"

"Some, but around the time the park was being built the police department began a heavier presence. That's what helps most."

Two officers walk in the front doors. After stopping by the desk, they walk around the main floor speaking or waving to people who look up. Brenda's eyes light up as they approach.

"Hi, guys."

The shorter of the two smiles, showing off perfect white teeth against his light brown face. As Brenda smiles, Evie notices the color come across her cheeks.

"Hi, Brenda." The shorter officer comes closer. Evie wonders if he even sees her there. "How are you and the little ones?"

"We're doing great!"

"Are they in there?" He motions toward the Children's Corner. Jimmy spots him first and gives him a fist bump. The girls run to him.

The officer left standing with the ladies puts out his hand to Evie. "Brenda seems a little preoccupied," he winks at Evie. "I'm Rip."

"Rip?"

"Family name. It's short for Ripley."

"Ah. I'm Evie. It's nice to meet you."

"Pleasure is mine."

When the other officer returns, Rip introduces him. "Evie, this is Giovanni."

"Hello." He shakes her hand.

"Hi. What a great name. I don't know another Giovanni."

He laughs. "My family is very Italian."

"Gotta move on," Rip says. "Will we see you again?"

“Oh yes. I’m in the city for work so I’m sure you will.”

Evie turns to Brenda, eyebrows raised and hands, palms up.

Brenda looks at her children sitting on the floor in front of a staff member who reads to them. “What?”

“What just happened? Don’t play coy with me.”

“He’s very kind to my children.”

“And their mom?”

Brenda smiles, tightlipped. “He’s been very nice the times we see him here.”

“And?” Evie waits expectantly.

“I can’t. He asked me to dinner, but no. I just can’t.”

“I understand. You have your reasons, and it seems he respects that too.”

Evie leaves it there. That he went out of his way to speak to the children melts Evie’s heart. She can only imagine what it does to Brenda.

“Hello. I’m Mark Stee, director of the library. Brenda and her children are some of our favorite people. She mentioned you are here on business.”

She nods. "Hi, I'm Evie. Yes, I'm in the city for work. This is a great library you have and very kind staff."

"Thank you. We are in the process of ramping it up to bring the people back. You know, help educate more people or at least offer them some enjoyment."

"Several people have said the city isn't what it once was. I can see for myself how depressed the city is."

"With all the trouble coming through here, I was determined that if the officials wouldn't do anything, we would maintain the integrity of the library. It has paid off this far. The park donor saw what we were doing and honored it not only by building the park and helping to restore the library, but also paying for the extra security."

Brenda and the children join them.

"What an inspirational story."

"We are making changes and learning how to make our library the best it can be, but it is a slow process. Lack of funding due to corruption and the city giving up on us doesn't allow us enough staff. I am determined though." He smiles. "It's nice to meet you, Evie."

"And you as well."

Father, Mark seems concerned not only with the growth of the library but about the people who need something good in their life. If there is something I can do to help, please show me. Bless him and the library to be the best it can be and for it to be a lighthouse for Your people.

On the bus ride back, Evie notices litter lines the streets against the curb and on the sidewalk. Pieces of broken glass shimmer in front of businesses. She counts four X-rated buildings, but only one church. As soon as Evie found a seat, Janie laid her head on her. With each bounce of the bus, Janie's head, resting on Evie's chest, rolls. What a contrast looking at this sweet little life on her lap and looking outside at the hopelessness and destruction all around.

Father, I know You have not forsaken them, but have they forsaken You? Has the evil one taken over this city? What can I do? Are there enough people here that care and can pull together to rebuild this city? I know hopelessness has taken over, but I am not hopeless. I am hopeful for this city and my new friends here. Direct me, Father. I may not see the results, but I am willing to be Your hands and feet in this city while I'm here. I will be the encourager, if this is what You want, as I tend to the two people You have assigned me. I am here for You and Your Kingdom. Your will, not mine, be done.

My daughter, it brings Me great joy to see your heart on fire. You will be a part of the change that is coming for this city. You must have missed your third person in this assignment. You will see him again soon. I love you.

Oh, Father, I'm so sorry. I have not done that since the early days when I was new. I have let You down. This hurts my . . .

Sweet girl. You never let Me down. I am proud of you always and love you forever. You are My child.

A tear falls on Janie's lolling head.

Thank You, Father, for loving me so.

Alfred pulls an article of clothing from a cart, as they pass Rose's house. Evie waves to him and gets a half arm raise in return. Jimmy asks how she knows him. She tells him that is where she is staying, and Jimmy looks at his feet.

Evie drops back and walks with him. "Something wrong?"

"He helped me one day when the boys were chasing me."

"That was nice of him."

"Yeah, but then the boys made fun of me and said my only friend is an old guy who lives in a box. I denied he was my friend and to prove it, I threw rocks at him and his house." Evie's heart softens for Jimmy and Alfred. "I feel bad every time I see him."

"I'll tell you what we can do. I'll come to get you tomorrow if your mom says it is okay, and we will go talk to Mr. Alfred and you can apologize." He blanches. She stops him and looks into his eyes. "Jimmy, when we do something wrong, that is on us. We did it, we need to own up to it. I'll let you think about it. It has to be your choice to go. Just let me know." She catches up to Brenda.

"You can go on to Rose's house if you'd like."

"Oh no. I don't mind at all. I'm enjoying the company." Brenda walks with downcast eyes.

Evie, you are correct. Brenda and the children have been through a lot. Do not be surprised if she is standoffish. It is a defense mechanism she learned early in life which she has never let go.

Yes, Father. Thank You for the insight.

Evie walks them to the door and Janie gives her a big hug and asks her to stay. Evie looks at Brenda and mouths, "So sweet." She hugs Janie again and tells her she will be back. Evie turns to Jimmy and cocks her head. Looking down, he shakes his head. He is not ready to apologize. She nods. She hugs Brenda and thanks her for allowing her to spend the day with them. The girls are still waving as she turns onto the sidewalk.

Eight

After setting her bag on the bed and washing her hands, Evie looks for Rose. One bowl and one set of silverware are on the table. Evie hears talking and peers out the back window. Rose is on the top step and Alfred is a couple of steps down. Empty bowls are stacked beside Rose, and her Bible is open on her lap.

Evie ladles soup over crusty bread. When Rose comes in, she starts coffee and asks about Evie's day. The kitchen smells like vanilla as Evie talks about Brenda and her sweet children, the park, the library, and all the good, fun things of the day. At the mention of the officers, the conversation changes to the not-so-great things.

"Rose, I know you understand when I say my heart is heavy for this area. I have never felt this way about a place, only people."

Like any host she stays with, Rose knows a little about what Evie does when she comes to "work" in a new town. When Evie replied to the ad she found in the local paper, she shared some information with Rose. Rose placed the ad the day before, hoping to find a good, reliable person to rent a room to for extra income. She told Evie that she considered the idea for a few months, but that day, she felt God told her to do it immediately. Evie shared with Rose that God told her she was going to Gidesha City and to look in the paper for a room to rent this time.

"Well honey, you know if it is heavy, God has a reason."

"Oh, how I know. I've already been talking to Him about it." She pauses. "I hope this is not too personal, but I notice you and Alfred sit out back and read the Bible. Why doesn't he come in?"

Rose laughs. "He is such a gentleman. He doesn't want anyone to think bad of me for having, 'not only a man in my home but a dirty homeless man,' in my home. I laugh, but in honesty, it makes me sad."

"That is sad."

Pouring two cups of coffee, Rose sets the pot back on the burner. "At one time, I helped serve dinner in the community kitchen. That changed one night. It was cold and we had more people than usual to feed so it was late when we left. I was offered a ride, but I don't mind my little walk to and from the church, so I declined. As I turned the corner onto East High Street, a man was in the shadows leaning against the building. He startled me and blocked my path, then I heard someone breathing heavy behind me. They taunted me and asked what I had in my purse."

Evie gasps. "Oh no! What did you do?"

"I was a little frightened, but I knew Jesus was with me. Then I heard another voice. It was strong and threatened bodily harm to those men if they didn't move on. When Alfred saw who they were, he called them by name and told them to go back to the city where they belong. The man in front of me stared Alfred down until the guy behind me told him to go and they left."

"Sounds scary. I'm glad Alfred was there."

"God always makes a way. I thanked Alfred. He grunted and told me I shouldn't be walking after dark by myself. He insisted on walking me home. Then he started sleeping next to my house and when I asked him about it, he said he is not going to let anything happen to me. Eventually, he asked if he could set up a box as shelter. Between the awning and the tarp, it stays fairly dry. I told him anytime I have enough dinner to share, I would. He would come around to the back and eat on the steps. After a while, I asked if I could join him for dinner. Not long after that, I brought my Bible to read after we ate. He agreed."

"What a sweet story! So he knows Jesus?"

"He met Him once." Rose's phone rings. She answers and puts it on mute long enough to tell Evie it was her son. Evie tells her good night and goes to her room.

Gracious, merciful Father, Rose is right. You have placed this on my heart, but what am I supposed to do about this city? I don't know the first thing about it. Where would I even begin? I can't. . .

Sweet Evie, shhh. You are correct. You can't, but I can. What is impossible for people is possible with Me. No man could restore this city. A committee, team, or anything else this world puts together, could not do it, but I can. I will use you and others who carry this same burden. As I have placed it on your heart, I have placed it on theirs as well. You are never alone. I am with You and so are the people passionate about seeing this city thrive again.

Evie drops to her knees, sobbing. *Father, forgive me. I know better.*

My child, you are forgiven. I love you.

Father, You promised to be with me always. Why do I think You would send me out there without a plan in place? I am listening. Where do You want me to begin?

Father MacKay. Talk to him. He hears Me and is My child.

Okay, Father. You are so kind.

As Evie prepares for bed, she remembers the little boy that went into the corner store by himself. If the bars on the outside of the windows are not bad enough, the posters encouraging cigarettes, beer, and lottery tickets taped to the windows offer a bigger glimpse into the problems of this city.

Nine

Evie gets up early to join Rose for Mass. Father MacKay enjoys the solitude of early mornings so morning Mass suits him. Rose would go regardless of who says it, but she likes it best when Father MacKay does.

They walk in silence. Evie thinks about the best way to approach Father MacKay about cleaning up the city. She looks at the rowhouses, some have plywood on the windows, others have wood planks across the doors and windows. Long forgotten buildings with bars and big red "For Sale" signs on them dot the road on the other side of the street. One stand-alone house on the corner has bright yellow "caution" tape wrapped around the house. It will take an army, but with God in the lead, it will happen.

On the grass next to the church, they see a man on the ground holding his side. He calls out for help. Evie goes as Rose stays back and warns her to be careful. She approaches him from behind and bends to help. He pulls a gun on her. When Rose sees the gun, she runs into the church for help.

The man looks down briefly as he stands, gun still pointed at Evie. When he looks back at her, he freezes. Eyes wide, mouth open, and hands trembling, he drops the gun.

A few men run out of the church to find the man on his face in front of Evie screaming, “Just don’t let them hurt me.”

The police sirens get louder as a patrol car comes to an abrupt rest and two officers get out. Evie points to the gun she kicked into the gutter. One officer, pulling on gloves, retrieves the gun, the other tells the man to put his hands behind his back and stay on the ground. The officer cuffs him and he and the other officer stand him up. The would-be robber stares at Evie, shaking and begging the officers to get him out of there.

The officers place him in the car as another patrol car arrives.

The officer jumps from the driver's seat. “Evie? Are you okay?”

It takes a second, then she remembers. “Rip. Um, I’m fine. I’m not completely sure what happened. I saw the gun and then the guy became afraid. He dropped the gun when he fell face down on the ground, so I kicked it into the street. He kept repeating 'Where are they?' I guess he meant the police."

The arresting officer approaches Rip and whispers. Rip tips his head.

"You sure you're okay?" Evie nods. "Give me a minute. Do you want to sit in the car and wait?"

"No. I'll be right here."

"Please don't talk to anyone."

Evie nods again. Everyone who came out of the church has gone back in except Rose.

A few minutes later Rip returns. Brows furrowed, he leads Evie to the church steps where she sits.

"You're okay? I mean you had a gun pulled on you. What you went through would scare anybody, including me. You're brave."

"I didn't do anything."

"You had the sense to kick the gun away when he dropped it."

She shakes her head. "He wasn't going anywhere. Why did he drop it?"

"Well, the story he's telling is when he turned to rob you, the two guys with you frightened him. He said their shiny, silver swords were as tall as you. Was there anyone with you?"

Rip can barely hear her. "Just Rose."

"Not two guys? Apparently, tall guys if the swords were as tall as you."

Oh, Father. You were protecting me. Your angels were with me. You'll never leave me forsaken. Thank You! You are good! Rip is my third person. How could I have missed that?

"Evie?"

She shakes her head as tears slip down her cheeks. Rip calls Giovanni over.

"I think she's in shock."

"No. I'm fine. I want to go." Evie points to the church. "What else do you need from me?"

"I need a statement and some personal information."

"Okay." She tells him what happened one more time and gave her present address and cell phone. Rip said to expect to hear from the prosecutor's office soon.

“Are you sure you don’t want to go home?”

She shakes her head. She needs to talk to Father MacKay. “I’m sure.”

“Okay. Take care of yourself. Be careful. This isn’t the safest town.”

“Thank you.”

Evie runs up the steps and Rose hugs her before they go into the church.

Rip shakes his head. “Man. Either that dude is on some strong stuff or something supernatural happened here.” He tells Giovanni what the guy said.

Giovanni laughs. “Could be either, but I like to think it was supernatural.”

“You would church boy.” Rip picks at Giovanni about his faith, but truth is, he remembers the days when he had faith too.

Father MacKay acknowledges Rose and Evie with a nod as he continues the Homily. When Mass is over, Father MacKay stands at the back door as parishioners shake his hand. Evie and Rose wait until everyone is gone to talk to him.

"Father, this is Evie."

"Evie, are you okay? I was in the back getting ready. I'm so sorry I wasn't around to help."

"Father, it's okay. How were you to know? I was protected and I'm fine."

"Still."

Evie doubts he realizes he still has her hand, so she pats his hand. "Father, I have more important things I'd like to talk to you about. This may seem odd, but are you doing something about the nature of this city? Do you have something in the works or on your heart? I was told to talk to you."

"How do you know that? Who told you to talk to me? Nobody knows anything because I don't know anything for sure."

Evie smiles. "A mutual Friend."

"Ah. Do you have time to sit?"

"I have all the time in the world."

He leads Evie and Rose to the kitchen where a pot of coffee is waiting.

"Please, have a seat." He pours three cups, pulls the creamer from the fridge, and sets the sugar on the table. Taking a sip, he peers at Evie. "Okay, so this mutual Friend, what else did He tell you? Better yet, start at the beginning."

"I've only been here a few days, but it didn't take long once I got off the bus to see a problem. Then I went downtown. Several of the church buildings are boarded up and others are in terrible physical shape. My guess is they are in terrible spiritual shape as well. The wicked places seem to be thriving as well as business on the streets. And if what happened to me this morning, is happening all over the city, it all adds up to trouble." Father MacKay nods. "My heart is heavy for this city and the few friends I have made already. I took it all to my Father and laid it down before Him. He directed me to you."

He laughs. "Sounds like something He would do. He brings His teams together, doesn't He?"

"He sure does. So, do you have something in the works? If you don't, I have a feeling it is coming soon."

“I believe I’m looking at my confirmation. It’s time. I know a handful of people who are committed to doing whatever they can to get this city rolling again. I’ll get with them, set a date, and call a meeting. I’ll let you know as soon as I know.”

“I look forward to it.”

Ten

Alfred is not at the house which prompts Evie to ask Rose what Alfred does when he is not home. Rose only knows he goes to the community kitchen, but other than that he does not tell her. Evie excuses herself to her room.

My Refuge, You rescue me, protect me, shield me, and shelter me. You promise to never leave me, never forsake me. Not that You need to, but You proved to me how very true it is. You are faithful to keep Your promises which are my armor and protection. I will forever keep my trust in You. Today could have turned out bad if it were not for Your angels guarding me. Thank You. So Father, how do I proceed with Alfred if I don't even know where he is?

My child, I want nothing more than to take care of you. My angels are all around but only seen when needed. Contact Toby. He drives all over the city. Tell him what you need.

Evie calls Toby who is between fares.

"I'm glad you called. Where are you going today?"

Evie chuckles. "I was hoping you'd tell me."

"Oh. I see. Who are you looking for?"

Evie was surprised but remembered who she works for. "Alfred. He is about five foot eight, with gray, unkempt hair and beard, and doesn't talk much."

"You know you described half of the male population here and some of the females."

Evie tries to contain herself. "Toby! That's not nice. Funny, but not nice."

"I'm just keeping it light, my friend. There are only two women that I know of." He winks. "Okay, let's go find Alfred. Tell me, is he homeless?"

"Yes."

Just past the library, he turns into the driveway of a corner store. He looks in, makes a call, then moves on. He backtracks to a gas station with a convenience store several blocks before the library. Evie sees Alfred picking up trash outside of the store.

She watches for a minute. "Do you know if he works for pay?"

"Probably. There are a few business owners who want to see change and are doing what they can for now. This gas station and the first place we stopped at try to employ as many struggling people as possible, who want to work. They don't drug test, ask for references, no background check, but he does ask them to come to work as presentable as possible. This place has showers for truckers, so he allows his employees to use them too. I heard that if things start to look up and jobs become available, this business owner will provide the homeless with showers and new clothes to look decent for an interview."

"Oh wow. Who is he?"

"I'm not sure his real name, but he goes by Smith Jones on paper. At least that's what I've heard. Do you want to get out here?"

Oh Father, bless these business owners who are taking care of Your children. They are following Your command wholeheartedly by loving the least of these.

Evie runs her fingers through her hair. "I don't think so. Would you take me to the library instead? I can take the bus back later."

"Or you could call me."

"You are so kind. Thank you, Toby."

He lets her out at the library.

"How much do I owe, and don't tell me you forgot to start the meter. Just make something up if you did because I am paying you."

"Yes ma'am."

She thinks about the business owner and wishes she knew who he was. As the door closes, the busy sounds of the city are swallowed up by peace and quiet. She waves to Mark and walks past the Children's Corner.

"Hey, Evie."

"Brenda! What are you doing here?"

"Frankie sent me and two others home because it was so slow. The children were..." Before Brenda could finish Evie hears Janie's sweet little voice, calling Evie's name.

"...climbing the walls."

The girls run to see her, but Jimmy strolls over. As Evie squats Janie grabs hold of her neck and doesn't let go. Evie laughs and falls on her bottom.

"Shhh. We have to be quiet." She tells herself as much as the children.

Brenda removes Janie from Evie's neck and Evie stretches her arms out. "Can you help me up, Jimmy?"

He grabs both hands and pulls. "You are strong. I see why you're a big help around the house." He stands just a little taller.

Brenda shoos them back off to the Children's Corner as she and Evie sit in their regular spot. Brenda leans forward as Evie tells her what happened earlier that day.

"Well? What did he see? What frightened him and made him drop the gun?"

Father, do I?

Yes, you can.

"He told the officers that when he turned to rob me, the two guys with me frightened him. He said their shiny, silver swords were as tall as me."

"Who were they? And swords?"

"Physically, no one was with me. Spiritually, two angels were with me."

Brenda sits stone-faced. "Angels with swords as tall as you? They must have been extremely tall."

Evie nods, hoping to learn if Brenda has a relationship with Jesus. But a commotion causes them to look towards the circulation desk. A loud man, with disheveled blonde hair, torn jeans, and a T-shirt with holes is holding money in one hand and the other palm up.

"I wasn't asking him for money. He called me over and gave it to me."

"Charlie, you know you're welcome in here, but you can't ask our patrons for money."

"But I wasn't. I promise. He's over here; I'll get him so he can tell you."

"Don't bother him. Leave him be or we'll call the police."

Brenda smiles and whispers. "I kinda hope they call the police."

Evie laughs and rolls her eyes.

The police were already coming in the door. They approach Charlie. Rip puts out his hand and Charlie places the money in it.

"I don't want your money Charlie. I want to shake your hand. You haven't forgotten how gentlemen greet each other right?" Rip puts the money back in his hand and Charlie puts it in his pocket. He puts his hand out to Rip, then Giovanni.

They step to the side, away from the desk. Evie listens as Charlie tells them he was not asking for money, but the man must have looked at his clothes and thought he needed it. Rip asks him if he needs it. Charlie looks down and explains he lost his job months ago and does odd jobs and he begs. He's trying to take care of his family. Rip tells Charlie about a job he heard about not far from here and to say Rip sent him. Charlie thanks him and apologizes to the staff.

"Ladies." Rip nods. "Evie, how are you doing after this morning?"

"Doing great. Thank you for asking."

Giovanni asks Brenda to walk with him to see the children.

"I wish those two would just get it together," Rip laughs. "It's obvious they like each other. Don't you think?" Evie smiles and shrugs. "Well, I know he's crazy about her and her children. Maybe she will come around. He's a super good guy."

They watch as Giovanni gets the same response from the girls and a fist bump from Jimmy.

Father, why is Brenda hesitant to date Giovanni? She is not opening up. Please soften her heart towards me and help her trust me. Also, what am I supposed to do with Rip? How does someone just find out a police officer's story?

"Listen, I know you say you're great, but what happened to you this morning is scary. Will you please get help if it bothers you?"

"I already sought help when I got home. I was protected at the time of the incident and comforted when I got home."

"Oh? Husband? Boyfriend?"

Father, this guy is going to think I am crazy. Please soften his heart and let him receive what I say.

"No. I'm talking about Holy Spirit, my Comforter."

"Gotcha. Well then, you were in good hands."

Giovanni waits by the stairs for Rip.

Evie smiles. "Have a good day and stay safe."

"Thanks, you too."

The children surround Brenda, asking about going to the park. Brenda invites Evie.

While the children play, Evie shares about her childhood and tells Brenda about the two-week discipleship camp that changed her life. After what seems like minutes, Janie comes over to the bench and puts her head on Evie's lap. Evie's heart rejoices and fills with love.

"Looks like they are winding down. Unfortunately, we just missed the bus. It will be another hour before the next one. Oh well, not the first time."

Evie makes a call and within ten minutes Toby pulls up.

"Hold on," Toby calls as he goes around to the back of the van and puts the stroller in and pulls out a booster seat for Janie. Brenda sits in the front with Toby, the two older children sit in the last row, and the two younger ones sit in the middle.

Brenda opens the passenger door. "Wait, what about you, Evie?"

Evie hands Toby money. "I have some work to do at the library. You're in great hands with Toby. I'll see you soon."

She waves to the children and walks back to the library.

Stack of books in hand she finds a table in the corner. Pulling a notepad and pen from her purse she sets them to her right and then reaches for the top book. As she pulls each book and skims the pages to take notes, she sets the most helpful to the side.

After reading about the Broken Windows theory, she sits back in her chair and thinks. She compares what she read to the abandoned properties, litter hiding like Easter eggs in the grass long overdue for a cut, excessive broken windows, and graffiti spread from one end of Gidesha City to the other. She realizes the downward spiral that begins if just one window is left broken. Then the grass grows out of control. It appears no one cares so another then another window gets broken. Then a beer can and a fast-food bag are thrown down in front of the place. The common thought is, who here cares? It spreads like a disease. Her thoughts drift to her people.

Father, it sounds like what happens to us. A repetitively broken, unhealed heart leads to a broken spirit. Hurt continues to heap on top of hurt until we are left feeling abandoned and hopeless. They just need to know someone cares. We, as Your children, must look beyond the destruction and brokenness to see the spirit which can be revitalized and made new again. I believe there are plenty in this city to care for the broken people here. It all goes back to loving You and loving Your people Thank You, Father, for showing me the connection and guiding me. I love You!

"Evie. You're still here."

She nods as Rip sits. "Yep. And you're still working."

"I'm covering a couple of hours for Phil so he can watch his daughter's ball game."

"That's nice."

"They know I like to pick up hours, and she needs her dad there. Are you planning to take the bus home? It's getting kind of late."

"Oh goodness. Is it? I was, but I don't think it'll be wise. I'll call a taxi."

"Or I can take you."

"No need for that. I have a friend who drives a taxi." He raises his eyebrows and cocks his head. She laughs as she gathers the books and puts her pen and notepad away. "I promise. I'll be fine."

Rip carries the books and slides them on the return cart. "If it's okay, I'll wait with you until he gets here." Evie nods and calls Toby. He is home with his wife who may or may not be going into labor, so he sends his friend.

Evie thought she had seen the worst of the city in the daylight, but so much evil lurks in the night. Neon dollar signs with half the bulbs missing blink on top of a building named The Palace After Hours which was also only half-lit. Women wearing very little line the streets and call out to passing cars. Evie witnesses a couple of drug deals out in the wide-open.

She is grateful not to be on the bus.

Father, this is terrible. It breaks my heart. I can only imagine what it does to Yours. Right now, I plead the blood of

Jesus over Gidesha City. I ask that hardened hearts be softened and that strongholds be broken. This town will be alive and thrive again in the Name of Jesus! I believe You have not forsaken this city, even though it is obvious they have forsaken You. The residents will be humble and honor their community and You will be pleased with them once again. It's just sad. Thank You for listening to me and allowing me to help before I have to leave.

Eleven

Evie feels like she hasn't even been asleep when the alarm goes off. She tries to remember why she set it so early. Gathering her thoughts, she sits up and turns on the lamp before reaching for her Bible. Alfred is on her mind as she opens her Bible and starts reading Matthew chapter 4. Two chapters later, she stops.

Evie, read that again.

Forgiveness? Alfred needs to forgive someone to get past this. His broken heart under all the hurt is unforgiveness. Oh, Father! Thank You! That makes perfect sense.

Hopeful after the guidance from her Father, she jumps out of bed and dresses quickly. Evie wants to catch Alfred before he leaves for the day.

Pulling the heavy curtain back, it's still dark. Not wanting to wake Rose, she sits in the dark living room waiting for the sun to peep over the horizon. She hears Rose shuffle to the kitchen and start coffee. Not wanting to scare her, Evie slides into her room.

Rose taps the spoon on her coffee cup as Evie comes from the hall. "Good morning."

"Good morning. You're up early today."

"Yes. I was hoping to catch Alfred and take him to breakfast before he wanders off. I peeked out but could not see his house."

"Honey, I'm sorry you got up early. Typically, when he is not around for dinner and Bible reading, I know he will be gone overnight. He doesn't do it often because he worries about me."

"Hmm. I'm too awake now to go back to sleep."

"Why don't you grab your Bible, honey, and I'll read my devotion."

Rose pours Evie a cup of coffee while she gets her Bible. She reads the devotion about family aloud, and then Evie reads the accompanying scripture. Rose talks about raising her children alone after her husband died. She had a good job as the supervisor over the cafeteria at the high school her children attended. When she retired, her co-workers joked that they would be at her house at least once a week for dinner.

Evie realizes how much Rose misses her children and wonders if they will move back when the city is thriving again.

When Rose leaves for church, Evie goes to her room and prays. Before long, Rose is back in the kitchen. Evie has no idea how long she prayed, but this does not surprise her; she had a lot to cover this morning.

***

Rose has not seen Alfred for a few days. He has not been home or to the community kitchen. She prays but shares her concern with Evie. Her Father would not send her here for him to disappear and not be changed. She tells Rose she will pray for him but if he does not come back soon, they will call the police. She leaves Rose in the living room to go rinse her cup in the kitchen.

"Evie, your phone is ringing."

Evie shuts off the water and comes to the living room. She looks to see who is calling. "Hello. Yes, hello, Father

MacKay." She looks for pen and paper. "Okay. Yes. A week from today at six p.m. Of course! I look forward to it. Let me know if I can do anything to help beforehand. Okay. Bye."

"Was that about the meeting for the city?"

"It was. I am very hopeful, Rose."

"Me too, honey. I will fix something for you to take to the meeting."

"Will you not be there?"

"No. I will let the wise and knowledgeable ones do their work in the beginning. I will volunteer when the time is right."

"Rose," Evie takes her hand. "You have lived here your entire life. You are a vital part of this city. I feel sure you have something to offer. Besides, Father MacKay said it will be a preliminary meeting to see who comes and shares in the vision. Just consider it, okay?"

"Such kind words. I will consider it."

Evie grabs her purse and a plastic bag. "I am going out for a bit. See you later."

"Be safe."

She takes a right at the bottom of the steps. Earlier this morning, Evie asked if she could have pizza delivered to Brenda and the children for dinner. Then asked if she could join them. Brenda did not think twice about it. They became friends fast, but Brenda has some solid walls. She is protecting herself or the children, or both. Evie knows God will make a way.

"Here she comes!" Janie squeals and claps her hands. Jimmy, excited, opens the door before she knocks.

"Hi, Jimmy…" She was ambushed from the girls. "Wow. All the love! Hey there, Brenda."

"Hi, Evie. They act like they haven't seen you in months. You girls know you're not starved for love and attention."

"They may not be, but I sure am!" Evie laughs as Janie pulls her by the hand to the color sheet and jumbo crayons on the table. "That is lovely!"

"For you." Janie glows.

Brenda joins them. She studies the finished product and jumps at the loud knock on the door.

Jimmy looks out the window. “Mom, it’s okay. It’s the pizza guy. Can I open the door?” Evie takes the drinks and Jimmy gets the pizzas.

“Since it is a fun night, you can sit on the floor and eat, and you can watch tv if you can agree on something,” Brenda says.

“Cool!” Jimmy suggests a show about sea turtles. Janie, who is obsessed with princesses, wants to watch a princess show, but the other two girls side with Jimmy.

Brenda picks at her pizza. Evie senses she wants to say something but instead, Evie tells Brenda about the time she had a job in the mountains in the fall. She admits it may have been her favorite, but that she has been blessed to go to some pretty amazing places.

“Until now.” Brenda rolls her eyes and laughs. “I would love to hear where this city rates.”

“I’ll let you know before I leave for the next assignment.”

Brenda puts up the leftovers and Evie picks up the children's plates and cups.

“Sit with me?” Evie can’t resist sleepy-eyed Janie. She nods, holds up her finger, and checks on Brenda who turns off the kitchen light. Evie sits on the sofa and up Janie climbs right into her lap. Janie’s breathing deepens so Evie carries her to bed. Before she gets comfortable, up climbs the next oldest and lays her head in Evie’s lap. Evie rubs her hair until she falls asleep.

“I’m getting a complex here. I’m boring your children to sleep.”

“You better be careful. I may move you in.”

Twelve

On the bus, her mind is on Alfred. Rose says she saw him last night, but he is not home this morning when Evie leaves.

Gracious Father, please let Alfred be okay. Rose said he has never been away from home as long or as much as he has lately. Keep him safe and if he is doing something bad, let me help him before it's too late. He may be the most elusive person I've tried to help. I don't feel like I'm getting anywhere with my people this time.

Time is an appropriate word, sweet Evie. Think about it for a minute. I love you, My child.

Yes Father, I understand. Your time, not mine. There is a time for everything. A time to be born and a time to die. A time to plant and a time to harvest. Your time is best. I will not rush or force anything. Your plan is always better.

Evie gets off at a stop a few blocks from the library. A vacant building, with a few busted windows and boards covering doors, catches Evie's attention. The front section has several floors, but at street level, the building is only one floor but it is as long as the front is tall. A couple of women are on the street in front of the vacant building this morning. Evie smiles and says hello. Another woman sits with her back against the building, head down in her hands. Evie checks on her. She holds her head up only long enough to see her empty, sunken eyes.

Oh Father, rescue these women. And this building, what wasted space. Maybe it can be transformed into something useful and beautiful.

Evie, dream big. With Me, all things are possible.

Feeling hopeful, she crosses the street to go to the library. There is an endless amount of trash strewn a full block in front of her. It looks like someone emptied a dumpster and spread it from one end of the block to the other. At the far end of the block is the Party Pit, where the majority of the trash is. It oozes from the Pit onto the walkway of other businesses.

My sweet Evie, please pick up the trash on this block.

Really Father? Is this You or am I thinking that? Oh, never mind. I know this is You because it would not have crossed my mind otherwise. But Father how can I carry it all?

I am not asking you to carry it all. Go back to the corner and look on the side street.

Evie goes to the corner.

Well. That's kind of random. Okay, Father. Definitely Your will, not mine. She laughs when she finds a pair of clean gloves inside each of the clean trash cans. *You are so good and funny too, but why two pairs of gloves?*

She places one can near the Pit and keeps the other one with her. Knowing this would not make sense to most people, she begins picking up trash. Passersby honk and some whistle at her. Undeterred she starts at the end opposite of the Pit. Before she finishes the area in front of the first business, she hears a man's voice behind her.

"Hey there. What are you doing?" She recognizes the voice immediately and cringes.

"Hey, Rip. Community service?"

"Uh-huh. Did you do something wrong for this community service?"

She continues picking up trash. "No. Not really."

Rip starts picking up trash and she hands him the other pair of gloves, which fit perfectly.

Outside the Pit, Evie stops. "I appreciate the help, but this is a big job. I can get it from here. This is my thing, not yours. And I'm guessing it's your day off because you're not in uniform. I'm sure you have plenty to do."

"Right now, this is what I have to do. What I want to do. If you are out here picking up trash, I'm sure you have a good reason. Besides, it will get done faster with two of us working at it so you can go on with your day too."

She cannot argue that and by the smirk on his face, he knows it.

"Okay then. Thank you."

"My pleasure."

It takes about twenty minutes to pick up all the garbage in front and on the side of the Pit.

"Well, that wasn't too bad, was it?" Rip moves the full trashcans to the curb.

"No. Not with two of us working on it." She smiles as she tosses the gloves in the can. "Thanks again."

"Do you have lunch plans?" Rip calls after her as she walks away.

It is good Evie. Get to know him. He is one of your people.

Father, I know You know what is best, but is that really a good idea. I mean, I. . .

Sweet child, You were so obedient to pick up the trash. That was not a fun job and you did not question Me, but now arguing with Me about going to lunch with one of your people?

Yes, Father. I'm sorry.

"Nope. No plans. Do you?"

"If you say you'll join me for lunch I will."

"Okay then, but you pick the place because I haven't a clue."

His car is parked around the block, but the restaurant is close, so they walk. He talks and Evie listens as she usually does so she can learn about her people. The sign on the door says, Louie's. The restaurant is one of his favorites but it has been difficult for him to eat here anymore. Evie wants to ask but decides to wait and see if he tells her.

They follow the hostess to a table in the back where there are fewer people. Rip looks down at the menu.

"Hi, Rip. How are you?"

"Hey, Zae. I'm doing well."

"It's weird seeing you on this side…"

"Yeah, I know." He laughs. "Ready to order, Evie?" Although he laughs, his eyes say something different.

As the server walks away, Evie takes a sip of her water. "I'm sorry for your pain. You're good at hiding your feelings, but your eyes can't hide it."

"I'm an officer. I can't let anyone know what bothers me and what doesn't. It could be the difference between life and death for me. You see it because you're different. It's because you care about people. But you're right. It's painful."

"We didn't have to come here. I would have been happy going anywhere."

"It may sound selfish, but I like this place and I thought maybe, having you join me, I could enjoy it again."

"Well then, let's enjoy it."

As they eat, he tells her about joining the Air Force right after high school despite his father wanting him to stay and learn the family business. He knew if he stayed around, he would not be good for anybody or anything. After four years of active duty, he came home and worked with his father, learning the business for the next four years. He was thankful for the education but knew he was not going to be satisfied doing that for the rest of his life. When he went to his dad about wanting to join the police force, his dad told him he was surprised he stuck with him as long as he did. So he was hired at the police department, went through the academy, and here he is ten years later. His dad still runs the family business and Rip helps him when he can.

Evie talks about her travels and how she stays away from home for long periods. That she helps people and has been blessed with the best job ever. The same canned answer every time, but now she adds traveling life coach. Rip says it would be tough for him to be gone for long periods, he likes to travel, but he enjoys coming back here.

Evie places her silverware on her plate and sets it to the side. "I don't think I've eaten that much in forever, but it was just so good."

"See why I like it so much? Do you want dessert? They are amazing."

"Ugh." She places her arms across her stomach. "I may have to come just for dessert sometime."

"Coffee?"

"Now that, I have room for."

He orders two and scoots his chair back. "So, I thought maybe you would've told me why you were picking up trash, but since you didn't, why were you?"

Father, what is wrong with me? I can't decide whether to tell him or not. Father?

"It's okay if you have your reasons."

"Well," She realizes she is fidgeting and admonishes herself. "Do you want the true story albeit difficult to believe, or a story that satisfies your ideals?"

Surprised, he chuckles. "Seldom am I speechless."

The server returns with the two steaming mugs. Evie wonders if her words were too harsh and decides to apologize when the server leaves. They both speak at the same time.

"I'm sorry. Go ahead." He nods at Evie.

"I'm sorry if my words sounded harsh. It's not what I intended."

"Honestly, I'm impressed. Most people sugarcoat or tell you what you want to hear. It's refreshing to be given a choice." He laughs. "I think I can handle the truth. Try me."

"I was on my way to the library and got off the bus a couple of blocks earlier and walked the rest of the way. I could see the trash from two blocks away. When I passed the first business, I was stopped." Rip nods. "I was stopped by my Father, God. He asked me to pick up the trash in front of those businesses, including the Party Pit." She stops and wonders if she should tell him the part about the trash cans.

He rubs his chin. "I'm going to guess you didn't have trash cans handy, so where did they come from?"

"He told me to go back to the corner and look on the side street. They were there, clean, new, and empty. Oh, and with a new pair of gloves inside each." She nods. "There you go."

"You're remarkable and I'm speechless again." He takes a big swallow of his coffee and stares at her. "Does this happen to you often?"

"Yes. I have been praying about the decline of your city since I got here. It's sad not just for the friends I have made, but for everyone. Father God uses people if they are willing and He knows I am His and more than willing. He had me pick it up for a reason. He never wastes anything."

"So, He just dropped the trash cans from Heaven?"

"Well, He could." Rip laughs. "But, more than likely He found an obedient person and asked them to buy the trash cans, new gloves and leave them there."

"People do that?"

"Yes, they do."

"That's a good reason to pick up trash. But why care about this city?"

"Because God cares about this city and the people. And I have asked Him to give me His heart. So, if His heart is for this city, then so is mine."

"Are you just going to do random acts of kindness while you're here?"

"I'll do what my Father asks. I am going to a meeting next week with some people who want to make a difference in Gidesha City."

"Really. Who are these people?"

"Father MacKay, from Saint Francis Church, is leading the meeting and others he knows who are on board."

"Father MacKay. He's a good guy. Do you think I could be there?"

"I don't see why not. Are you interested?"

He laughs. "Oh yeah."

"Tuesday night at six at St. Francis Church."

"I'll be there."

"May I ask you a question now?"

"Of course."

"What happened that you don't come here to eat?"

The sadness in his eyes returns and she feels bad for asking.

"That's fair. You were honest with me. Four years ago, my fiancé died. I proposed here."

"Oh. I'm so sorry."

"Thank you. It helped coming here to eat today. You being here made it easier and better."

"I'm glad. I enjoyed it." Evie finishes her coffee. "I need to get going, and I'm sure you have things to do. Thank you for lunch and for helping me clean up the trash."

"Thank you for joining me. I'll see you Tuesday night, if not sooner."

Thirteen

Evie waves to the staff and goes to the catalog computer. Looking for anything on marketing, building community, library growth, and anything unique, she writes down several titles and pulls a few books from the shelf. Finding an available computer, she types "how to attract people to the library" in the search bar. After a few clicks, she finds herself on a page about children and the library.

This library already does story time. After more reading, Evie realizes how important coming to the library is to a child's growth and how Brenda brings her children here which makes her research more relatable.

She digs around and takes notes. Some libraries use their program rooms for exercises, some do bounce houses once a month, and others offer popcorn or snow cones in the parking lot. She jots down several more ideas for children and adults and then skims the books.

Setting the books on the return cart, she asks for Mark.

"Hi, Evie."

"Hey. Looks like a few more people around here today."

"A few. We will take what we can get for now."

"I know you told me you are understaffed and it's difficult to find time to research right now, so I thought since I was here and had a few extra minutes, I would look into it for you."

She hands him her notes.

Shocked, he takes the papers. "You took your time to do this? That's kind."

"You know your library and staff better than I do, but maybe some of those will work."

"People in our city haven't tried to help us. Well, except for the donor, that is."

"The people feel hopeless and probably don't realize they have options. It's time to shake them a little. Change is coming, Mark! I just know it!"

"Your attitude gives me hope. Maybe you need to run for office here in Gidesha City."

She waves her hands in front of her. "No way! Talk to you later."

Evie barely catches the bus. About halfway home, she looks out the window and sees Alfred. She gets off at the next stop to walk with him.

"Hi, Alfred!"

"Your dad wouldn't like you being out here by yourself."

Evie, though a bit taken aback, keeps talking. "I was on the bus going home when I saw you. I thought it would be nice to walk with you."

"Why?" He looks down at the sidewalk as he talks.

"Because you're my friend."

"Not a good one."

"Why would you say that?"

"Something bad happened a long time ago and if you knew, you wouldn't be my friend."

"I think I would. Want to talk about it?"

"No."

"Okay. Let's talk about something else. Where are you coming from?"

"Work."

"That's great! Where are you working?"

"Gas station."

"Okay. What do you do there?"

"Clean."

Father! This is painful. He doesn't want to talk.

Sweet Evie. So don't. Remember, sometimes saying nothing speaks the loudest. Just be there.

She quietly walks home with him.

"Bye." Alfred turns and goes toward his house.

"Bye, Alfred. I enjoyed walking with you."

He grunts as he ducks inside his house. Evie is disappointed that she was unable to reach him. When she walks in the house, clanging pots greet her. Not wanting to startle Rose, she calls out from the hall.

"Hey, Rose."

"Hello," Rose turns to face Evie. "Oh, my. What is it, dear?"

"Something has been more difficult than I expected. I need to try something different."

"Life can throw some curveballs, can't it? You know what I do? I ask myself what would Jesus do or what did He do."

She smiles and sets a steaming bowl of soup and French baguette slices in front of Evie. "You know the Bible. Think of Jesus in a situation like yours and read it again. You will know how to apply it to what's going on."

Evie blows on her soup and thinks about what Rose said. People are supposed to live their life like Jesus. They have everything that Jesus had because they are joint-heirs with Him. What God gave Jesus, He gives others.

As Rose prepares bowls for her and Alfred, it's a labor of love. Rose ministers to Alfred every time she feeds him and shares the Word of God with him.

"Rose, this is delicious."

"It's one of my favorites. My grandma had me in the kitchen with her from an early age."

"I'm grateful for your grandma."

"Me too, hon." She slides a can of soda into each pocket. "Would you mind opening the door for me?"

Evie opens the door and closes it behind her. As she eats, she hears murmuring but cannot make out the words. She cleans her dishes and goes to her room.

Gracious Father, Rose is right. What would Jesus do? I believe He would forgive Alfred and heal him so he could be free. He has done nothing to me, so I have no reason to forgive him, but I can help him see that Jesus forgives, heals, removes shame, and brings freedom. But how do I do that if he won't talk to me or spend time with me?

Sweet child, you are right, but what else does My Son do? Before all of that?

He loves. Please show me how to love him.

And what is love? It is patient. Try to remember, My child, sometimes saying nothing speaks the loudest. You must meet people where they are, just like My Son does. You know if they come as they are, you and all My other children must meet them, love them, and lead them to eternal life with Me. I work out the kinks and they do not stay where they are if they enter into a true relationship with Me. Sometimes people are tough to reach. You cannot blame yourself because I created humans to have free will. Not everyone will come to Me.

Oh, Father. That would break my heart. I want Alfred to know You. Thank You for comforting me and sharing Your wisdom. I love You.

Evie reaches for her Bible and turns to 1 Corinthians chapter 13.

Fourteen

Evie calls for Alfred and notices a car across the street. It strikes her as odd that the person in the driver's seat is hidden behind a newspaper. Alfred pokes his head out of his house.

"I'm here, Evie."

"Great! Want to join me for breakfast at Frankie's?"

His eyes brighten and he nods. As difficult as it is for Evie, they walk in silence.

"Welcome to Frankie's. Table for two?"

Frankie watches Alfred but says nothing.

"Yes, please. In Brenda's section if she's here."

Alfred sits. "He's watching us."

"I know, but we aren't doing anything wrong. Order what you'd like and enjoy."

Another server comes to their table. "Hi. Brenda will be over in a minute, she asked if I would get your drinks."

"Great! Thank you. Coffee for me, please." Evie looks at Alfred.

"Same and orange juice."

Brenda brings their drinks and gets their order. Silence.

Alfred stares out the window and clears his throat. "People have secrets. They can be pushed down, but they resurface throughout a lifetime. They get pushed down again and maybe people almost forget about their secret, but then it happens. The secret bites them." That is the most Evie has heard him say. He looks at her. "You're nice. Your dad would be proud."

"Thank you for your kind words." Evie fights to keep quiet.

Brenda comes up. "Phew. What a morning so far. Everybody woke up hungry."

"How are you, Brenda?"

"I'm good. The children are too."

"Wonderful." Evie nods toward Alfred. "Brenda, have you met my friend, Alfred?"

"No. We haven't officially met, but I waited on you the last time you two were here."

"Well, this is my friend Alfred. Alfred, this is my friend Brenda."

Alfred nods, "Nice to meet you."

"Nice to meet you too, Alfred." Brenda looks back to Evie. "I'm off tomorrow and the three older children will be at a camp at St. Francis Church. Do you want to do something? I'll have Janie, but she won't be a problem."

"Sure. Any ideas?"

Brenda shrugs. "I'll call you later and we'll figure it out. Let me check on your meal."

Sliding the plate in front of Evie, Brenda says she will be back with refills. Alfred is quiet. After breakfast, he thanks her and leaves for work. Evie pays and waves to Brenda. She goes to the church to help serve lunch.

This time she finds her way to the volunteer entrance and avoids a scene with the guardian. Coming through the door, she hears a thud.

"I'm so sorry, Father MacKay. What are the chances?"

"No worries, a little knot on the head is minor in my line of work. Come in."

In the kitchen, two people are cutting onions and have the volunteers around them in tears. Another is opening several cans of green beans as another pours them into a large pot. Rose waves her over.

"Here, honey." Rose hands her a rubber spatula. "It's easier to pour the batter into the tins when I have help."

They place the filled tins in the oven, clean, and wash their dishes. Another volunteer asks Evie to check the silverware containers and napkins. While she is in the dining room, she straightens the chairs and picks up trash. Savory smells fill the room. When Evie walks back into the kitchen, several people are slicing pork tenderloins. Others are scooping the side dishes into the large serving pans. Rose has the cupcakes sitting on the counter to cool.

"You are just in time. Next, we get to frost them." They finish and set them at the end of the serving line.

"I had no idea how much work goes into preparing a meal for this many."

"Some days there is more, some not so much. But the pay is all the same." Rose winks.

"You know where your reward is Rose. It'll be big." They laugh and take their spots on the serving line.

People get through the line quicker this time. As he did the first time she met him, Bud waits to be the last person. He has a smile and a kind word for every volunteer.

"Hello, Bud."

"You remember my name. Evie, right?"

"And you remember mine."

"I don't forget kind, genuine, special people."

She blushes. "Thank you."

He wanders to an empty table. Evie gets a towel and cleans the tables.

Bud watches her. "So, what do you think of our city?"

"There are some wonderful people here."

"Oh. Is that so? But what about the city itself?"

She pulls out a chair and sits. "Your city makes me very sad. My friends tell me what a beautiful place this was. That it was once a healthy, thriving, safe community, years ago."

"That it was. Money was made here, legally, and people worked hard. We were friendly and helped each other. We worked together, played together, and went to church together. It was a wonderful city. Then corruption found its way in and with it came nasty businesses, gambling, drugs, bars, and clubs. They got fuller and churches got emptier. The violence got out of control, and everything went downhill from there. And here we are."

"I'm sorry. It's very sad."

"It is. I have a crazy question. By any chance were you downtown cleaning up trash this week?"

Her cheeks flush. "Yes. That was me."

He smiles. "Interesting. Well, young lady, I am holding you all up. Have a nice day."

"Thank you and you too."

Father MacKay calls after Evie and Rose. "Don't forget tomorrow night at six."

Evie grins. "I wouldn't miss it for anything."

Going back to the house, the same car that was sitting outside the house this morning passes them. Evie does not get a look at the driver because she did not realize it was the same car until it passed. She says nothing about it to Rose.

"Rose, do you ever take care of children?"

"I help in the nursery at church when they are in a bind, and I have my grandchildren although I don't see them much. Why?"

"Brenda is off tomorrow, and we talked about doing something. The older children will be at camp, but Janie, the four-year-old, will have to come with us. Janie is great and I love her to pieces, but Brenda has no one here and probably does not get time to herself very often."

"Oh, I see. You want me to watch Janie while you go do girl things?"

Evie grins sheepishly. "Yes?"

"Do you think Brenda would be okay with that?"

"I'll ask her to stop here on her way home from work. I'll introduce you and suggest it to her. All she can say is no, right?"

"I'd be glad to do it."

Fifteen

After some convincing, Brenda agreed to let Rose watch Janie as long as it was at Brenda's apartment. On the way to the apartment, Evie tells Rose that eleven-year-old Jimmy tries to take care of the family since he is the only guy in the house. Jill, nine, is a mini mom. She helps Brenda and gets carried away with her role sometimes. Brenda has to remind her she is not the mom, just mom's big helper. Jess at seven, is smart and takes everything in like a sponge but says very little. Then there is Janie. Four and full of life. She is smart and independent unless she is tired then she is all cuddles. She has a very sweet spirit.

Waving fervently, Janie watches out the window. Her smile says all they need to know. Brenda opens the door and Janie runs out barefooted and in her pj's.

"Aunt Evie!"

Evie, eyebrows raised, picks up Janie and looks at Brenda. "Aunt Evie? I've graduated."

Shaking her head, Brenda shrugs.

"Janie, this is my dear friend, Ms. Rose." Janie buries her face in Evie's neck. "Ms. Rose, don't let Janie fool you, she is shy for only a minute."

Brenda takes Janie to get her dressed. Janie, with only a shirt and shoes on, comes running out and jumps on Evie. "Um, Janie, I think you forgot something."

Brenda sighs and retrieves Janie. "She escaped. It's the old run while mom puts the toothpaste on the toothbrush trick. I've seen it a hundred times and still fall for it." She rolls her eyes.

Evie has Janie sit between her and Rose and holds her hand as she and Rose talk. Janie listens then tells Rose, as she holds up four fingers, how old she is.

"Four years old? My goodness, you are so smart for four." Janie nods and Rose laughs. And that quickly, they are friends. Sweet spirits cannot be kept apart.

Brenda stands near the table fidgeting, watching Rose and Janie interact. Rose leans in, hands folded on her lap as Janie describes her favorite princess.

Oh, Father. Comfort my friend. Where there is fear, replace it with peace. Please help her. I want her to enjoy her day. Being a busy mom it's seldom about her, but today will be. Thank You for caring about the little things as much as the big things. It is an example of how You love us and how much You love us. Help me show Brenda Your love and goodness so she will want to know You. I love You.

Evie assures Brenda that Janie will be well taken care of and she can always check on her.

Brenda nods. "Janie, sweetie, Mommy and Evie are leaving now. Listen to Ms. Rose and be a good girl. Okay?"

"Okay, Mom" Janie half-heartedly waves still telling Rose all about the princess dress she wants. Rose gives them a thumbs-up as they leave.

Brenda sighs heavily as she shuts the door behind them. "The only time I leave my babies is when I go to work. Nova is the only one who stays with them or is close by next door. The only reason the big ones are at camp is that Nova is there."

"Do you worry about their safety because of the violence in the city?"

"Yes and because...yes."

"Understood. Toby will pick us up at Rose's house within fifteen minutes. Did you think about what you want to do?"

"No. Not really. I don't know how to act or what to do if I'm not going to the park or library or someplace for the kids."

"We'll stop by The Vintage Cup first, then go to the mall. We have a manicure and pedicure appointment shortly. Have you heard of Louie's?" Brenda shakes her head. "I ate there the other day. It was good. So, unless you have somewhere else in mind, we'll eat there."

"Oh, man! No fast food?"

"Uh. No."

Toby picks them up, makes the coffee stop, and drops them off at the mall.

Father, please let her know I am safe to talk to so she will open up. This is prime time for her to share. No interruptions from the little ones, or fear of them overhearing, just adult time. Let my words be from Your mouth and help her trust me.

Both women are quiet during the manicure. Brenda looks like her mind is elsewhere. Lavender fills the air as the pedicurists fill the foot bath with warm, scented water.

"I miss my Janie-girl, but this is amazing. This is a first for me."

"Oh? Your first pedicure?"

"And manicure."

Oh, Father, I had no idea. Wow. Thank You!

Outside the nail shop, Brenda stops Evie. "Thank you so much. I have never felt so pampered. My children are my only concern. I don't even remember the last time anything was done for me. It feels great!"

"I'm glad. It's my pleasure! Okay. I think Louie's is a few blocks that way. Are you good with walking there?"

"Of course." Waiting at a stoplight, Brenda chews her bottom lip. "I have been considering going to dinner with Giovanni. We have been talking just about every night for a few weeks. He is just so kind."

"And adores your children. I think it's a wonderful idea."

"I'm still not sure. Can I count on you and Rose if I decide to go? You have become the closest friend I ever had."

Evie's heart swells. "Absolutely! We'll be glad to help in any way we can. You have become very dear to me and those precious babies too."

"Hey ladies!" The patrol car stops to their left. "Where are you heading?"

"Evie kidnapped me for the day and is taking me to a new place she tried the other day, Louie's."

Evie, smiling sheepishly, peers in the car window past Giovanni. Rip gives a thumbs up. Giovanni turns and says something to Rip.

"Mind if we join you? We were trying to figure out where to go ourselves."

"It's up to Brenda. Today is all about her."

Brenda turns her back to the guys and mouths, "Gee, thanks."

"Sure. We would enjoy the company."

They walk half a block further to the restaurant and meet them at the door. The conversation is casual and light about the children and who is watching them. As they drink coffee after the meal, a call comes over the radio about a shooting a couple of blocks away. Rip responds on the radio and Giovanni tells them to leave the check at the cash stand and that they will get it later.

They rush out the door and the server comes to the table. “Don’t worry. Happens all the time.”

Evie opens her wallet and hands her a hundred-dollar bill. “Really?”

“Oh yeah. I can take the officer's check to the cashier. They will settle up later.”

“It’s not necessary. For all they do in and around the community and to keep us safe, this is the least I can do. Keep the change. You did a fantastic job and have a beautiful smile.”

“Thank you so much!”

They finish their coffee then Evie calls Toby. She wants Brenda to be home when the children get back from camp. Waiting outside for Toby, Brenda takes Evie’s hands.

“I can’t thank you enough for today. I don’t know how I got so lucky that you care about me and my babies. It’s been a long time since anyone treated me so kindly. I felt like a real woman today. It has been a wonderful day. Thank you.” She hugs Evie and makes her tear up.

“I am so thankful for you Brenda. It makes my heart happy to know today made you happy and feel good about yourself. You deserve to be treated well. That is why I think you should spend more time with Giovanni. Do it for yourself. Do it for your children. He is a nice guy.”

“I think I will.”

Toby gets them to the apartment in plenty of time. Evie tips Toby graciously for stopping at Vintage Cup and taking good care of them. He tries to argue, but she tells him to spend it on the new baby, shuts the door, and waves.

Brenda is waiting for Rose to open the door when Evie catches up. She was so excited she left her key on the counter. Evie senses some anxiety when she has to knock a second time.

"Hold on. I had to get up off the floor." They look at each other. "Who's there?"

"It's us, Rose," Brenda says.

"Mommy!" Janie comes running from the other room. "We played a game all day!"

"What game was that?"

"When Ms. Rose sang, we cleaned something."

Brenda looks around the apartment. "Oh, Rose. Now I know I'm a princess, at least for the day. Thank you both so much." She rubs Janie's cheek. "Did everything go okay?"

"Yes. You have a wonderful young lady here. There is one thing." Brenda froze. "A man came to the door. I left the latch on and cracked the door. He was looking past me asking if this was Izzy's apartment. I told him no but noticed he was trying to see behind me."

Brenda's hands shake. "Where was Janie?"

"I told her to stay in her bedroom until I came back for her."

"What did the man look like?"

“Taller than me, medium length, wavy dark hair, green eyes.”

Brenda’s shoulders drop.

“Brenda,” Evie reaches for her arm, “What is it? Is something wrong?”

As she searches Evie’s eyes, Evie sees fear briefly appear.

“No. It’s just weird. Izzy could be short for Elizabeth, right? I received mail for Elizabeth Stewart so I figured she lived in this apartment before me.”

Father. When! When will she trust me enough to confide in me?

In time, sweet child.

“Yes. It could.” Evie opens the door as a church van drops off Nova and the children. “If you’re sure you are okay, we’re going to leave.” The children run up the sidewalk toward the apartment. Evie gets hugs before they go in and hears Jimmy asking for a snack as Brenda closes the door.

“Something is wrong there, Evie.”

“Yes. I know. I guess she doesn’t trust me enough to tell me, so I pray for them. You didn’t happen to see the vehicle he was driving, did you?”

“No. The door wasn’t open enough and when he left, I went back to playing with Janie.” Evie thinks of the car sitting outside Rose’s house and tells herself to stop being paranoid.

Sixteen

Evie walks into the little room. People are already seated, and others are standing around talking in small groups. She counts ten people, mostly men but a couple of women too, but no Father MacKay. Rip comes in and smiles when he sees her. Father MacKay follows in behind him. Rip hugs Evie and sits down.

Oh, Father. Was that just a friendly friend hug or. . .Oh no.

Sweet child, relax. Everything is fine.

Father MacKay welcomes everyone and starts.

"First, this meeting is about improving the city, if you are here for the Bible Study on the book of Luke, that is downstairs in room 10." No one leaves so he explains he is only the facilitator and not running the show. Then he opens the floor. There is concern that someone needs to be in charge or a few people working together. There are a few who are adamant that they are too busy to head it up, but definitely are interested in being involved.

Two men, one a retired judge and the other, dressed in a three-piece suit, and one woman, who is well versed in legal jargon, are interested in leading this venture. Everyone agrees and offers their assistance in whatever way they can.

The judge wants to make sure everyone understands this is to be a group effort and all input is welcome. He suggests anyone who has thoughts on where and how to begin to bring their ideas to the table. Everyone agrees they will share ideas during this meeting and come back with thoughts and where to go from there at the next one.

It was almost nine-thirty by the time they finish. Rip and Evie walk out together.

"Where's your car? I'll walk you to it."

"I don't have a car. I plan on walking. It's not too far from here."

"May I give you a ride."

"I'm fine. I walk here all the time."

"In the dark? Please, I will feel better if you don't walk."

"Well, if it will help you sleep tonight, I'll take a ride."

They talk excitedly about the meeting. Rip is surprised that people did some homework and had good ideas. Evie agrees.

He pulls up in front of the house and she asks if he has a minute for her to share an idea with him. He turns off the car and turns toward her.

"I always make time. What's up?"

"I have a friend. He's homeless. I wondered where he went on the days he wasn't hanging around here. That's his home." She points to Alfred's house. "I asked my taxi friend if he had seen Alfred. He sees a lot of people, you know? He asked if he was homeless and took me by two businesses that hire homeless people. They do not drug test or do background checks; the owners just put them to work. He told me there were a few businessmen who are employing the homeless."

"Okay. And?"

"I love this! I want to invite them to the next meeting, but I don't know who they are or how I'd find them." He stares at her with such soft eyes that she has to look away.

"I'm one of them."

Her jaw drops. "You are?"

"Listen. I probably need to go. Early shift tomorrow. I'm off the day after tomorrow. Can we finish this conversation then?"

"Oh. Sure."

"I'll call you that morning to make plans, okay?"

"Sure." He opens her door for her, and watches as she makes her way into the house. The house is quiet.

Father. What have I done? I was so shocked that he is one of the businessmen that I agreed to see him again. And his eyes. What was that look in his eyes? He looked at me so tenderly. Father, I do not want to mislead him. I must tell him I can't be alone with him, but how will I help him. Oh, Father, I'm so sorry. I'm making a mess instead of fixing things. Forgive me, Father.

Evie dries her cheeks.

Evie, My sweet child, listen to Me. It is okay. Everything is fine. You are not messing anything up. You are amazing! You are being obedient! I gave him a glimpse of My heart through you. He needs to know so he will open up. He trusts you, completely.

Oh, Father. I trust You to work everything out. Thank You.

Seventeen

Tapping snooze, Evie pulls the covers up over her head. Reliving the conversation with Rip makes her stomach uneasy. What was she thinking? She pulls the covers back and sits on the edge of the bed. Elbows on her knees, head in her hands, she encourages herself to get moving. Talking herself into focusing on Alfred today helps her get motivated.

Good morning, Father! I love You!

Evie picks up her Bible. After reading a few scriptures and meditating on them, she is ready for the challenge.

"Here, honey." Rose hands Evie a mug.

"Thank you. You are on it today."

Rose chuckles as she pours herself a cup. "To be honest I was pouring it for myself when I heard your door squeak. You got in late last night and I thought you may need this more than me. How did everything go?"

Evie gives her the details. Rose knows the judge and says he is a fine man. He was always on the side of the laws and presided as well as he could alongside the crooks that were easing into every area of town. Although he made it to retirement, she feels he would have stayed on, but she believes he was squeezed out.

She thinks she knows the guy in the three-piece suit and the woman as well. If he is who she thinks he is, he is a CEO of a respectable company in the city but only because he was forced out of the church he was pastoring when evil became larger than good in this town. She is not sure what the woman does, maybe a lawyer.

"Honey, if I think about something to share would you mention it to them?"

"Of course, but why don't you join us? This is going to grow. More people will get on board."

"Well, I will just wait until then to join you, but you can share my ideas. I'll let the smart people get things started. I'm no leader, I just like to serve my Lord." She pats Evie's hand.

Evie rinses her cup and sets it in the drainer as she looks out at the back steps. Sensing she should go out front, she thanks Rose and goes down the hall. Alfred sits on the step with the paper cup of coffee from Rose.

Just sit with him, My precious daughter.

She sits one step below Alfred and waves. Feeling a little awkward, she looks up the street. It is still early. Sirens can be heard off in the distance.

"Thanks for the company." Alfred stands and crumples his cup. "Stay safe today." He picks up his bag and starts up the street.

"You're welcome. Have a good day." Without turning around, he just raises an arm.

Ugh, Father.

***

Evie calls Toby to come get her. She takes a pen and a notepad from her purse and sits on the step waiting. An insistent car horn causes her to look up. At the crossroad, she catches a glimpse of the tail end of a car resembling the one she has been seeing. She starts down the steps with the intention of going up there, but Toby pulls up. She gets in the van instead.

"Where to today, Evie?"

"How much time do you have?"

He turns off the meter. "As much as you need."

"Oh, no. If you're going to run me around, I'm going to pay, but thank you. If my bank account starts getting low, then I'll take you up on it." Knowing that will never happen, she feels a little guilty pulling that one.

"Deal!" He starts the meter.

"I would like to see the churches around the city."

"You know probably seventy-five percent of them are defunct, if not more."

"Yes. I have seen. Some of them may have needed closing. I would like to see what we are working with though."

"So, you went to the secret meeting last night?"

"Apparently, you mean not-so-secret meeting." Evie laughs.

"Eh, taxi drivers have the opportunity to learn a lot, they just have to listen." He turns and offers her a cheesy smile.

Toby drives around the city, points out churches, and tells Evie what he knows about each. After about thirty churches, she asks if he takes lunch breaks and offers to buy him lunch. He suggests an old favorite that has made it through the decline and is thriving.

As soon as she steps inside the door, she realizes why they are thriving. Not only is there an enormous sign hanging behind the hostess stand which reads, "But as for me and my house, we will serve the LORD," but the friendly welcome is the best Evie has experienced. Evie watches the owner make his rounds, checking on people, and laughing with them. She recognizes him as soon as she sees him. As Toby starts to introduce Evie, the owner recognizes her.

"Evie! Welcome!"

"Sal. Hello. I would not have guessed you as a restaurant owner."

"Well, here I am. How was your lunch?" Sal pulls the check off the table.

"Very good. Great atmosphere, friendly, and relaxing."

"Good. I walk through praying over every employee and guest before I open each day. Lunch is on me, my new friend. Come back again."

"Aww. Thank you. I sure will. See you at the next meeting."

Toby opens the van door for Evie, and she slides in. "Sal told you about the meeting, didn't he?"

Delivering his cheesy smile again he starts the van. A light mist covers the windshield. They spend a couple more hours looking at churches as it sprinkles on and off. They call it a day, once big droplets pelt the roof of the van. Just in case Alfred is off work, Evie asks Toby to drive the route Alfred walks home. They spot him walking off the parking lot as they drive by.

"Please stop. I'd like to see if he'll accept a ride."

Toby pulls into the next driveway and Evie jumps out, doubting Alfred would take the offer but she needs to try anyway. "Alfred. Hi. I'm heading to the house would you like a ride?"

He gets into the van.

Gracious Father, why do I doubt. Thank You always for making the impossible possible.

Evie introduces Alfred to Toby and then it's quiet the rest of the way home.

Alfred gets out. "Thanks." He saunters to his house.

"Thank you, Toby. I appreciate your time today. Here is the fare and a little something extra for your time and kindness. Be blessed, my friend."

"Thank you. I'm here when you need me."

Running from the car to the house she shouts in the direction of Alfred's house. "Have a good night, Alfred!"

As Evie opens the door, she hears a man's voice coming from the kitchen. She also hears Rose's happy voice. The smell of tomatoes, garlic, and a variety of spices welcome her into the kitchen.

"Rose, this can only mean one thing, gravy!"

"Oh honey, you're home! This is my son, Antonio. He is working about forty minutes north of here and surprised me. He said if I fix gravy, he'll stay the night. I hope you like dogs, since the upstairs is full of years of stuff, he will stay on the sofa."

"Um, the dog or your son?"

Antonio laughs as he stands. "Nice to meet you, Evie. I'm Antonio, the son and this is Champ, the dog. I will be sleeping on the sofa and Champ will sleep next to me on the floor."

"Pleasure to meet you both." She puts out her hand to Antonio and pets Champ, a striking yellow Lab.

Antonio tells Rose at least three times how he is thrilled to have a home-cooked meal. Evie tells Rose she is cleaning the kitchen so she and Antonio can visit, and Rose concedes. Champ lays on the living room floor by Antonio's feet until he hears Evie putting the pots away in the kitchen. Evie starts a small pot of coffee. Finished in the kitchen she brings a couple of cups, sugar, and creamer to them.

Rose takes her cup. "Will you join us?"

"No. You enjoy your visit. I have some things to work on in my room."

Rose smiles. "It's okay. We would like for you to join us.

Evie hands Antonio his coffee. "I'm sorry, not tonight. In case I don't see you again, it was nice meeting you."

He nods. "You too."

Evie shuts the door behind her. She pulls out her notepad, stops, and listens. Through the gap under the door, a yellow paw reaches into her room accompanied by soft whining. She laughs and opens the door.

"Hi, Champ." She walks to the kitchen, pours a cup of coffee, and goes back to the living room. "Champ decided I would like to join you."

Sirens go by the house twice and can be heard on the street over. Antonio grimaces each time. Finally, after the third time, he suggests she move away. Rose smiles softly at her son who shrugs and gives up.

Evie collects the empty cups and loves on Champ. When she goes back to her room, Champ sniffs and snorts with a subtle whimper. Antonio comes to the door as she opens it.

"He has taken a liking to you."

"He's welcome to stay in here tonight. I love dogs, but travel so much I don't have any."

"Are you sure?"

"Yes. What time are you leaving?"

"After breakfast." Champ finds a good spot on the rug by the bed, curls up, and closes his eyes.

"Well. I guess it's settled."

Evie sits on the floor by Champ wondering what tomorrow will look like.

Father, thank You for being with me today. You are always working on my behalf and behalf of Your children. You are so good to answer us as we bring our needs to You. You know before we even ask. I ask You to help them in their disbelief. Give me wisdom in choosing my words as I discover where each one of them stands with You. Let my words be life-giving and refreshing to them. Let my words be kind and sweet to their soul. May they listen to instruction and prosper. And Father, You have already told me everything is fine with Rip, but help me help him quickly so he can go about his life and I can go about mine. You are kind and merciful. I love You, Father.

Eighteen

Champ stirs when he hears Antonio talking. Evie rolls on her side to pet Champ and smells coffee.

Good morning, Father. Today is the day. Protect my mind and be with me so I can remember who I am and that what I am doing is for You and Your glory. Today would be a great day for Rip to come to You and go on his way.

Daughter, be still. I have been at My job for a very long time. Trust Me.

Sorry.

She throws off the covers and scratches Champ's chin. "You are blessed to be a dog."

Evie lets Champ out. Brushing her hair, Champ slides his paw back under the closed door and whines. When she opens the door, Champ's entire body wags. He escorts her to the kitchen where Rose and Antonio are sitting. After breakfast, Evie excuses herself from the table.

Berating herself for telling Rip yes, she gets her Bible from her room and turns on the living room lamp. She doesn't have room for anxiety in her life so she finds scriptures that help comfort her.

"Okay, Evie." Antonio puts out his hand. "You take care and if I ever need a sitter for Champ, I'm calling you."

Smiling, she gets down to hug Champ. "Deal! Safe travels."

Rose wipes a tear as Antonio assures her, he will be back soon.

The ringing phone makes Evie cringe. "Anxiety, you have no place in my life."

"Hello, Rip. Yes, that's fine. I'm ready. Bye."

Rose sits with her open Bible on her lap, staring off into space. Evie leans down and hugs her.

Rose smiles weakly. "Even at his age, it's difficult to see him go. I miss my children."

"Maybe one day they'll be back."

"I sure hope so."

"Me too. I'm not sure when I'll be back tonight. A friend is coming to get me."

"Be careful. Do you know this person well?"

“Yes. Thank you for your concern.”

Hearing a car stop out front, Alfred comes out of his house. He scowls as Rip goes up the steps and Evie comes out. Rose peers out the window and Alfred glares so she smiles and waves to hopefully reassure them.

Rip waves as he opens the car door for Evie. Rose recognizes him from the day of Evie’s attack and waves back. Evie goes to Alfred and tells him that Rip is an officer and was in the military. He peeks around Evie and glares at Rip. Just before she gets in the car, Alfred tells her that her dad would want her to be careful. She nods and tells him she will.

Rip raises his eyebrows. “Everything okay?

“Yes. It’s fine. He’s harmless.”

“Does he know your father?”

“No. Well, not that I know of.”

Rip leaves the city behind as Evie tells the story of taking Alfred to breakfast and how she shared her childhood. Alfred’s knowledge of what she was talking about made her think he was a submariner too.

"I'm sorry you lost your dad when you were so young. That must've been rough."

"It was, but my mom, her family, and my dad's family did a great job taking care of my brother and me. I would have liked to grow up knowing him."

"I understand. I hope you don't mind the drive, but I need to check on something and thought we could finish the conversation from the other night."

"Do we have to leave the city for this?"

"I didn't want to leave you hanging today to take care of this. I thought it would work. I apologize. I should've asked if it was okay."

"No. It's fine. I get to see more of the area this way. I just don't want you to get the wrong idea."

"Don't you have male friends?"

Her cheeks felt hot as she chuckles nervously. "I don't really have friends. Men or women. I travel so much that I don't stay anywhere long enough for that."

"I guess that goes the same for a boyfriend then. So, good, we can be friends. At least while you are here." He glances at her.

"Friends it is."

More trees and open fields replace buildings and traffic. Their first stop is an A-Frame log cabin restaurant about ten minutes up the mountain. The wooden sign hanging over the steps to the entrance read Kitchen Corner.

"Are you hungry? Best pancakes around or if you are ready for lunch, the potato soup is good."

"Sure. Soup sounds good."

Rip opens the door for Evie. The adorable restaurant distracts her from hearing more than one person call out to Rip or Mr. Rip. The hostess tells Rip about her baby taking her first steps and shows him a quick video on her phone then leads them to their table. Before they get there, Rip stops at two tables and shakes hands with the men. One table of young women waves flirtatiously.

As he pulls out Evie's chair all the ladies bend in toward the table and whisper to each other. Evie grins.

"I'm sorry."

She shrugs. "No biggie. You're a popular man." This time he shrugs. "You must come here quite a bit."

"I try, but crime in the city keeps me busy. I'm so popular because..."

A young girl with shiny silver braces and a big smile stands next to the table.

"Mr. Rip, guess what!"

He laughs. "What?"

"Do you notice anything different about me?"

Overdramatically he rubs his chin. "You dyed your hair?" She places her hands on her hips. "Um. New shoes?" Wide-eyed, she puts her teeth together and smiles hard at him. "I'm teasing. I noticed immediately. You got contacts." Her shoulders drop and she scowls. He smiles slyly. "Your braces look great on you!"

"I know! They do, don't they? I had to get used to them but now I'm good and excited that I only have two more years to go!"

"That's fantastic. You're going to have the best teeth around."

"Thank you. What can I get you to drink?"

Rip puts his hand out toward Evie who orders water and Rip makes it two.

Evie reminds him that he was explaining why he is so popular when a man in overalls stops at the table.

"Howdy, Rip. Ma'am. Good to see you. How's business down there in the city?" Rip starts to answer but the man continues. "Best thing I ever did was leave the city and come up here. I don't regret it one bit. That crime, gosh, I'm glad you've been safe. So, when are you gonna get up here? Well, good to talk to you. Hope you move sooner than later. Take care."

When the man walks away, Rip turns to Evie. She covers her mouth so she does not laugh.

"Maybe coming here was a mistake. I don't recall this many interruptions, ever, but maybe that's because I usually eat in the back." By this time the young girl is back with their meal.

Evie suggests they finish the conversation after they leave. They make it through the meal with choppy conversation as more people stop to speak or holler out as they leave. They manage to make it out the door from the cash stand without further interruption.

He opens her door and laughs. "Hurry, get in before they see us."

Instead of going down the mountain toward the city, Rip climbs higher.

"One more stop. I promise."

Twelve minutes later, Rip turns off the main road and slowly makes his way along a narrow gravel road. He stops in front of a modest cabin with a cute front porch and two white rockers to the left of the front door.

"Should I wait here?"

"Of course not. Come in."

Father, it is a good thing I know and trust this guy. I would have been frightened if we were this far from the city. I'm still not exactly comfortable with the situation, but I trust him and more than that, I trust You.

"Coffee?"

"Sure."

He takes her on a tour of the cabin. The large main room is split with the living room in front and the kitchen in the back half. A small table with four chairs sits in the corner. The shades are drawn, but Evie imagines how beautiful the view must be. There are two identical bedrooms on either side of the house with a small bathroom with a shower. They also have tall windows on the back wall. By the look of the décor or lack thereof, Evie guesses a man lives here.

They go back to the kitchen where he hands her a cup of coffee and opens the kitchen door. She stops and gasps. Rip stops behind her. When she realizes how close he is, she steps to one side.

"Beautiful, isn't it?"

"Much more so than I imagined."

He walks to another set of white rockers facing the mountains and the city below and motions for Evie to have a seat. "We have a better chance of finishing our conversation now."

"I sure hope so." Evie laughs.

"I'm so popular at the Kitchen Corner because I own it. The young girl with the braces is fifteen and home-schools around her work schedule. Things are tough at home. Her dad was in an accident and her mom is doing what she can, but there are three younger children than Sissy at home. I put Sissy to work."

"How does a struggling family afford braces these days?"

"Her teeth are crooked, as you probably saw. She needed them." She raises an eyebrow.

"Yes. I did, but they don't know that."

Father. This man's heart is amazing. He is so kind.

Yes, Sweet daughter. He is, but he is not good with Me.

"That's nice. And your other businesses?"

"Where to begin? I'm sharing this because I trust that you'll keep it between us."

"Of course. Thank you for trusting me."

"I saw it in your eyes the other night and knew. So, I was engaged to the most loving, strong, and amazing woman. We knew we were meant to be, but God decided otherwise, I guess. Maybe he didn't think I was good enough for her pure heart. She died after a brief battle with cancer. There were no signs until about three weeks before she died. If there was anything I could find to be thankful for, it was that she didn't suffer for a long time. I know you have your faith, but mine died the night Ava died." He pauses. Evie feels his pain. "After her death, all I did was work and save. Anything the department needed, I picked up, and then there were special assignments too. I did not spend money because all I did was work. That allowed me to buy several businesses that were struggling. Since I own them, I hire who I want."

When he stops, his gaze drifts somewhere far beyond the mountains. She looks down at her hands.

"I'm sorry your fiancé passed away."

"Thanks."

"Ava is a beautiful name. I'm sure she was lovely."

He nods. In their silence, a bird sings and something under the porch rustles the leaves.

"So, I have to come clean on something. Brian, uh, Father MacKay had already invited me to the meeting before you told me about it."

Evie raised her eyebrows. "Hmm."

He grins. "I'm sorry. I wasn't ready to share my secret life until I saw your compassion. Father MacKay and I have been friends since high school. He knows about my businesses, and we work together on what we can to help others. I had to invite myself to the meeting to keep from explaining. I wasn't trying to be deceitful. That's why I wanted to talk to you."

"It's okay. You didn't know me, and you have to do what's best for you."

"You are gracious."

"I do have a question about the gas station. Why doesn't Alfred recognize you if you are his employer?"

"I don't want to be known. They haven't seen me."

"Okay. Anything else you want to share?"

Rip thinks about it for a minute. "Oh," he laughs. "Louie's is my father's restaurant where I learned the family business and Giovanni is crazy about your friend Brenda and her children."

"I already knew the last one."

Rip brings the coffee pot to Evie and asks if she is in a hurry to get back. Enjoying the tranquility, she tells him she has time. When he comes back out they sit quietly enjoying the nothingness of life.

To the right of the house, a hawk leaves his perch with a screech that slices the silence.

Rip checks his phone for the first time and sees a message from his father.

"I would love to sit here all night, but dad left me a message asking if I could help out tonight."

"So, wait a minute. You said you hadn't been to Louie's in some time. Was that a lie?"

"No, I said I haven't eaten there in a long time. I go, but only to help and then I leave."

"Oh. I see. It's okay. Yes. I need to get back. Besides, I'm sure the owner will be here soon, right?"

He looks at her like she made a joke and then realizes she is not joking.

"This is my house. I plan on retiring here."

Her cheeks flush. "Oops. When you said you had to check on something I thought you were helping someone."

When they get in the car. Rip starts it and faces Evie. "Thanks for listening about Ava and forgiving me for deceiving you."

"No worries." Evie pauses, listening to the crunch of the gravel. "What does Father MacKay think of your lost faith?"

"He respects where I am, but he is a priest and tries to get me back on track. I don't blame him, he loves me. My problem is not with Father MacKay. It's a little higher up than that."

Father. I could cry right now, but I wouldn't dare. He is upset with You. He thinks You took Ava because he wasn't good enough for her. Oh, Father, I know that's not true. Help me find the words to soften his heart toward You. He is a decent man, he just needs to find his way back to You. I'm sorry he's angry with You. Please forgive him. He's just hurting.

She wipes away a tear.

Precious daughter. Many are hurting. That's why you and others like you are sent. I hear your pleas, but He needs to be the one to ask forgiveness for himself. It's not your place. I have given him free will just as I have everyone. He needs to decide.

Another tear escapes. *Yes, Father.*

Rip tells her about Louie's and shares a couple of funny stories about encounters with different people. He has her laughing so hard she holds her sides as he tells about the day a guy he arrested applied for a cashier job. Rip walked into the room to interview him. He said he was not sure, but he felt they both had the same look on their faces. He sat across from the guy and asked if he was seriously there for the money handling job. The guy knew what he was getting at but said yes. In case the guy forgot, Rip reminded him that he was arrested for stealing.

He told Rip he had been going to church and doing his best to live what he was learning. Rip talked with his dad and although he did not get the cashier job, he was hired as a cook and is already the Assistant Kitchen Manager.

Rip parks in front of Rose's house and opens Evie's door.

She smiles. "It was a nice day. See you at the next meeting."

Nineteen

Evie places the plate she is drying back in the drainer and quickly dries her hands. She grabs her phone on the last ring.

"Hey, Brenda. Slow down, I can't understand you. Yes! Of course, I can. I'm not going to let you miss this. Saturday at four. I'll be there."

Aww, Father. I am so glad Brenda said yes to dinner with Giovanni. He is one of Yours and cares so much for her and the children. Thank You, Father. Still, something isn't right with her situation. Please continue to protect Brenda and the children. Protect Giovanni as well and let him be a blessing to her. Let them have a great first date and if it's Your will for them to be together, let everything work out for them. Although, I have a feeling Giovanni already knows something Brenda doesn't. You are so good. Thank You, Father, for allowing us enjoyment as we live this life.

She locks the door and leaves for the church. Alfred is half a block ahead of her, so she calls out to him. Surprisingly, he waits for her.

Alfred clears his throat. “Where’d that guy take you that took all day?”

“We went up the mountain and had lunch. We’re just friends. I don’t have time to be seeing anyone. I travel way too much for that.”

She decides it is best not to tell him she was alone with him at his house. Which, when she thinks about it, does sound bad.

***

Rip calls the night of the meeting and asks if he can give Evie a ride. She tells him she will walk and see him there. On her way, she says hello to a man at the bus stop who has his head down, engrossed in a magazine. At the church, Rip is leaning against his car.

“Good walk?”

“Mmhm.”

They enter the meeting room where several people are in groups talking and others sitting. There are more people than at the last meeting. Rip hands Evie a cup of coffee and then fills his.

He looks at his watch as they find a seat. "So, I hear Brenda is giving Giovanni a chance. Dinner on Saturday."

"Yes. I'm so happy. I think our girls day helped her realize it's okay to have a life and raise children. Plus, now she has Rose and me to help her."

"Are you watching the children for her Saturday?"

"Yes. It should be fun."

"Would you like me to come to help?" She is shocked at the effort it takes to tell him no when everything inside of her is saying yes.

"No. They are so well-behaved. I think I got this."

He nods.

Several more people enter the meeting room as surprised Father MacKay follows them in.

"Welcome everyone. We will begin with a word of prayer, then I will turn the meeting over to the judge. Lord, You are the creator of Heaven and earth. This is Your city before it is ours, but You brought us together for such a time as this.

Finding enough righteous people in this city You have chosen to show mercy upon us. Thank You. Lead us in the way we should go. Show us favor as we take back Your city and give ownership back to You. And as the city is restored all glory and honor is Yours. Amen. All yours, your honor."

Before the judge opens the floor for discussion, he tells them that they need a prayer team.

"I was a judge for many years, but long before I was a judge, I was a Christ-follower. My parents raised me to pray and read my Bible from an early age. As my relationship with Jesus grew, my prayers changed. I matured and realized how vital prayer was to my everyday life. By the time I started law school, I had a strong prayer life. For every decision I made in my personal life and professional career, I prayed and waited for God. I've been praying about our city for a long time. The only way we will take back our city is through prayer."

A lady close to the front raises her hand. "I would like to be a part of the prayer team."

"Great! Anyone who wants to be a part of the prayer team, we will meet for a few minutes after this meeting."

The judge then opens the floor for discussion. Every suggestion is written down. Once all the ideas are shared, they decide if it fits. If it fits, they discuss it until it is a working piece of the plan. By nine-thirty, it becomes obvious this process needs more time. The directors decide on a meeting twice a week until further notice. Before closing the meeting, the judge reminds them of the prayer team meeting.

Rip opens the car door for Evie. "I guess walking home is a thing of the past."

"Sorry. What kind of man would I be to let you walk at night?"

"Mmm." Evie concedes.

"That was productive. It may be challenging, but I'm looking forward to it."

"Like Father MacKay said God has found some to be righteous and He honors that."

"I'm sure I'm not on His list of righteous men anymore, but I still plan on being a part of restoring this city."

"You know Rip, God is in the restoring business. Not just cities, but relationships too."

"Mmm."

As Rip waits for Evie to go in the house, he rolls down the window. "If you change your mind about Saturday, give me a call."

She gives him a thumbs-up as she sees Alfred pop his head out of his house.

"Good night, Evie."

"Good night, Alfred."

Twenty

After the third ring, Evie's call goes to voicemail. "Hey, Brenda. It's Evie. I thought about coming to get the children and taking them to the playground so you can get ready for tonight. Let me know if that works for you."

Brenda calls back almost immediately. She could hardly hear the phone ringing and finally found it in the basket of toys Janie collected. Her only concern is that it will be four against one. Evie admits she is not brave enough to take four children on the bus by herself and tells her Toby will pick them up. To put Brenda's mind at ease, Evie adds the park is their only stop. She will be there just before three.

Once her plans are set, Evie pulls the drape to the side and peers out. Alfred is sitting on the step. She checks her watch then goes out and sits on the step below him.

"Hello, Alfred."

Eyes downcast, he picks at his fingernail. "I know you worried about me that time I was gone for a while. I'll be gone for three or four days so don't worry about me."

"Okay. I won't worry, but I'll pray for your safety on the trip."

He nods, grabs the gym bag next to him, and starts up the street. Evie watches him and then turns in the opposite direction, down the street.

Father, Alfred seems especially sad today. You know what's going on with him. I ask You to protect him on his trip. Keep him safe. As he travels, soften his heart, and speak to him. Comfort him as only You can do. Whatever situation he is going into, go before him and prepare the way. Be with him throughout and bring him safely back. I ask for him to find the joy You have tucked away for him inside his heart. You are kind and generous to Your children and I thank You. I love You.

My precious child, your beautiful heart fills Me with joy. I will always love you.

The love of her Heavenly Father has sustained her through life without her earthly father.

Perched at the window, the children wait for Evie. Brenda opens the door and children pour out. Brenda gives Evie a key and tells her they can stay up until she gets home because she does not plan on being late. Evie assures Brenda they will be fine as they hug her goodbye. Evie reminds Brenda to have fun.

Toby beeps and they load into the van. "Looks like the gangs all here. Where's Mom?"

"She's going out tonight and Aunt Evie's watching us." She smiles at the addition of Aunt by another sister.

"Well, where to?"

The children say, "the park!" in perfect unison. Before they get out, Evie asks Toby to come back in about two hours.

Evie sits on the bench watching them run wild. She admires that the children look out for each other. Whoever designed this park must have children. There is only one way in and out.

"Aunt Evie, push me," Janie calls out. She pushes her a couple of times but when her siblings run by playing tag, she wants to go. In the two hours there, Evie feels like her name is called seven hundred times by one or another of the children wanting to show her something or be pushed, but she doesn't mind. She feels the love.

When Toby comes back, she herds the children toward the van. Jimmy helps Janie into her booster while the other girls buckle up. Evie watches, making sure everyone is situated. She turns quickly sensing someone watching them. A man, with his ball cap low waiting at the corner, turns and crosses the street. Thinking nothing more of it she asks if chicken nuggets sound good for dinner. The children cheer.

"Toby is it possible for you to run us by to get nuggets? I don't want to put you out though."

"Of course! Anything for the littles."

The smell of nuggets and hot fries fills the van. Janie rubs her tummy. "I'm hungry."

"Almost there sweet, girl. Then we can eat."

"And sleep?"

Evie laughs. "Yes, and sleep if you want."

Not long after they eat, the two youngest fall asleep, and Evie moves them to their beds. An hour later Brenda comes in.

Jimmy and Jill are engrossed in a documentary about rare animals and give her a quick hi.

Evie follows Brenda to the kitchen where they talk in whispers.

"Well?"

"Oh, Evie. It was wonderful. He is too good to be true. There is no way such a gentleman is still single."

"There is a way if God wants you two to be together. He is waiting for the right woman; the one God has chosen for him."

"Ha. As if God would choose me for anyone, let alone a man of his character. He is perfect."

"He would. You deserve a man of his character. I'm happy for you."

Brenda looks down. "I don't deserve someone as good as him. I'm good for nothing and will let him down. It won't take long before he realizes how unstable I am. He will see how I mess everything up. He will quit coming around real quick."

Evie's heart aches for her friend.

Father, my friend has been hurt, deeply. Emotionally, mentally, and I would guess physically as well. I don't know what to say, but You do. Give me Your words. Help me please.

"Brenda, I have known you for just a short time but in this time none of those things have ever crossed my mind about you. Quite the opposite. You are amazing. You're raising four wonderful children on your own. You go to work every day and pick up extra shifts. The love you have and show your babies is undeniable. Making sure they are clothed, fed, and entertained is never an issue for you. The reason I stole you away the other day was that I'm sure you never care for yourself. And you deserve to be taken care of and loved. You are worthy of true love and happiness. It can happen to you, especially if God wants this. Contrary to what you think, God loves you and wants good things for you."

Cupping her face in her hands, so the children do not hear her weeping. She shakes her head, unable to talk as Evie holds her.

"Thank you, Evie. Thank you for your kindness and friendship."

Evie can tell Brenda did not believe a word she said.

***

Before turning out the light, Evie gets on her knees beside her bed.

I don't know if I can sleep, Father. Tonight, I saw a glimpse of the broken, beat-down woman Brenda is. When will she tell me her story? What will it take? How much more can I do to win her trust? My heart hurts for her. She needs to be set free from the lies she has been told and the way she views love. Oh, Father. She deserves to be loved.

Evie weeps as she is overwhelmed with compassion for Brenda.

Sweet daughter, your compassion and desire to help Brenda touches My heart. To answer your questions: In time, she will tell you her whole story. It will be tough to hear. It will take something big for her to tell you. But she trusts you completely. Now you need to help her trust Me. Therefore I have brought you and Giovanni to her. Giovanni is much stronger than he lets on. We are very close. She will be set free if she chooses Me.

If?

Free will My child.

Something big?

Yes. Trust Me. My peace I give you. Good night Evie, rest well. I love you.

I love and trust You, Father.

Twenty-one

Alfred comes through the serving line several days later. Evie is relieved to see him but asks no questions.

"Hi, Alfred. I'm glad you're back."

"Thanks." He takes his plate and finds a seat by himself.

Bud comes through last.

"Not a very talkative fellow, is he?'

"No, he's not."

"But it does not stop you from trying, does it?"

"No. I can't be responsible for what others do, but I am responsible for me, and I know what my Father in Heaven wants from me."

"Ah, yes. Fine Father, He is."

"Yes, He is. So, you know Him?"

"Very much so. He has been better to me than anything I could have imagined."

Evie places beans on his plate. She cannot help but marvel at the fact that he is wearing clothing that is at least one size too big for him, if not more, and that he eats at the community kitchen.

That right there, Father, is a fine example of contentment. Learning to get along happily whether we have much or little. Thank You for Bud in my life.

Wiping the tables in the dining area, Bud tells her he would enjoy talking with her more when she has time. When Father MacKay walks by, Evie asks if she and Bud can stay longer and talk. He tells her to pull the door tight behind them when they leave. As the volunteers leave, Evie sits.

"Father MacKay said we can stay if this works for you?"

"Oh, yes, it is perfect."

His blue eyes sparkle as if an overflow of joy escapes from them.

"Good. So, what's on your mind?"

"I would like to hear about you. There is something different about you."

She laughs. "I was thinking the same about you."

"You first, young lady."

Evie shares that her father died when she was eight. She was brought up with faith, but then had an experience of her own one summer at an intense youth discipleship camp when she was fifteen. She travels for work and helps people. Her bio well-rehearsed for what she wants people to know.

He asks her a few questions about her childhood and her faith and asks one more question.

"Why do you care about this city?"

"I am very fond of several people in this city and since I got here, all I hear from everyone is how great it once was. It can be great again with the right people in place. Of course, some things will take money, so it may take time. The two most important things are welcoming God back in and lots of love."

Evie shifts in her seat as he looks into her eyes. He sees all he needs to see.

"Thank you, for taking time to sit with an old guy like me. Sometimes I get lonely for good conversation."

"You're welcome, but what about you? You didn't tell me about you."

"Next time, okay? I am missing my nap."

Moving quickly for an "old guy" he hurries to the door and is gone. Evie wonders what that was all about. It was not an exciting conversation, but he left happy. She turns out the lights and pulls the door tight behind her. There is no sign of Bud. He must have needed that nap.

At the house, Evie sees Alfred's house moving. She turns the knob to go in and Alfred calls out. "Hey."

"Hey, Alfred."

She goes in and finds Rose in the kitchen. Evie sits at the table and Rose pours her some coffee. She tells Rose about the odd, one-sided conversation. Rose says he looks familiar, but she does not know why.

As Rose tells Evie about the call from her daughter, they hear sirens approach. Nothing new in this area, but they do not go past.

"Rose, they are close," Evie runs to the door and Rose follows.

She opens the door to see an officer over Alfred's crumpled body with blood splatters all around him on the sidewalk. Horrified, she cannot speak. Evie goes down the steps to him.

An officer stretches his arm, palm out in front of her. "Ma'am I am going to need you to stay back. The ambulance is on the way."

Oh, Father! No!

A fourth patrol car pulls up and Rip jumps out. "Evie!" He looks up and sees Rose in the doorway hands over her mouth, tears in her eyes. The officer steps out of Rip's way so he can get to Evie.

"Alfred."

Rip turns back to the officer tending to Alfred.

"Evie, don't repeat anything. He has a pulse and the officers are doing what they can until the ambulance arrives. Officers were patrolling the area. They were up the street when they spotted a man violently kicking something. They got closer and the man took off running. An officer ran after him and hasn't come back yet. Another unit is in the area with him assisting."

Sirens get closer. Rip checks on Rose where she sits on the step and then goes back to Evie as she prays for her friend.

"Can I go with him? He has no family."

Rose comes down the steps. "He does have family. He has a daughter. I'll call her."

"Really? Well, I can ride over and stay until she gets here."

"Hang on." Rip talks to the EMT as they prepare to load Alfred into the ambulance. "They said you can, but you need to ride up front in the cab. Why don't you let me drive you and we will follow them? Giovanni can hop in the back." Giovanni nods.

Evie looks at Rose. "Would you rather go?"

"No. You go on. I will call his daughter and wait for her to get here."

"Okay then. Thank you."

Alfred wavers between consciousness as they get him in the ambulance. The EMT tells Giovanni that Alfred needs prayer.

"Evie, let's pray now." As they follow behind the ambulance Giovanni prays for Alfred. Rip pulls a napkin from the glove box for Evie to wipe her eyes.

"That was powerful." Evie dabs her eyes again.

Rip stops behind the ambulance and tells Evie he will be back when his shift ends. She tells him there is no need. Evie follows behind the stretcher, but a nurse who met the EMT tells Evie to go to the waiting room and that someone will talk to her soon.

Oh, Father. Lead them to the evil man who did this. Why would anyone want to hurt Alfred? He has nothing of value. He doesn't bother anyone. Please minister to him. Let there be no brain damage or other internal injuries. Help him remember well enough to describe the man who beat him. Bring his daughter here safely.

Shortly the nurse leads her to Alfred's room and tells Evie to prepare herself because he looks much worse than he is and he is heavily sedated. Evie gasps when she walks into the room.

Both eyes are swollen and red, with some dark purple at the bottom of the bruising, pieces of stitching stick out under his right eye, and from under a white wrap around his head, part of a knot on his forehead is visible. Most of his ear is under the wrap, but what can be seen, reveals a torn earlobe. A cast on his arm covers from just under his fingers past his elbow.

The nurse tells Evie his body is bruised. Once they get his results, they will know if there is any internal damage. Evie thanks the nurse and sits beside Alfred.

"Alfred, it's me, Evie. I'm here with you. I am going to lay my hand on you and pray. Gracious, Heavenly Father, You are the only one who can heal Alfred. You are with him now and always and I ask You to comfort him and begin the healing process in his body. Internal organs line up with the Word of God and work the way you were created to work. You are rejuvenating as he rests and all results will be normal. None of this will cause any lasting issues, and Alfred you are healed and whole. Father, when he is able, he will recall, with complete clarity, what happened and describe the man. Alfred,

I speak life over your body and believe you will have an amazing testimony to share about the goodness of God. In Jesus Name, Amen."

Evie squeezes his hand when Rose calls to tell her that his daughter should be in town in a few hours.

"Alfred, Rose called. Your daughter is on her way."

Both Brenda and Father MacKay visit in the next hour. Father MacKay hugs Evie.

"Rip called. I'm here to pray for Alfred and keep you company. I see how he is, but how are you?"

"Concerned."

"Okay, let's pray."

The authority by which Father MacKay prays calms Evie. She knows Alfred will be fine. Father MacKay shares about his first encounter with Alfred when he met him at the community kitchen.

Rip comes in and hands Evie a bottle of water. She opens it, takes a sip, and nods. Rip walks with Father MacKay as he leaves.

Evie was ready for him when he came back into the room. "You told him to come here for me as much as to pray for Alfred, didn't you?"

"You were upset when I last saw you. I thought he would be good company for both of you."

"Mhmm, thanks. You have plenty of other things to do. We are fine. You can go."

"We? He doesn't look fine. Besides Evie, he's my employee, remember?"

"Oh. Yeah."

Father, why does he have to be so kind and thoughtful?

"Well, I know Alfred is going to leave this hospital healed and whole."

A woman, a little younger than Evie walks into the room.

"I hope so. Evie?"

"Yes. Alfred's daughter?"

She nods. "I'm Willow. Thank you for sitting with him."

"It's my pleasure. He is heavily sedated and not responding right now."

Willow stands beside the bed and looks down at him. She wipes her eye with her sleeve.

"Alfred. Can you hear me? I'm here with you."

Evie and Rip exchange looks. Evie walks to the door. "I guess I'll go and leave you to your dad. Did you drive to Gidesha City?"

"No, I rode the bus and then got a cab to Rose's house. I rode the bus to the hospital."

Evie gives Willow her contact information. "If it is after dark, please call me. I have a friend who drives a taxi."

Willow nods. "Thank you."

Rip touches Evie's arm. "I know you haven't eaten. Would it be okay if I drive you and we pick up something on the way to the house? If I'm still there when Willow calls, I'll come back for her." When she hesitates, he adds, "Sound good, friend?"

She half-smiles. "Sure, friend." She turns to Willow. "Are you okay? Is there anything I can do for you?"

"No. I'm fine."

"Okay. If your dad wakes up will you let us know?"

She nods and sits by his bed.

Rip talks to the officer sitting outside the door. As they walk to the car, he asks if Chinese is good. She is hungry, tired, and agreeable. He calls the order in, then glances at her bloodshot eyes in silence.

Back at the house, Rose is in the living room. As she asks how Alfred is, she sees the bag of food and points to the kitchen and tells him to help himself. On the way to the kitchen, Evie updates her.

Rose sits at the table with them and gives every detail from calling Willow to her leaving for the bus stop. Rip hangs on her every word.

Evie reaches for a Crab Rangoon. "Do you know what kind of relationship Alfred and Willow have?"

"No. Alfred tells me very little. Today was the first time I met Willow. Alfred gave me her number and her my number, in case of emergency. I never used it until today."

Rip's police instincts kick in. "You don't know this person and you're letting her stay here?"

"Of course, I know her. She's Alfred's daughter." Evie giggles and Rip looks at her.

"I'm sorry. I know it's not funny. It must be the exhaustion catching up with me. We'll be fine. You met her Rip. She didn't seem like a murderer."

"And what does a murderer seem like? What if she's a thief."

"Oh, honey, nothing worth stealing here. She can have it if she wants it."

Rip shakes his head.

"I've already cleared a spot and set up a cot upstairs. It's not a big spot, but I don't need much room. Willow can have my room."

"Oh no, Rose. I will stay upstairs while Willow is here. It won't take me long to move my things."

"Now honey…"

Evie shakes her head. "No disrespect, but I will be sleeping upstairs on the cot while Willow is here."

"Well okay."

"The reason I ask about their relationship is that she called him Alfred. That seems very impersonal, but she was crying. She asked him if he could hear her and said she is here for him. It almost seems like she cares about him but does not know him."

"Excuse me while I take this call." Rip goes to the living room and comes back in a flash. "Come on Evie! He's awake and frantic looking for you. They had to strap him to the bed."

"Oh, no!" Evie grabs her purse and hurries behind Rip.

Waiting for the elevator seems like an eternity. When the door opens, Evie makes a beeline to Alfred's room. Evie pleads with the nurse to remove the straps as she makes her way to Alfred's side.

"Aww, Evie! You're okay." He lays back, as his body relaxes tears roll down the sides of his face and onto the pillow. Rip asks the nurse if she is authorized to release the straps then steps into the hall to make a call. He asks the officer outside the door to step into the room in case Alfred says anything of importance. When he comes back everyone is in the same spot and Alfred is calm from the meds.

"The investigator's on his way. He'll need to talk to everyone who was in the room when Alfred woke. Including you and me, Evie." Her face is pale and there is a crease between her eyebrows. Rip sits by her.

"Why would Alfred be worried if I am okay?"

The nurse removes the straps and leaves. Rip told Evie earlier in the day that the investigator is one of the best. The investigator sets up in a vacant office and begins the interviews with the nurse and finishes with Rip since Alfred is groggy from the medicine.

"Your friend looks shook up."

Rip paces. "She brought up a good point. Why is he so concerned about her?"

"We'll figure it out. You know it."

"Yeah, but will we get the guy?"

"You know as well as I do. I wish I could tell you yes, but we know how that goes too."

It is late when the investigator finishes. Evie, realizing Willow is torn about staying, tells her that she will stay because Alfred will wake up looking for her again. Rip offers to take Willow to Rose's house. Evie's heart drops just a little but then she reminds herself that her friend has a life and career he needs to tend to and her Father is here for her.

Evie hugs Willow who seems surprised but hugs back. Evie thanks Rip.

When everyone is gone, except the officer outside the door, she kicks off her shoes and rests on the sofa. Exhausted, she sleeps.

Disoriented, she wakes to Alfred shouting her name and trying to get out of bed.

"Alfred. I'm here. I'm right here. I'm okay."

"Evie. You're okay. He didn't get you."

"No one got me. I'm right here with you." Evie takes his big calloused hand in hers. She wants to ask a million questions, but she knows he needs to stay calm. She looks across Alfred and sees Rip who looks like he is recording.

Alfred closes his eyes for a long moment. "Evie, I'm glad you're okay. He wasn't going to get to you. I felt something burn my chest, which stunned me. Then maybe a rock hit my face. I tried to get up, but he kept kicking me and then I don't know what happened."

Evie covers her mouth as emotions flood her. "But you did save me. Here I am. On this side of the bed, not in it like you." She sobs knowing whatever happened, Alfred took what was coming for Evie.

Father, why? This innocent man took this beating so I wouldn't suffer. Who am I to him? Why would he do it?

My precious daughter, sounds like another familiar story, doesn't it? Alfred loves you. I will take what the enemy has done and make something beautiful from it. You are loved and I am with you always.

Yes, Father. It is a familiar story. I thank You for all Jesus has done for me. Thank You for Alfred and what You will be doing next. I love You.

Rip continues to record until the investigator gets there.

"I just sent you a video of him waking up." Rip hits send and then stands by Evie.

The investigator nods. "Alfred, hey. I'm Doug. I'm working on your case. Do you feel like answering a few questions?"

"Did you get him?"

"No. He ran. The officers went after him, but he got away."

"Then Evie's still in trouble. He was looking for her." Evie tenses and Rip puts his arm around her shoulders.

Doug asks a few questions but Alfred gets agitated. "Okay. How about you just tell me what happened? Don't leave anything out because it may be important to finding the guy and keeping Evie safe."

"I was at my house and this guy starts up the steps. I have never seen him before. I got between him and the steps. He said he was here for Evie, so I asked who he was and what he wanted with her. He was taking her on a date. I asked where his car was and he got short with me. He said they were taking the bus downtown. I told him Evie never said anything about you and he pushed me aside. I didn't like his attitude. She travels too much. I knew Evie wasn't going on a date because she said she doesn't have time for that stuff when I asked her about him." He points at Rip. "I was worried for Evie because his face got distorted. When he tried to go back up the steps, I grabbed him by the back of the shirt and he hit me in the chest with, I guess a taser. I never felt one before, but it was burning my chest. When I bent over, he slugged me in the face with something hard like a rock and I went down. The last thing I remember is he was kicking and punching me."

Doug looks over his notes. "Did he call Evie by name?"

"Yes. He said he was here for Evie."

"Can you describe him? When neither of you was on the steps, was he your height?"

Alfred focuses on a spot on the wall and squints. "I don't remember. I'm sorry Evie. How can I keep you safe if I don't remember?"

Evie takes his hand again. "You kept me safe and now I know I must be more careful. That's all."

"I owe it to your dad to keep you safe. He wouldn't like it if something happened to you, and neither would I."

Rip steps closer to the bed. "You're a hero, Alfred. You already did the most important thing. You didn't let the man get Evie. We'll catch him, but until then we'll keep her safe. I'm sorry this happened. Thank you for protecting her."

Doug asks a few more questions as Evie and Rip step out of the room. Out of Alfred's sight, she weeps into Rip's chest as he holds her. Her breathing slows and she steps back.

She looks up at Rip. "Why is someone after me? Does he want to hurt me?"

He shakes his head. "I don't know. Has anything happened since you've been here? Have you made someone angry?"

She pauses for a moment, then her eyes widen. "Well, it may be just a coincidence, but one day there was a car sitting out front of the house. The person in the driver's seat was behind a newspaper. I never saw their face. Then I thought I saw the same car crossing the intersection near the house. It may not be anything though."

"Do you remember anything about the car?"

She half-smiles. "Um. It was green and older."

He grins. "Okay."

Doug comes out of the room. "I'm through. He is asking for you, Evie. He's worried something will happen to you."

She nods. "Okay. Thank you." Rip waits for her to go back into the room.

Evie holds Alfred's hand. "Listen, I'm not afraid. I talk to my Heavenly Father all the time. I am protected by Him. He is my refuge, my place of safety. My trust is in Him."

"I knew Him once."

"He still knows you and is waiting for you to return to Him."

"How do you know that?"

"I told you, I talk to Him all the time. We talk about you."

He turns his head and looks out the window as a tear rolls down his chin. She squeezes his hand.

"He loves you, Alfred. He's right here waiting for you to decide."

Willow comes in with Rip following.

Ugh! Father, He is so close to turning back to You. He knows You are what he needs. In Your timing. You are always working. Thank You for the time I spent alone with him and the opportunity to talk about You.

"Alfred!" Willow hugs him.

"What are you doing here?"

"Rose called. I came right away. How do you feel?"

"Sore. Thanks for coming. I love you."

Willow chews on her bottom lip. "You're welcome. I was worried about you."

When Willow does not return his love, Evie realizes their relationship is definitely strained. Evie suggests leaving so they can visit, but he objects and tries to get up.

"Okay. I will sit here on the sofa."

Rip in officer mode, tells her he will be back and makes it clear she is not to leave the hospital at all and not to leave the room alone. She nods and appreciates his concern. There is very little conversation between Willow and Alfred which makes Evie sad.

Daughter, it's time for you to get involved. Talk to Willow. Ask her how long it took to get here and what she does for a living. You will know where to go from there.

Alfred has his eyes closed.

“So, Willow, did it take long to get here?”

“It was five hours by bus. I have a car, but I’m not sure it would make it. I started a new job not long ago and hope to get a better car soon.”

“What do you do?”

“I help veterans get the help they need to live a successful life.”

Willow waited for the opportunity to work at this company for over a year. For the first month she was in training, then had a small caseload to start. Her eyes sparkle when she talks about helping them find stability in their mental health, housing, and community. Once they are established and all their needs are met, they can stay with the program or go their own way.

“That sounds amazing. Did your dad and his situation have anything to do with your decision to work there?”

“Not initially. But all veterans, in general, deserve the best. They leave everything behind to defend our country. They have a deep affection and dedication for this country and shouldn't suffer when they need something. Alfred served his country. He paid his dues and it cost him everything. I want to help him, but he doesn't want to move there."

"Is this a local company?"

"They have branches around the country but want to add more as they can."

"Are you tied to where you live?"

She frowns and tears rim her eyes. "No. Not anymore. Mom passed away a couple of weeks ago. Alfred was by her side and stayed with me for the service, but I couldn't convince him to stay. I have a few friends, but nothing keeping me there. Well, except my job."

"I'm sorry to hear about your mom. It sounds like you have a great job."

Alfred's voice makes them both jump and he flashes Willow a rare smile. "I'm so proud of you. Thank you for taking care of my brothers and sisters."

"I could be helping you too if you come back with me. There's nothing here for you."

He shakes his head and looks back out the window.

Twenty-two

Laughter in the hall lightens the mood inside Alfred's room. Janie breaks free from Jimmy's hand and comes running to Evie.

"Janie, what are you doing?" Evie laughs as she picks her up. Brenda rolls her eyes and apologizes for Janie rushing into the room.

Alfred moves his bed up so he could hold Janie's outstretched hand. Evie introduces everyone, but Jimmy stays in the doorway. Evie approaches, whispers, he looks at her. In his big sad eyes, she sees a faint twinkle as he mumbles. He nods and goes to the side of the bed.

"Mr. Alfred. I'm sorry for being mean to you and throwing rocks at you after you helped me with the mean boys," he whispers.

"Takes a lot of courage to apologize. I forgive you."

Alfred puts out his hand to Jimmy. "Thank you for keeping Aunt Evie safe too."

Evie looks at Brenda. "We stopped by Rose's house looking for you. Little ears must have been listening. Are you scared?"

"Not at all."

"Really?"

"My Father is my refuge and place of safety. I trust Him."

"Still, that's pretty brave."

When the nurse brings Alfred his meal, Willow says she is going down to the cafeteria.

"I'm hungry." Janie rubs her belly.

Evie decides to stay. She does not want to cause Alfred any more stress. Instead, she asks Brenda if she wants to take the children and go with Willow and bring something back for Evie. She gives Brenda money and mouths "my treat." Brenda agrees, but Jimmy stays with Evie.

Oh, Father. The love of all these men wanting to protect me. I know You are the only One who can keep me safe, but it is so sweet and kind. Thank You for placing all these sweethearts in my life.

My brave girl! I love you. Alfred is ready. He has so much running through his head right now, but his heart is soft.

"Are you not hungry, Alfred?" He shakes his head, staring out the window. "What is it?"

"It's you, Evie."

"But I'm okay and will be okay because…"

"I know! God is your protector."

"Exactly."

"Where was God when your dad died and left you fatherless? It should have been me!"

Surprised, Evie steps closer to the bed, takes Alfred's hand, and looks at Jimmy sitting on the sofa. Not sure if she should ask him to leave, she lets him stay. She wonders if the medicine is causing him to talk like this.

"I wouldn't want you to have taken his place. It was my dad's ordained time to go."

"No. It was mine. I was the reason your dad was asked to stay on the sub."

Alfred draws back his hand and stares out the window.

Evie walks between Alfred and the window and looks in his eyes. "What do you mean?"

"I, it was me. I was the sick person who couldn't go to sea. I got your dad killed. You should hate me, and I understand. I'm so sorry."

Evie gasps. "You know this for sure?"

"Yes."

Alfred explains he got orders that he was to leave in two days. Knowing he would not see land again for some time, he and his friends went into the city. It was getting late, and he was ready to go, but his friends were not. Since he didn't drive, he decided to walk and then catch a cab. He accidentally walked up on a drug deal. Before he knew it three more guys came out of the shadows behind him.

After they beat him and one of them stabbed him in the stomach, they threw him into a dumpster and left him for dead. If was not for a kid looking for food in the dumpster the next day, he would have gone to the dump that evening. Officers never found Alfred's wallet, so there was no one to contact and he laid up in the hospital for two days after Evie's dad left in his place.

Help me, Holy Spirit.

I'm here, My daughter. My peace is yours. Rest here a minute.

It felt like hours that she stood in the presence of her Father. She felt a sweeter love than she ever experienced, and peace overpowered her heart and mind.

Precious Evie, love Alfred. He has lived in torment and despair since the day he heard the news of the loss. It's time for him to heal and it will begin with your response today. Alfred thinks your dad died that day, but he didn't. He is alive and well here with Me. My children don't live then die; they live then live even better.

My daddy is alive and well. Thank You, Father.

Only a few minutes had passed. Alfred looks toward the window with tears soaking his hospital gown.

Evie takes a deep breath. "Alfred..."

Saying his name opens the floodgate. She can barely make out his words.

"Evie, I'm so sorry. I want to protect you, but I did the most to hurt you."

Evie rubs the top of his hand, and he tries to draw it back, but she holds on instead. "Alfred, my dad's death was not your fault. You didn't do anything to the submarine. You did nothing wrong in going to the city before your deployment. My dad could have said no, and they would have found someone else. I'm not mad at you. You are my precious friend and I love you."

"How can you?"

"Oh, Alfred. How can I not? My Father in Heaven has been slow to anger, patient, kind, gracious, and loving to me. Who am I not to show that same grace to others? Especially my friends."

He looks at Evie and slowly nods his head. "I don't understand but thank you."

She pats his hand and lets go. "You're welcome. But Alfred, now you need to forgive yourself."

Alfred nods and sits his bed up straighter. "It's time."

“It sure is. Begin by asking forgiveness for walking away and ask God to restore you to right-standing with Him. Surrender your whole heart to Him and ask Him to help you forgive yourself. I’m proud of you!”

Alfred closes his eyes. As he spends time with Jesus, tears stream down his face. He opens his eyes, nods, and smiles at Evie.

She hugs him. “The angels in Heaven are rejoicing!”

Rip walks in. “Hey, Jimmy. You driving now?”

“Naw. Mom and my sisters are here. They’re getting food.”

Rip nods. “You good, Evie?”

“Absolutely!”

“And you, Alfred?” He gives a thumbs-up. “Well, good then.”

The others come back and Jimmy tears into his sandwich. Evie sets hers to the side as the room fills with chatter. Evie is hopeful the attacker left the area, but she doubts it can be that easy.

Twenty-three

Rip turns off the car in front of the house. Convincing Alfred that Evie would be safe was a battle. Rip told him he would watch over her as much as she would tolerate.

"As much as I will tolerate, huh?"

"For my friend, I would live on the sofa at Rose's house to keep you safe."

"Yes. I believe you would. Please don't take this wrong because I know you are a man of honor, but you are just a man. As much as I trust you, I trust my Father to protect me so much more. He has been faithful and constant in my life and since He tells me He will never leave me, He won't stop now."

"I know and understand, but it's difficult for me since I prayed and Ava died anyway."

Compassion floods her. "I know. But did He let anything happen to me when the guy pulled a gun on me outside of the church? Did He let this guy get me when he tried? I call Him my Father for a reason. Just as a natural father would protect his child, my Father does too, and more. In the book of Matthew chapter seven, it talks about the sinful, that's us, giving good gifts to our children, and how much more our Father gives good gifts to us if we ask. I ask Him for everything, including protection."

Looking out the rear window, Rip watches as a patrol car pulls up behind him.

"I still won't rest easy."

"If anything happens to make me uncomfortable or fearful, I will let you know, and then we can discuss other measures. Will that work and help you rest easier?"

"It's a deal, but I won't be resting easier until this guy is put away. Hang on a minute." He gets out to talk to the officer behind him then walks around and opens Evie's door. She tells him bye and walks towards the steps. She does not hear his door close, so she turns around. Her nose in his chest.

Rip smiles. "Too much?"

Stepping back, she looks up into his eyes. How can she be aggravated with someone so concerned for her safety? "That officer has our back right now, right?"

"Yes."

"Follow me. Not that I must tell you that, but anyway." She stops on the top step. "Give me your hands. Gracious, Heavenly Father. Thank You for placing my wonderful, brave friend Rip in my life for such a time as this. He is dedicated to keeping me safe, so I ask You to place Your angels around him. To go before and behind him and protect him on all sides. Give him the wisdom to do his job well. Now Father I ask that You calm him. May he feel at peace knowing that I am Your precious daughter, and You love me more than anything and will protect me always. Help him receive this so he does not worry and can do the job that You created him to do and do it well. You are good and faithful, and I trust You Father. I love You. I ask this in Jesus' Name. Amen."

When she opens her eyes, he is staring at her. He hugs her, tells her good-night, and stops by the patrol car one more time before he waves and drives away.

***

In the two weeks since Alfred's beating, things return to normal, except for Alfred who is recovering inside Rose's house. Even Rip relaxes some after Evie prayed for him. It may have helped that she promised to stay close to home more than usual. Brenda, the children, Rip and Giovanni came to visit several times and Rose loved having the house full. Willow left after the first week and Alfred wanted to go back to his house, but she persuaded him to stay the second week with Rose.

***

Knowing Evie is tired of restrictions, Rip invites Evie, Giovanni, Brenda, and the children up to the mountain house for the day. Evie rides with Giovanni, squeezed between Jess and Janie in the second row of seats.

Leaving the town behind, Evie says, "Wait until you see the view from his back porch. It is stunning." Both Giovanni and Brenda turn to look at her.

Brenda's right eyebrow arches. "What are you not telling me?"

"It's not like that. We, um." Brenda cocks her head. "Brenda, stop. It's not like that. He wanted to finish a conversation we had to end because it was late. He asked if I minded talking while he took care of some things. I had no idea the things were going to be out of town and up a mountain."

Evie sees Giovanni's eyes in the rearview mirror and knows he is smiling. Brenda crosses her arms as she looks at Evie. "Mmhm."

Evie pauses between each word. "We are just friends. That's all we are and all we will ever be. So, keep all those matchmaking ideas out of your head."

Janie looks at Evie who is not laughing. "Mommy, what's so funny?"

"Aunt Evie, sweetie. Your Aunt Evie is so funny."

Janie looks back at Evie. She kisses Janie on her head and whispers, “Your mommy is the funny one.”

The children run and play in the woods. After a while, they drag into the house to see what is going on. Realizing nothing fun is happening, they race out the back door to sit on the porch. They never had so much freedom to run before.

Janie is nominated spokesperson and sent back into the house. “Um. Excuse me.” She dramatically rubs her stomach. “I’m hungry.”

Brenda rolls her eyes at Evie. “Janie, sweetie, poor thing. You look so pitiful; it must have been all that playing.” They hear giggles at the back door.

Rip takes Janie’s hand and walks toward the front door. “Well, Janie, since you’re hungry, I’m going to take you to a favorite place of mine for lunch.” Janie’s eyes get wide. This was not the way they planned it. “There is lunch meat in the fridge for when everyone else gets hungry.”

The three older children almost knock each other down trying to get in the back door. Talking over each other they announce they are hungry too.

Rip regains his composure. "I know just the place."

Heading down the mountain, he leads them to the Kitchen Corner where they have lunch with fewer disruptions. After lunch, they go back to the house where Rip puts up a badminton net and sets out a corn hole game. An intense game of cornhole ensues between Brenda and Rip while Giovanni plays badminton with the three older children. As Evie and Janie follow a trail into the woods, Evie hears Rip tell her not to get lost.

"Aunt Evie, do you know who God is?"

Evie tries to keep a poker face but is joyful about the conversation. "Yes, sweet girl, I do. Do you?"

"Yep, but Mommy doesn't. Ms. Rose read me stories about Jesus."

My child, you are right. I've planned for Janie to have an encounter like yours when you were young. This is all a part of My plan.

Oh, wow, Father! My heart! I knew she was special. Thank You for this sweet blessing.

"That is wonderful. You are going to grow up knowing how much Jesus loves you and you will do great things. And we will be in Heaven together one day. Your Mommy will know Him too someday. We better get back, so they don't worry."

Walking out of the woods they hear cheering and Janie scampers ahead. She joins in cheering Brenda on in the final minutes of the cornhole match. There is silence as she throws, then the crowd erupts into cheers as Brenda makes the toss. Rip puts out his hand to congratulate his opponent and humbly accepts defeat. The children drag Rip and Giovanni to the badminton game while Evie and Brenda sit on the rockers on the front porch enjoying the afternoon breeze. Janie climbs up in Brenda's lap as the gentle sway of the rocker puts her to sleep.

Brenda makes sure Janie is asleep then whispers, "I'm scared, Evie."

"Scared? About what?"

"Giovanni. I, I really like him."

"What about it makes you scared? He loves your children and more importantly treats you with such tenderness and affection." Brenda looks away. "What is it? You can tell me."

Jess trips over a tree root and falls. Bleeding, she starts to cry. Brenda places Janie in Evie's lap and follows Giovanni as he carries Jess into the house.

Rip strolls over to the porch. "It might be a good time to put steaks and hot dogs on the grill and start a movie."

"Maybe."

Rip pulls up the poles of the badminton net and Jimmy helps gather the birdies, rackets, and bean bags for cornhole. Rip decides to have him help with the grill, along with Giovanni.

Jess unnecessarily props her leg with a tiny band aid on it on a stool as they watch tv.

"Do you have a relationship with Jesus?" Evie asks as she cuts onions while she and Brenda get things together for dinner.

"Wow. Where did that come from?"

"Well, I figure you can either answer that question, or we can finish the conversation started on the porch."

"No. I don't. I've been through a lot." She avoids eye contact with Evie. "I don't believe God would make someone go through all that, but after becoming friends with you and seeing your faith, I might consider hearing what you have to say…someday."

Giovanni pops his head in the door. "Onions and mushrooms ready yet?" Brenda hands them to Giovanni and leaves with him. Evie shakes her head as she follows.

This is a tough crowd, Father. Just when I think I am getting somewhere, I'm thrown a curveball.

Standing by the railing, Brenda looks out over the city below. "It's been a nice day, Rip. The children have never experienced such freedom to run and roam. It seems like the perfect place to raise children." Rip glances at Evie as Brenda pauses. "Thank you for having us."

"My pleasure. It's one of my favorite places to be."

After dinner, Rip looks at the children. "How about ice cream?"

Brenda is barely audible over the pleas of the children. "Sure, why not? We don't do this very often, so let's celebrate."

As they eat their ice cream, the sun dips behind the trees.

Looking at her watch, Brenda herds the children into Giovanni's car. After seeing them out Evie helps Rip straighten the house. On the drive back, Evie closes her eyes, wishing she was in bed.

Rip pulls in front of the house and turns off the car. "I'd like to come in for a minute if that's okay."

"I'm really sleepy. I was fighting to stay awake."

"No. The way you were snoring, I'd say you were asleep."

Eyes wide, she covers her mouth. "Nah-uh."

He starts to laugh. "I'm playing."

"Why do you want to come in? Rose would have called me if there was a problem." She sighs. "You're not going away, are you?" He shakes his head slowly. "Come on then."

Rose and Alfred look up as the door creaks open. In the middle of the coffee table, sits a deck of cards.

"See, Rip. Nothing going on here but a friendly game of cards. By the way Alfred, I like seeing you in the house."

"Thanks, but don't get used to it. I'm feeling almost as good as new." He winks at Evie.

Rose stands. "Would you like to stay for coffee? Alfred, don't look at my cards. Evie, watch him. Come on in the kitchen, Rip."

Evie shakes her head. "It's a conspiracy."

"What's a conspiracy, honey?"

"You two. I just want to go to sleep."

"Oh honey, then just go to sleep. He is here to play cards with us anyway."

Rip balls up his fist and places his knuckles across his mouth to keep from laughing.

"Uh." Evie starts laughing with them. "Goodnight."

"You said you like seeing me in the house. Stay with us. Sit here." Alfred pats the cushion next to him.

"You're in on this too? Unbelievable."

Twenty-four

Rip comes by the house and takes Evie to the meeting. Tonight, they are breaking the city into different sections and looking for leaders and teams to work inside each section. At the bottom of the steps, a sign says the meeting has been relocated to the sanctuary since they outgrew the meeting room.

Rip finds a seat near the front. “This is a good sign.”

“Yeah. A very good sign.” Evie looks around. “I’d say word got out.”

Father MacKay opens in prayer and turns the meeting over to the judge.

The lights dim. On the screen behind the judge appears a map of the city, broken into four sections.

“Welcome, everyone! Good to see so many interested in taking back our fine city. Let’s get right down to business. As you see we have lines drawn dividing the city. These are not set in stone. With as many people as we have here, we could make smaller sections and accomplish more. If you live in one of the sections and would like to lead a team, you are more than welcome. Of course, there will be strictly non-residential areas as well, so keep that in mind too. I am going to ask this question then as judges like to say 'take a fifteen-minute recess and reconvene' at seven o'clock to discuss your thoughts. If you are interested in leading a team, I will ask you to come to the front. Please keep in mind how much work will be involved and decide accordingly. See you back here at seven."

Evie stands. "Would you like a refill? I'm getting one."

"That would be great, thanks."

He watches Evie, wondering what kind of woman would spend her off-hours from work at a meeting to better a city where she does not even live.

"Thank you," he says as she slides back in the pew.

"It makes it easy since we drink it the same way."

Evie knows she cannot lead a team. She could wrap this up and be gone within days. She doubts Rip would lead a team, but then again, he has been involved in this long before these meetings started. It seems important to him, but then again this is home.

Father, move in the hearts of those You want to lead this city into Your plan of restoration. Place a passion within that burns so deep they cannot remain sitting when the judge calls for leaders. Then guide them. Thank You for caring about this city and its people. Thank You for not giving up on this city. Thank You for revival! Soon You will be in Your rightful place here and not squeezed out by the corrupt and evil ones. I love You.

The judge comes back to the front. "Okay folks. Let's take our seats and prepare to take back our city." When everyone settles, he begins. "Hopefully you had some time to think about the kind of a commitment it will take to be a leader. Remember, we don't know exactly what this will look like, it's new to all of us. Anyone interested in leading, please come to the front."

As she turns to say something to Rip about a third of the sanctuary heading to the front, she finds herself talking to the back of him as he joins the others. The judge turns to the other directors. Palms up, the woman shrugs, and the man smiles.

"Being a judge all my life and seeing and hearing many things, I don't think there was a single time I was speechless, but right now, I'm pretty close." He wipes his eyes. "Excuse me. I've gotten to be a softy since having grandchildren." The audience laughs. "But seriously. This is a blessing. We were concerned we would not have enough leaders for the four sections and now we can make smaller ones."

The man in the three-piece suit sits down at the computer and removes the map from the screen. As he quickly reworks the sections according to the number of leaders, the judge sends everyone back to their seats. He tells them once the sections are reworked; team leaders will be chosen and before they leave they will know which of the three directors they will report to.

"Our goal is to bring people in our assigned sections together as a community. This, in turn, will make us stronger to remove the corruption and filth from our city and return this city to God. Find new ways to bring people together. Have your team go out and pick up trash. Wave to those that look at you and talk to those who talk to you. Tell them what you are doing. Tell them you want to be proud of your city again. Ask if they want to help. That's just one idea, but I know we have some creative geniuses here. Also, if you can stay after the meeting to set up your teams, that would be great. Please email us team information once you have it together."

The man in the three-piece suit turns the screen on and steps away from the computer. After the judge takes a minute to look at the updated areas, he turns back to the crowd and begins at the northwest area and asks whoever wants that section to stand. Once a leader is established, he or she goes to the female director and provides contact information. If there are two or more for the same area, he asks them to decide amongst themselves. This continues until only one area is left; the northeast portion of the city, where Rose lives. Rip stands and is appointed leader.

When he comes back to his seat, he smiles sheepishly at Evie. "Will you be my second in charge? I know you will be gone when your job is over, but I am taking into consideration how much you care about a city that does not belong to you."

"Um."

"I need help and you would be perfect."

Yes, My sweet daughter. The answer is yes.

"Of course. I'd like that."

It is decided that even though each section has a leader, they will continue to meet as a group once a week, at least in the beginning. They can share ideas, talk about what they are doing with their team, and encourage each other. The judge also encourages teams to work together or help other teams. When everything is done, Father MacKay asks Evie to pray.

"Heavenly Father, You are good and gracious. We know 2 Chronicles 7:14 says, 'Then if My people who are called by My name will humble themselves and pray and seek My face and turn from their wicked ways, I will hear from Heaven and will forgive their sins and heal their land.' We know that if the people humble themselves, pray, and seek You, You will hear them, forgive them, and heal this city. We know if they don't You will protect us, Your faithful followers, and deliver us from the minions of evil who will fight us for what they think is theirs. Place Your angels around us as we bring the light that cuts through the darkness covering this city. Produce in us a boldness to do what You need us to do in this city as we stand against the evil one. Have them see there are more on our side than theirs. We stand before You in agreement that Gidesha City belongs to You. It is all Yours and we are Your vessels. Direct our steps, give us Your wisdom, and allow Your goodness and love to flow through us to the people of this city. In Jesus' Name. Amen."

Even though it is late, very few leave once the meeting is over.

"Hey, Brian. Uh, Father MacKay, are you going to join our team?"

"I'd like that. Rip, Evie, this is Sean and Patrick, they are my two oldest altar boys. They serve well and would like to be on your team. Is that okay?"

"Definitely." Rip shakes their hand. "Nice to meet you guys."

Rip sees a few people not talking to any team leaders and asks if they need a team. When they say yes, he invites them over. He sets a meeting for Friday night at six at Louie's.

Evie looks at the boarded windows in the houses they pass. "Rose would probably like to be on our team. Would that be okay?"

"Oh yeah! She'll win people over with her cooking."

Evie laughs. "Wonderful."

"So, do you have any ideas where to start?"

"You know I do, that's why you asked me to help."

***

Evie convinces Rip to let her call Toby for a ride to Louie's. There is no sense in him coming from his house past Louie's to pick them up just to go back to Louie's. Besides, she already knows he will fight her about calling Toby to take them home. They wave goodbye to Alfred and get in the van where Evie introduces Rose to Toby.

Toby shuts the doors and gets in the van. "So we're having dinner at Louie's tonight?"

"Why do I feel like you already know what we're doing?"

"Because you are a wise woman." Toby laughs.

He pulls into the parking lot and right up to the door where Rip is waiting for them. He opens the van door.

While Evie looks for her wallet, Rip hands Toby money and tells him to keep the change. "Thanks, Toby. Stay safe out there."

Evie walks past him through the open door. "You have got to stop."

"What? I was paying Rose's fare and you happen to be in the van too."

Rose opens her mouth and Evie, hands on her hips, says, "Don't even Rose. You two always gang up on me when you get together."

"Well, honey, I don't know what you're talking about." Rose takes Rip's arm, and he leads her to the meeting room leaving Evie shaking her head. He looks back and winks.

Introductions are made and they place their order. By the time the food comes, the ice has been broken.

While they eat, Rip mentions that Evie has an idea of where to start and asks her to share.

"Thank you. Because I haven't heard your ideas yet, I'm not sure if this is where we want to start, but on the drive home after the meeting, I saw boarded window after boarded window. I am sure that the houses were occupied. I am not sure how difficult it would be to do some home repairs for people, but apparently, God has supplied us with a team member with construction experience. This would be good to build trust with the people and make the neighborhood look better too."

They all agree, but question who will pay for it. Evie assures them God will supply every need. The construction worker says it is doable and he would get some buddies to help when they can. Another person suggests a block party, which they all agree is a good idea as well.

Evie speaks again. "One other thing I noticed on my first day here, is the convenience stores. They have posters promoting cigarettes, beer, and lottery tickets. What a person decides to do is their choice, but if this is all children see, it is what they believe everyone does as adults. I would like to ask if they would exchange some of the signs, but maybe we should wait until things change before approaching the owners. Who knows, if we get the area cleaned up, they may make the changes on their own."

They plan the block parties, deciding three should cover their territory. Two members of the team have family who have an additional lot beside their house. They offer to check with them about setting up a block party there. Evie suggests talking to the owner of the apartments Brenda lives in and asks if that would be in the middle of the other two places. Rip suggests email between meetings. He asks the team to work on what has been discussed, and for everyone to share thoughts and ideas about the block parties. They will meet back at Louie's in one week to finalize plans and discuss repairs. Rip thanks them for coming and picks up the check.

Evie pushes in her chair. "Great meeting. Very productive. We have a good, solid team."

"May I give you ladies a ride home?"

Rose responds, "Honey, you sure can and since we didn't have any dessert you can come in and have some fresh tiramisu. That is if you have time."

"For your fine Italian dessert, of course I have time."

Twenty-five

Alfred's incident has softened him, but he seems uneasy around Evie at times. She hopes she never gave him a reason to feel that way. Finding Rose in the kitchen, she asks if they can cook a nice meal and invite Alfred to dinner. Maybe he will open to her.

"Now Rose, I can't tell you who you can and can't have in your home for dinner but, if possible, can it be just the three of us? I know how much you like to play matchmaker between Rip and me, but I would like to spend time with Alfred. And by the way, Rip and I are friends, and he knows it will never be more than that."

"Okay, honey."

Evie rolls her eyes. "So, when can we have dinner?"

"How about tonight?"

"Great! I'll go ask Alfred."

Evie starts out the door and sees Alfred walking up the street. She calls out as she runs towards him. "Hey! Are you going to work?" He nods. "Rose is cooking tonight, and we would like you to join us. Will you?"

He looks at her feet and finally looks up at her, briefly. "Yes. Evie, please be safe today."

"Great. I'll tell Rose and I will."

Bless our time together tonight, Father.

Rose sits at the table with her closed Bible in front of her.

"He said yes. So where do we start?"

"I have it all planned out, but need a few things. Can you go to the store?"

"Of course. Do you have a list?"

"Yes. It's just a few things." Rose hands it to her. "Wait, you shouldn't go alone."

Evie sighs heavily. "I can't live in fear, Rose, you know that."

"Will you call Toby instead of taking the bus?"

Dearest daughter, these people love you. Please remember that.

I'm sorry for getting frustrated, Father. Yes. I know they do.

"Sure, I'll call him." Evie goes to her room to make the call. "Okay, he'll be here shortly."

Toby drops her off and asks if she expects to be long. She shakes her head. He says to call and that he will be in the parking lot.

She tries to be quick, but she is unfamiliar with the layout. As she reaches for a clove of garlic, she hears her name being called from the speaker overhead. Thinking she misheard it, she grabs the garlic. She stops when she hears her name being called to the front for a second time.

Father, I know You are with me. I refuse to be afraid. You are faithful! You make me strong and always protect me from the evil one.

"Hi. I'm Evie. Is someone looking for me?"

The girl at the counter looks around. "Yes. There was a man here a couple of minutes ago."

"Was he here the second time you called me?"

"I'm not sure. If someone doesn't come the first time, we announce it again."

"Can you describe the man?"

“He was tall. I remember his eyes were a pretty green color, but his dark, wavy hair was dirty.”

It was not Toby because he is not much taller than Evie.

“Okay, but you don’t see him around now, right?” She shakes her head. “Okay. Thank you.”

Evie quickly gathers what she needs, pays, and calls Toby. She waits inside until she sees him pull up.

“You need to go anywhere else?”

“Nope. Just home.”

Father, thank You for keeping me safe. I know I have nothing to fear because You are with me always, but it still freaks me out a little. I love You.

And I love you, My child.

Evie unloads the food while she tells Rose what happened. She nervously rubs her hand but let’s Evie finish the story.

“This is not a coincidence. Evie is a beautiful name, but not very common. Let Rip know what happened and he can decide if it’s important information. Maybe the guy is on video.”

About the time Rose convinces her to call him, Rip calls, his tone professional.

"Evie, stay in the house. You're not in immediate danger but just stay inside. We'll be there soon."

Evie hangs up.

"I didn't get to tell him what happened."

There is a rap on the door. "Evie, it's me, Rip."

"Hey, guys. Come in."

"Did you go to a store downtown today?" she nods. "Did anything happen?"

"Yes. I was about to call you. My name was called over the paging system. I wasn't paying much attention the first time but thought I heard my name. I didn't know who it was, so I kept shopping. They called it again, so I went."

"And?"

"No one was there. The girl wasn't sure when he walked away or if he was there the second time she paged me. I got what I needed and called Toby. Why? How do you know I was there? Wait." Evie paused. "What is going on? The girl didn't know how to reach me."

"We were called to the store because an envelope was left at customer service. It was addressed to Evie. The manager thought it odd that a man paged someone named Evie and disappeared. The girl found the letter on the counter after you left. She described you and we knew it was you. She also described him, so we have an idea of who we are looking for."

"Oh. I guess you opened the letter?" He nods slowly. "It's not a round-trip ticket to Bora Bora, is it?"

"No. Not at all. I would have preferred that. The original has been sent to the lab, but I took a picture." He hands her his phone.

"Evie, such a beautiful name, until those bratty kids repeated it over and over at the park. Yeah, I was the guy crossing at the corner that day and the person behind the newspaper in the car in front of your house. I was the visitor your roommate wouldn't let in. You know, the one looking for Izzy at the apartment where the brats live. Oh, and my favorite, the one who came to take you on a date. So sorry about your friend; he got in my way. Haha. But now I'm through playing with you. I hope you like fireworks. Watch out!"

"Can you describe him from any of those incidents?"

"I never got a good look at him." She hands him the phone. "Well. Now we know where he stands."

Rip sighs heavily. "Do you ever worry about anything?"

"I try not to. God tells me not to worry about anything but to pray about everything. All He asks me to do is tell Him what I need and thank Him for all He has done. I try to live by that. Less stressful."

Giovanni hits his arm and grins. "It's the Bible and you can't argue with that."

"Now I feel ganged up on." He goes to the kitchen where he knows there is always coffee. "Rose, what are we going to do with her?"

"Well honey, she will do what you tell her to keep her safe, but her faith in our Lord is so strong that you might worry more about the man bothering God's beloved child."

"True. God doesn't like someone messing with His own. I wonder what it's like to have that kind of faith."

“You can find out.”

Rip puts up his hand and rolls his eyes. “I know, Rose.” He motions to Evie. “You won’t let me stay here when I am not working will you?”

Looking into his eyes, she sees concern, but what concerns her more is how she feels looking into his. Struggling to find her words, and flustered, she feels her face warming.

She gets herself together. “I understand the severity of the situation, really I do. But if I can’t trust in my Father’s protection in these situations, do I even trust at all?”

He crosses his arms. “Are you going to continue as you normally do?”

“Yes, but I will do what you suggest to stay safe.”

“Okay. I suggest you don’t go anywhere alone and be aware of your surroundings at all times. I could say so much more, but I respect your faith.”

“Thank you.”

“But don’t think for one minute I won’t be around more.” Evie rolls her eyes, and he hugs her. “There may be more questions, so don’t leave town, ever.”

Giovanni hugs Evie. “Sorry. I can’t do anything with the man.”

Evie giggles and shuts the door behind them.

“Okay, Rose. What can I do to help with dinner?”

***

Evie opens the door and steps back.

“Alfred! Look at you! Come on in.” A perk of working at the gas station is the showers.

“Thanks.”

He follows Evie to the kitchen where Rose is at the sink with her back to them.

“Alfred is here.”

She turns and smiles tenderly. “You look so handsome, Alfred.” Evie thinks he blushes.

“Thank you.”

Rose taps the back of the chair. “Come, sit down. Dinner is just about ready. In the meantime, enjoy the antipasto. What would you like to drink?”

"Water, please." Evie places his drink in front of him. He is a different person from when

she found Alfred under a trash heap. It was an interesting start to this assignment. After everything he has been through, she sees a man who Father God loves dearly healing and learning how to not only live again, but walk in more and more freedom. She is grateful to be a part of his story and thankful that Rose was faithful in showing him the love of Father God.

Evie picks through the antipasto. "So, we're all friends here. What made you cut your hair and shave? The goatee makes you look younger. I like it!"

"Haha. Thanks, but I wasn't going for younger. I'm not sure I can ever go completely clean-shaven again. God is cleaning the inside of me, and I thought it was time for the outside to catch up."

Rose sighs. "That is so beautiful. I saw your kind heart, which made you beautiful to me."

He looks down. "Thank you."

Father! Is this what I think? How sweet! But so like You. You are amazing and so gracious!

Evie sets the gravy on the table next to the sweet sausage. For the first time, she realizes how close in age they must be. Of course, Rose is older, but by how much?

Rose shares some stories about growing up in an Italian family and has them in tears. When Rose was a child most of the family still lived in the area and they gathered often. At one such gathering, Uncle Lorenzo was responsible for getting Rose's Mom Mom, her mother's mother, to a family wedding. The bride was close to her and wanted her to sit in the front where she could see her should she get nervous.

The bride was searching for her Mom Mom, before coming down the aisle, and could not find her. She refused to go down the aisle until someone went to get her. Uncle Lorenzo was never responsible for her again. When he married and his wife was expecting, the family teased him mercilessly about not forgetting the baby. Rose chuckles and adds it was funny by then, but the family was so angry with her uncle for forgetting Mom Mom.

After dinner, Rose sets the coffee and dessert on a tray. "Come, let's move to the living room."

Alfred fidgets as Rose hands him the cup. "What is it, Alfred? Something's on your mind. Remember, we are all friends here."

"I have been working a lot and saving almost all the money I make. I am sorry to leave you and you Evie, but I am getting a real place of my own."

Tears pool in Evie's eyes. "Congratulations. I am so proud for you."

Rose places her hand over her heart. "Alfred! Congratulations! Don't be sorry. I'm surprised you stayed this long."

"I didn't want to leave you here alone. It's not safe."

Alfred knows nothing about the newest incident but needs to be in a place of his own, especially with winter not far off.

"Are you staying in Gidesha City?"

"Oh, yes. My job's here. I'd like to be near Willow, but I won't leave my city again or you Rose. Besides someone asked me to be a part of a group cleaning up the city. I want to be here to see that."

Rose pats his hand. "I'm so proud. I'm glad you're staying. When do you move in?"

"Next weekend, but there's really nothing to move in. I'm not keeping anything from the old place. I don't have anything but a used mattress a coworker is giving me. But you know what? It doesn't matter to me because I'll be in a place of my own. I'll save and buy as I can."

"Before you leave tonight, let's look around the kitchen for a few essentials to help get you started."

Father, let's bless Alfred. Can we? Maybe a gift card so he can have the fun of picking out what he wants. He's done without for so long, let's not have him wait to save money. He doesn't need to know it's from us, well me. He needs to know You blessed him. Oh, this would make my heart so happy! And I'm not sure what is going to happen, but I am all for Alfred and Rose being together. Just saying.

Of course, My daughter. You know I enjoy nothing more than blessing My children. Be sure to get one for furniture as well as the others you choose.

Thank You. You are kind and generous.

"Thanks. I'll clean my things out of your front yard that weekend too."

"It's going to be difficult to come home and not see your house, but you know where I live. Don't be a stranger."

"I'll never forget you." Tears fill his eyes. "You have been so kind to me. You fed me and talked to me about Jesus. Most of all though, you never treated me like I was less than you because I was homeless and lost."

Evie gets the tissue box and passes it around.

Rose stands up. "Look at us. You are going across town, not across the globe. I'm going to clean up the kitchen."

Evie stays with Alfred. "Would Willow consider moving here?"

"Possibly, since her mom died, but she enjoys her job."

"Why does she call you Alfred?"

He looks down into his coffee. At twenty-one years old, without a care in the world, he was eager to leave Gidesha City for good. It was his first leave since joining the Navy and he was home visiting his mom before leaving for Washington state. He and some friends leave the city to find some real fun. Back then, Gidesha City was an upstanding city, not the center of moral decay. On the outskirts of the city, they stop for something to eat. The first time he saw her, she served him and his friends, who were being disrespectful. He tells them not to talk to her like that. Her olive complexion and shimmering green eyes took his breath despite the hideous uniform she wore. Her nametag read Katalina. He was done. He no longer wanted to go out on the town and act crazy once he met her. Instead, he wanted to get to know her. When they finished eating, he told them to go on and he would find a way home. He was going to sit at that table until the end of her shift just to get to know her.

Katalina's mom spent her entire life making sure nothing happened to her daughter like it had happened in her childhood, so she always waited for her in the parking lot fifteen minutes prior to the end of Katalina's shift. Since Katalina was friends with the manager, she let Alfred's table be her last. Behind the building, backs against the wall, they talk until just before her mom gets there. Every day she was at work, he was there. Three days before he left, he rented a car. He still feels bad that she lied to her mom about working, but they met up and spent time together. The day before he leaves, they spend her shift together one last time.

"I asked her to come to Washington state with me. That's when I found out she was graduating that June, from high school. She was eighteen, thank goodness or I would have been done in the military, amongst other things."

He shakes his head. "I didn't know I had a daughter until six years ago. She was already grown by then. Poor girl looks nothing like her mother, and everything like me. Katalina could never shake the control her mother had over her. Once Willow's grandmother died, her mom told her about me. It took some work, but Willow found me. She told me the story Katalina told her, which was all true."

"That must have been a tough time." Evie hands him a tissue.

"I told her I would wait for her. I tried to call, but her mom would call me nasty names and hang up on me. I never knew why. After so many times of that happening and my career taking off, I let her go."

Rose leans against the wall, listening.

"After a year of Willow coming here to see me and spending time together, she convinced me to visit her and see her mom. I'm glad I did. That's where I went when I would disappear. We never got back together, just remained friends. We had a few good years until her mom got sick. I spent her last days with her and helped Willow with the arrangements. I was with Willow through it all. That helped our relationship, but it's still weird for her to call me dad."

Evie dabs her eyes. "Maybe someday, Alfred."

Rose sits beside him and pats his leg. "I'm sorry your life has been a difficult one, but now you are free from all the shame, guilt, and heartbreak. You are a new creature in Christ. Don't ever forget that."

"I know. Thank you. I've got to go."

Evie stands and hugs him. "Good night, friend."

"Good night, Alfred." Rose hugs him.

"Thanks for dinner."

Evie closes the door behind him. "I love that man."

"Me too, honey."

Twenty-six

"Hey, Evie. It's Brenda. Frank told me not to come in because he's overstaffed today. I'm thinking about going downtown. Call me back if you want to go with us."

Evie listens to the message and cringes. She wants to go with them but does not think it would be wise. The window-rattling rumble followed by the rain pelting the window makes her jump. "I guess that takes care of that."

Before Evie calls Brenda, she asks Rose if she has any games from when her children were young.

Rose nods. "But honey, they are upstairs, and you know it's not been used for much of anything but storage for years. You can go on up and search if you feel brave. I don't mind."

Evie runs up the stairs. Feeling the wall for the light switch she flips on the light and understands why her cot was in the small hallway outside the large room. She is immediately met with things. Chewing at her bottom lip, another crack of thunder helps her decide to make a path. As she sets aside a baby swing, she realizes she is standing in the middle of

Rose's life. Picking up a white shirt box with Antonio written in black marker, the rain thuds overhead. She pulls out an orange shirt with First Bank across the front and turns it over to find the number four on the back. Rose kept his old sports jerseys. Another box has several porcelain dolls from around the world. Hanging in a corner under plastic is a wedding gown. Once white, it now has a yellow tinge, but Evie can imagine how beautiful Rose looked. She finds an aged brown chest with a splotchy golden latch and opens it. There she finds a treasure of games. She finds a basket sitting on a dresser, places several games inside, and carries the basket downstairs.

She sets it on the sofa and calls Brenda to suggest a game day. Brenda loves the idea.

Evie finds Rose in the kitchen where she is placing something in a brown bag. "I enjoyed seeing the special parts of your life while I was searching for the games. Do you have a picture of your wedding day?"

"Honey, you know I do." Coming out of her bedroom, she looks down at the silver frame surrounding the newly Mr. and

Mrs. and smiles. As Evie suspected, the smile Rose wore was as lovely as the white laced wedding gown on her petite frame.

"Beautiful! I saw your wedding gown and just knew how happy you were."

"Oh yes, and tiny too. Those babies and my wonderful husband made me happy and, um plump. Of course, the macaroni and bread I love so much didn't help either."

"You still shine, Rose."

"You and I both know that is the love of Jesus coming through."

"Well, that too. I'm going to Brenda's to spend the day with them. Do you happen to have an umbrella?"

Rose hands Evie the umbrella and the brown bag. "Goodies for the babies." Rose smiles. "Do you think it's okay to walk there by yourself?"

"I should be fine, especially with the spy Rip thinks I know nothing about, watching me."

Rose covers her mouth. "I didn't know."

Basket of games, goodie bag, and umbrella in hand she is thankful the storm has passed, and it is only raining. For the benefit of Rip's private spy, she opens the door, looks around, then steps out. As she walks to Brenda's apartment, she continues to be obviously cautious. She is grateful Brenda does not live far.

"Aunt Evie!" Janie wraps her arms around Evie first, followed by the others. Jill takes the basket from her and looks inside. She squeals.

"Okay. Let me say hi to your mom and then we'll pick a game." She hugs Brenda. "Hi. Can I put this in the fridge?" Brenda takes the bag from Evie. "Okay, kiddos let's decide on a game."

Being the oldest Evie lets Jimmy pick. Pieces rattle inside the box as he pulls it from the basket. Janie sits on Evie's lap and helps her. She is surprised to hear Jimmy and Jill are the only two who have played board games in school.

In his excitement, Jimmy tells Evie they were not allowed to have toys at the old house. Brenda sternly calls Jimmy's name. Evie reassures Jimmy that nothing is going to stop them from playing games today.

Jill's shoulders drop as she counts six spaces and her player lands just behind Jimmy's final player. Jimmy rolls two fives and wins the game.

Evie gives Jimmy a high five and consoles Jill. "This is just the first game, girlie. You still have plenty of opportunities to win. Come on. Let's see what goodies Ms. Rose sent for you."

Opening the goodie bag for the children, Evie shows them the cannoli.

Janie scrunches her nose. "What's that?"

"Cannoli, it's an Italian dessert. Be right back."

Evie opens the fridge to get the milk. "What was Jimmy talking about earlier? No toys?"

Brenda chews her bottom lip while she plates the cannoli. "My ex-husband wanted a clean house, and it was close to impossible to have toys, four children, and a clean house, so something had to go. As much as I think he would have rather kept the toys and gotten rid of the four children, we removed the toys."

"Ah. Not a pleasant man, huh."

"No." Brenda carries the cannoli to the children followed by Evie with their drinks.

They go back to the kitchen while the children eat. "Wanna talk about it?"

"No."

"Okay. Understood. I didn't get to tell you the latest about the guy that beat Alfred."

"Oh, did they find him?"

"No, but he found me, again."

Evie tells her about going to the store, being paged, the letter, and what Rip wanted to do.

"Oh! That's scary. I'm so sorry this man is harassing you. What did you tell Rip?"

"I have work to do. Besides, I don't live in fear. I can't. You know the story of the guy outside the church. My Father is my protection."

"You are so strong. How do you do it?"

"On my own, I'm not strong. My strength is from God. Plain and simple. I really can't do it by myself."

Brenda hugs her.

"Aunt Evie!" Janie tugs at Evie's shirt. "Ready?"

"I can't wait! Which game this time?"

Chutes and Ladders. They laugh and bicker. Brenda watches with a heart full of love for her babies and for Evie being a part of their lives. Evie gives Jill a high five for her win.

By noon, Evie orders pizza and Brenda puts on a movie. When the doorbell rings, Evie cautiously peers out the window.

She places the hot boxes of pizza on the counter, they fix the children's plates and get them situated. Then they fix theirs and then join them on the living room floor.

Thinking lunch should be settled by the time the movie is over, Evie pulls out a large plastic mat with red, blue, yellow, and green dots. They laugh and fall over each other until they are tired of playing. The girls had enough of games and ask to watch another movie.

Evie packs the game in the box. “Jimmy, how about you? Have you had enough?”

“Nope. I could play 'em all day.”

“Okay, good. I doubt the girls would like this game so come to the table and I’ll teach it to you. My grandfather taught me how to play Cribbage when I was about your age. I haven’t played in a while, but I’m sure it’ll come back to me.”

By the second game, Evie realizes just how smart Jimmy is when he starts playing better than her. He finally beat her in the third game. They play Cribbage for hours until Brenda tells them she needs the table for dinner. Evie packs up the games, gets hugs, and leaves before dark.

Evie senses she is being watched and is grateful Rip cares about her safety.

Father, bless my friends. Keep them safe. Let them see You in all I do and say. Continue to open their eyes and soften their hearts. Draw them into You and love on them the way You loved on me until I completely surrendered my will for Yours. Until I fell so deep in love with You that nothing else matters. Until I was anchored in You and knew I would never look back. Continue to heal Alfred's wounds and renew his mind. You have great plans for him that You have already begun. Finish that work in him and may all the glory be Yours forever. Lord, if it fits in Your plans, can Willow open a branch here to help veterans? Having her and Alfred together would be beautiful for them. Oh, and what's up with Rose and Alfred? I know how I want that to turn out, but only You know what's best for them. Thank You for the fun day with the kiddos. I love You.

Precious daughter, you are a living, tangible example of My faithfulness, goodness, and love. You make Me proud.

After dinner, Rip calls to check on Evie and asks if he can pick them up for the meeting tomorrow night. She concedes, knowing he is just looking out for them.

Twenty-seven

The first block party was a success. More than expected came out. They stayed and ate and talked to their neighbors. It was a great first step toward being a community again. A few of the people asked why they were doing it and asked to help at the next one.

In the three weeks before the next block party, Evie goes to the meetings, both the team meetings and corporate meetings. At the corporate meetings, there is an urgency in rebuilding the local churches.

Father MacKay knows of a few pastors present and tells them to seek God for what they should do next. "If we expect God to work in our city and the hearts of our people, we need to be ready for them. If we believe people are going to repent and seek God with all their hearts, then we need to provide a place for them to come and do that. He encourages them to be expectant. God needs to be let out of the box we tend to keep him in. He does not belong in a shoebox. This is His city, and He deserves full reign."

***

Brenda tells Evie how much she enjoys her friendship. The only women she had in her life were the ones brought over by her ex-husband's friends and they seldom brought the same girl more than a couple of times. Unfortunately, the women were not in the best frame of mind when they arrived and even worse by the time they left.

Alfred moves into his new place and carries everything from his former life to the dumpster. Evie asks Rip to leave the envelope full of gift cards at his gas station for Alfred. After he furnishes his home, he invites Rose and Evie to dinner to show off his cooking skills. Alfred casually mentions that God left him gift cards and a thousand dollars cash in an envelope. Evie's heart swells.

***

At the next team meeting, they double-check that everything is ready for the block party on Saturday.

Rip asks Evie to bless the meal.

"Gracious Father, thank You for this meal set before us tonight. Bless it, this business, and the staff. May all they do glorify You. Bless this meeting. Give us wisdom and direction so every part of it gives You the glory You deserve. Prepare the neighborhood. Soften their hearts. Open their eyes and minds to what we are doing and help them to be receptive. In Jesus Name, Amen."

Rip stares at her when she finishes praying. As the others eat, Rip leans over to her.

"I could listen to you pray all day. It is soothing and peaceful, and you talk to Him like we would talk. It's nice."

"Thanks. It's because I have a relationship with my Father, God. It's a lot like our friendship. We talk and the more we are around each other, the better we know each other."

"Mmhm. I think we should spend more time together."

She flushes but says nothing.

Rip stands to get everyone's attention. "Okay people. Everyone good? Got everything you need before we start?"

Several people nod. He begins with the person to his left and asks to be reminded of what his responsibility is and where he is with it. The third person, a shy, young lady, seems to shrink with all eyes on her.

She keeps her eyes on Evie, seemingly encouraged, and speaks louder. "I was able to get a, oh, sorry, I was asked to find some games and other entertainment. I was able to get a dunk tank donated for the day, several carnival-like games, and a live band."

Rip sits back in his chair. "Well done. That's impressive."

"I do better talking to people one on one than in a group. That's how I did it."

"Well, you did great!" Evie says. "How fun will that be?"

The girl grins in embarrassment.

Rip rubs his chin. "So, with a live band, I guess we'll need a stage of some sort and electricity. Can we get that together by Saturday?"

One guy raises his hand. "I've got the stage covered. I have access to one that is fairly quick to assemble. It's nothing fancy, but it should work."

Another offers to investigate electricity access at the location and find a way to make it work.

Rip closes his book. "Block party number two is ready to roll out on Saturday. We'll meet at 8:30. And the forecast looks perfect."

Driving back to the house, Evie asks if any officers would be willing to be dunked to show that they are friends not foes. He responds with a firm 'not this officer.' They laugh and Evie thinks Giovanni would do it.

Twenty-eight

With no new incidents concerning the mystery man for weeks, Evie wonders briefly if he found someone better to bother. Then she quickly adjusts her focus as they approach the church.

Evie stands behind the pan of green beans as Father MacKay blesses the meal. Alfred is talking to Bud at the end of the line.

This is so nice to see, Father. Alfred smiles and tells people about You. What a conversion! Thank You for Your goodness and mercy. I love You so much.

"Alfred, it's nice to see you. Is everything okay?"

"Yes. I just wanted to say hi to everyone."

"Aww. That's nice."

He smiles and takes his plate.

"Hello, Bud. How are you today?"

"If I were any better, I am not sure what I would do."

"That's wonderful."

"Listen, Evie, I was wondering, did you have anything to do with Alfred's transformation?"

"Now Bud, you know one person cannot change another. Jesus must do that."

"I know that, but Jesus has helpers, you know."

She giggles. "I see. He does, doesn't He?"

"Mmhm." He wags his finger at her, grins, and walks away.

Thinking about Bud, she lifts the pan from the warmer and takes it to the kitchen. She wrings out a towel and cleans the tables.

It's okay Evie. He is a smart man, and we are very close. He knows without being told.

Father, he knows?

Yes, Daughter, he figured it out. I gave him the gift of discernment and he has strengthened that gift like a muscle for such a time as this. He knows who to trust and who not to. He is fond of you.

For such a time as this, Father?

Watch and see, precious girl.

I will, Father. Thank You for sharing this with me.

Alfred throws his plate away and hugs Evie. She reminds him of the block party Saturday, but he is scheduled to work. He asks when the last one is and promises to ask off that day so he can be there. When he writes it down, she hugs him again. As she wipes the table next to Bud, he asks her if she has free time to buy him a coffee tomorrow at Frankie's at nine o'clock.

***

Bud is sitting in the lobby when Evie gets there. Evie hugs him. If it were not for his oversize clothes and the fact he comes to the community kitchen, Evie would not know he is homeless. She asks for Brenda's section.

"Hey, Brenda! This is my friend, Bud."

"Brenda, the pleasure is mine." He nods.

Brenda leaves to get their drinks. "She is another one, is she not?"

Evie knows what he means. "One what?"

He laughs. "It is okay. You do not have to admit anything. I asked you for coffee because I like you, Evie. Not in a creepy old man way, but I see the love of God flow from you."

"Thank you, Bud. I like you too."

"In the community kitchen and wandering the streets, I hear a lot of stuff. Some of it I believe, some of it I discard, and some of it I am not sure. I can usually figure it out, but this one stumps me. I feel sure that if it is true, you will be a part of it. Is there some underground group trying to clean up our city?"

She laces her fingers together to cover her smile. "I wouldn't say underground. We're not keeping it a secret, but we are not necessarily calling it a takeover. We are subtly rebuilding relationships and asking spiritual leaders to pray about opening the churches."

"I knew you would know."

She tells him how it began with a handful of people meeting at St. Francis' Church and how it has grown with teams working towards building relationships and community. Excitedly, she explains that before her job here ends, she would like to see a safe place for women wanting to leave the sex industry and the streets. Plus, a place for abused and homeless women to go to help them get on their feet. She thinks that the building for sale not far from the library would be perfect because it already has rooms. Of course, she wants to see a nice facility for homeless men, especially veterans, so they can get help getting back into society.

Brenda leaves the coffee and two warm blueberry muffins. Evie raises an eyebrow.

"Frankie says it's on him this morning."

"Wow. I've come a long way in his book. Please thank him for us."

Evie explains the first time she and Alfred went to eat and the hoops she had to jump through to have breakfast.

"Bud, I have no idea why I told you half of what I did today. We are not publicizing why we are doing what we are doing, so please don't share what I told you."

"You know why you are so comfortable with me and don't worry about me saying anything. I am honored you discussed this with me and would like to help in any way possible."

Her heart is full. This little man whose clothes do not fit wants to serve, so serve he will.

"Well, we're having a block party in the section Rip leads. If you can make it, we will put you to work, or you can be your kind self and just talk to people."

"I will be there."

Evie writes the address and slides it across the table. Brenda refills their coffee and Evie asks Bud about his life. He tells her very little and asks about her friendship with Brenda. She tells him how they met here at Frankie's and hit it off. She grins as she tells him about the children. Since her work keeps her traveling and busy, she has not settled down to have children, so she enjoys Brenda's.

Evie hugs Bud. He says he will see her Saturday. She waves at Brenda as she leaves.

Twenty-nine

Evie wakes and runs her hand under her pillow. Finding her phone, she quickly silences the alarm, so it does not wake Rose. The smell of coffee slithers under the door. Rose must be as excited about the block party as Evie.

Sausage biscuits and an excitable Rose greet her. As they have breakfast Rip calls and tells Evie someone will pick them up shortly and that he is working on the dunk tank, stage, and other things.

"Rip says he'll have someone pick us up shortly. I guess this means I need to get moving."

"Me too, honey. I pulled myself out of the bed this morning and started breakfast."

Thirty minutes later Evie stands on the top step watching for a car. A fire truck comes up the hill and stops in front of the house. Evie cocks her head.

"Good morning, ladies. It's a fine day for a block party, isn't it?"

"Good morning. Yes, it is. Are you our ride?" Evie starts down the steps.

"Yup. You're Evie right?"

"I am. And this is Rose."

"Hop in," he laughs. "They asked us to bring this 1953 beauty out for everyone to see. Cleanest vintage I've ever seen. There should be other emergency vehicles for the kids to check out too."

"That's going to be fun. Rip must have set all that up after the meeting."

"He said you gave him the idea."

"I did?"

"Yeah, when you suggested an officer in the dunk tank, it made him question what else he can do to help emergency personnel relations."

Evie grins. "That's a wonderful idea."

The firefighter on the passenger side hops out to help Rose into the truck. Then Evie. Then he stands on the back.

Rose leans in toward Evie. "I'm glad this truck isn't any taller. Goodness."

Evie has not been in a fire truck since first grade when her class was given a ride around their town. She wonders how many children will want to be emergency personnel after today.

All eyes are on them when they pull up, especially after the driver turned on the siren. Rip looks up from building the stage and hands the hammer to the guy next to him.

Grinning, he walks over and helps Evie out of the truck, then Rose. "How was the ride?"

Shaking her head, Evie laughs. "You couldn't find anything bigger and more attention-getting than that?"

"Well, the helicopter was taking someone to a meeting in Denton today, but I tried."

Evie swats at the air. "Okay, where are we needed?"

"Rose, are you still good helping with food today?"

"Honey, you know I am."

"Great. See Janice from the meeting. She's over there."

"And me?"

For a long second, he looks into her joyful blue eyes. "Would you be opposed to sticking close to me? I may be mighty bossy today sending you off to do various things."

Okay, Father. I'm trusting You.

"You? Bossy? Say it isn't so." She brings her hand to her chest in mock surprise.

"Listen, you said okay to being the first in command, which translates to an assistant, gofer, or anything else that is needed."

"I know. I'm teasing. What first?"

"Finishing the stage."

As it creeps towards 11, everything begins to line up. People are already wandering around. Evie asked Rip at the last planning meeting if they can open the party with prayer from Father MacKay.

Rip hands Father MacKay the mic.

"Good morning! How is everyone? We have quite a crowd already. On behalf of the neighbors who are putting on this party, we welcome you all! Let's pray. Lord, this is the day that You made. We rejoice because You go before us and prepare the way. Thank You for the beautiful blues skies and the puffs of clouds that provide us with shade from the beating sun. We ask You to be the center of this party and that You keep Your hand of protection over us and help us to have a wonderful time. Bless the food and Lord, thank You for those who fixed it. Everything we do here is for Your glory and honor. In Jesus' Name. Amen. Have fun, everyone!"

Evie follows Rip as he checks with his team leaders to make sure everything is running smoothly. When he finishes, they go to the dunk tank. Rip gets three balls and waves to Giovanni who provokes him.

"Look at the wannabe ballplayer. My very own partner." The first ball hits high. "Ha. I knew it. Noodle arm." The second ball hits just below the target. "Man, you're not looking so good in front of Evie. You should just give it up." Evie blushes. The last ball misses and hits to the right. "Haha! I knew you wouldn't dunk me. Evie, you can do better than that, can't you?" Several people have gathered around by this point.

"I don't want to dunk you."

“Is it because you throw like a girl? Don’t be ashamed for being a girl.” Brenda and the children cheer Evie on.

He flaps his arms and clucks at her. “I never took you for a chicken. Cluck, cluck.”

“Aunt Evie,” Janie looks up at her. “You can do it. I know you can. You’re strong.”

She shakes her head and throws. The crowd is still applauding when a wet Giovanni gets back on the plank.

Evie shrugs. “I guess I should have warned you I was the star pitcher in town league softball back in the day.”

After that people line up and Giovanni goes down, again and again. Evie sees Bud when she turns around, then waves him over.

“Hi. Are you ready to help?”

“As long as I do not have to get in there.” He points toward Giovanni.

“Not at all. Rip, do you know Bud?”

Bud puts out his hand. “Hello.”

“Hi. You look familiar. Have we met before?”

“Hmm. Possibly.”

Evie jumps in. “Rip is a police officer here in the city and team leader of our section.”

Bud smiles at Rip. “Well, I can assure you that you never arrested me, that is for sure.”

“Well, that’s good. So where would you like to help? Food, face painting, or water balloon toss?

“I like children. Face painting will be fun.”

Rip introduces Bud to the face painting leader and watches as she gets him situated. His first child sits and asks for a tiger on his cheek. They watch as he paints.

“That’s impressive.”

Janie runs over. “Me next?”

When the boy turns around, people compliment the detail. Evie lifts Janie into the seat and reminds her not to touch her face until the paint dries. Rip and Evie check on team leaders.

Rip asks about Bud since he can’t shake the feeling he knows him. Evie shares what she knows, including meeting him at the community kitchen. They watch as Bud laughs as he paints their faces.

The sun works its way across the sky, passing behind clouds and back out again. The band sets up and checks sound as blankets and chairs dot the grass in front of the stage. Rip is pleased nothing out of the ordinary happens and keeps Evie within arm's length.

Giovanni drops the tailgate when the band starts and lets the children hop in the back. Brenda and Evie sit on the tailgate and the guys lean against the truck. Bud comes over and Evie makes room for him.

He shakes his head. "Thank you for letting me help today. It lifted my spirits in ways you cannot imagine."

"Are you kidding? Thank you! I am glad it brought you joy, but what a blessing you have been today."

"I had fun. Makes me feel young again."

"Aww. You're welcome."

As the band plays the teams begin tearing down other equipment. Rip walks around to see who needs help, but his team gets the job done. When the band finishes all that will be left is to tear down the stage and pick up trash.

The band thanks everyone for coming and tells them if they enjoyed the block party to be sure to be at the next one in three weeks at the Rundell Apartments. The street clears quickly and clean-up begins. The lack of trash on the grounds shows a sign of respect and that gives Evie hope.

Rip gathers those who are left. "That's a wrap everybody. This was great! We did this together and that's the only reason it went so well. One more. We can do it." As they left, there were high fives and fist bumps all around.

Evie smiles at Rip. "We couldn't do this without you. You're a great leader, a hard worker, encouraging, and fun. It's a pleasure to work alongside you."

He raises his eyebrows. "We really do make a good team, you and me."

"You two!" Rose nods her head. "Are we riding in an ambulance for the trip home?"

"Haha. I'm taking you home. Hop in."

Thirty

As Evie and Rose walk to Mass, there is an alarming crash behind them. Evie jumps, and Rose cries out. They turn to see a dog, head deep, in the trash can he toppled and two trash can lids nearby.

"Honey, that about scared me to death! This old heart is about to beat out of my chest."

"Me too! I was too deep in thought for all that."

Father, I need to calm down. I jumped out of my skin. You are my refuge. Who shall I fear? No one! I know this. I must remember not to listen to what the world says because this world is ruled by darkness. You are my light. Thank You for Your promises which I continue to stand on. I love You, Father.

Evie is not sure, but it seems like more people are at Mass than usual. Hopefully, the community is coming together.

Father MacKay hugs Evie after Mass. "There have been more people than usual for at least three weeks. I believe what we are doing is making a difference."

"I believe it is, Father. Let's keep praying, loving people, and watch what God does next."

On the walk back, Evie mentions how more people go to Mass on Sunday versus how many go in the mornings. Rose tells her even morning Mass has a few more people than usual. Crossing the street, Evie notices a dark blue car waiting on the light to turn green. They are halfway down the block when the car pulls up next to them.

"Evie." A man's voice calls out. "I'm sorry to startle you, have you seen Rip?" The man asks as he gets out of the car. "I have great news and he's not answering his phone."

"Hey, Rick. Do you live in this section?"

"Yes. That's why I was excited when Rip asked me if I was on a team."

"That's good. I'm not sure where he is today."

"The way you two stuck together at the block party, I thought you might know where your boyfriend is."

"Oh, he is not my boyfriend. Just friends."

"Sorry for assuming. Anyway, I want to share some awesome news, but I can wait until the meeting, I guess."

"Would you like to share..." He holds up a finger as he reaches into the car for his ringing phone.

"Rip, hey. I'm standing here talking to your girlfr...I'm sorry friend, Evie. Now I can tell you all." He puts the phone on speaker. "I was a pastor of a small church before I moved here. I left because the company I work for transferred me here. I had no plan to start a church, but I have been praying since the last corporate meeting. I know God wants me to start a church. He told me almost immediately, so I made some calls, talked to a realtor, and it looks like I can buy the old church on Walnut."

"Man, that is fantastic! That's in our section too."

"Yes. And a couple of blocks from my home."

Evie congratulates him.

I see You Father. You are faithful.

The man hops in his car and talks to Rip. Evie and Rose wave and go to the house.

After lunch, Evie goes to her room to read her Bible and pray before she goes to Frankie's.

Reading her Bible, she finds a promise of restoration in Amos chapter 9, verses 14 and 15.

"I will bring my exiled people of Israel back from distant lands, and they will rebuild their ruined cities and live in them again. They will plant vineyards and gardens; they will eat their crops and drink their wine. I will firmly plant them there in the land I have given them," says the LORD your God. Then they will never be uprooted again."

Gracious Father, You restore everything that has been stolen by the enemy. You prepare a feast for us in the presence of our enemies. You make our cup overflow with blessings. How wonderful is Your love for us? Thank You! All glory and power and honor are Yours Father. I love You.

As she rests in the sweetness of Holy Spirit, He reminds her that she is victorious because of Jesus and how deeply she is loved. All she needs to do is ask and she will receive according to His will.

***

Evie waits outside of Frankie's. Earlier, when Evie told Rose she planned to meet Brenda and walk home with her, Rose cooked noodles with her famous gravy. She packed it, bread, and a small salad for Evie to take for dinner. Brenda, removing her apron, came down the steps where Evie was leaning against the building.

"Evie! What a nice surprise. What are you doing here?"

"Since we haven't been able to sneak off for girl time, I thought I would sneak some in on your walk home. Rose sent dinner."

As they approach Rose's house, Brenda suggests sitting on her steps for a few minutes.

Evie sits. "Will the children be okay?"

"Yes. Nova is close by and checks in on them often. I'm so thankful for her. With what is happening with that guy, I would hate to leave the children with no one around."

"That's a good plan. Is there a reason you worry? It seems he was targeting me."

"You know, just in general." Brenda tugs at her sleeve.

Evie faces Brenda and takes her hands in hers. "I love you and your sweet little family. I don't even want to think of the day I have to leave. Our friendship is important to me. You are important to me."

Brenda runs her sleeve across her eyes. "I feel the same. Like I said before, I never had this kind of friendship or relationship where the other person is so kind, selfless, and loving. You and Giovanni have shown me something I never experienced, even as a child. I am overwhelmed."

"You know, we could not love the way we do if it weren't for God. I cannot speak for Giovanni, but I know it has not been easy to love and forgive. Through the years, Father God has shown me love and grace. How could I not show that to others?"

Brenda weeps. "I was young when my father died. It devastated my mom. I was told she was not an independent type, you know, the kind to take care of herself let alone children. There were different men at our house. I was too young to understand. I was Janie's age when my mom moved a man in with us. He was evil and hurt us, but Mom stayed with him. When I was ten, an elderly neighbor asked my mom if she could take me to Vacation Bible School at her church. By this time, Mom was numb and just functioning. She let me go the first two nights, but then that man came back to the house after being gone several days and refused to let me go. He said awful things about God and made me repeat them. He was pure evil. I got to hear about God for two days. Just enough to think He might help me."

"I'm sorry. That hurts my heart."

"Through the years, I would call out to Him or talk to Him, but it didn't help. At sixteen I couldn't take anymore and left home with a man six years older. He was a great guy until I turned eighteen and married him. We went to the courthouse with promises of a big wedding in the summer." She half laughs as she wipes her face. "He had no intentions of a wedding, being faithful, or anything else good for that matter.

Each time I got pregnant, he got meaner. He didn't interact with the children and only abused me. I decided I could live with that but swore if he ever hurt our children, I would be gone."

Brenda stops. Staring far away, she shakes her head. "One day, I came home from work, and Jimmy's eye was black and swollen as was his lip. My husband was on the sofa watching a game when I asked Jimmy what happen. Before Jimmy could respond, my husband said some kid at school punched him. Trembling, Jimmy nodded. When I mentioned calling the school, my husband told me boys will be boys. Then when I said it a second time, he jumped up from the sofa and got in my face. Jimmy flinched and covered his face. After I left him, Jimmy confirmed what I had suspected. He threatened to hurt me and the girls if Jimmy told."

"What a monster."

"I left him, Evie. He wouldn't sign the papers and finally the judge gave me a default divorce. He could do what he wanted to me, but not my babies."

"Oh, Brenda. My heart. Those sweet children."

They sit in silence until Brenda says she needs to get to the house.

"Would you still like company?"

"Of course!"

At the house, the children run up to Brenda and shower her with love. Janie runs to Evie.

"No one is loving you."

"I knew I would get my turn. Mom needs all that sweet love first."

"What's in the bag, Aunt Evie?" Janie peers in the bag still in Evie's hands.

"Ms. Rose sent some of her yummy noodles and gravy."

"Yes!" Jimmy and Jill high-five. Janie dances in circles. Evie looks at Jess who smiles. At seven, she is more serious than many adults Evie knows.

"Are you ready for me to warm dinner while you change clothes?" Evie pulls the meal from the bag.

"That would be wonderful. Thank you," Brenda sighs in relief.

After Evie cleans up. It is Janie's turn to pick a movie, and she surprises them all by asking for a dog movie. Brenda searches for a movie about a puppy who strays from his mom and gets lost in the city.

During the movie, Evie's mind wanders. Brenda's life has been anything but peaceful, but she has determined her children will be raised in a peaceful home full of love.

Evie runs her hand over Janie's hair and pushes it back behind her ear. She wonders what her child would look like if she had chosen the path of a wife and mother. Would she have blue eyes and brown hair like Evie or would she look more like her father? Evie does not even want to dream about what the father might look like but thinks it would be okay if he looked like Rip.

Father, my mind just ran away from me. It ran to a place that I have never even considered. I'm sorry. Well, this is a great reminder to set my mind on things above and not to copy the traditions of this world. Thank You for this beautiful family. Even though it has made me wonder a little, I am blessed to have them as one of my people. I pray blessings upon blessings for Brenda and the children. My desire is she continues to listen to me about You, but I need Holy Spirit's words because she is deeply hurt. Please place Your angels all around them and this apartment so no more evil infects their lives. You are awesome and I thank You for always hearing my prayers.

After the movie, the older children sit on the floor with piles of blocks competing for the tallest building. Janie falls asleep on Evie's lap, so she carries Janie to Brenda's bed and tucks her in. Turning to leave, Janie groggily whispers, "I love you, Aunt Evie."

Evie bends down and kisses her hair. "And I love you."

Evie looks at her little body in the big bed and wonders once more what it would be like to be loved by her flesh and blood. She shuts the door and sits back down.

"Fifteen minutes until the children go to their rooms. Can you stay a little longer?"

"I sure can."

Evie helps the children clean up the blocks and Brenda gets them to their rooms.

"If Jess doesn't become a doctor or something like it, I'll be surprised. All she ever wants to do is read, especially before bed."

"That's great! I see you encourage her to play too, which is vital."

"Definitely! Each of them is so different. Take Janie. She talks about God like she knows Him. I didn't teach her about Him." Evie knows Rose has talked to her but wonders if Nova is a follower as well.

Brenda sets out a box of tissues on the table next to her.

"I don't know if you truly understand how wonderful it is to have you, Giovanni, and Rip, of course, in my life. Never have I been surrounded by such love, and yes, I know Giovanni loves me, he told me. Despite having four children and an ex-husband."

Evie places her hand over her heart. "Aww."

Brenda reaches for the first tissue. "Giovanni told me that Rip lost his faith," she shrugs, "when he lost his fiancé. I guess that means he stopped believing in God."

"Yes. Sort of."

"Well, he knew God and it shows. You and Giovanni have shown love I have never known. I guess you guys have learned how to love by the way God loves you?"

"That's it. We're created in the image of God and that is how He sees His children. As we grow closer to Him and learn more about His ways, we want to be more like Him. It's like the way children want to do what they see Mom or Dad do."

Brenda grabs another tissue. "For that reason alone, I should have gotten out sooner."

"You did what you thought was best. Don't live in what's behind you. The enemy, Satan, the Devil, will feed you lies and bring up things to keep you feeling ashamed and worthless. He is evil like that. We never find true freedom if we continue to believe the lies."

"I'm not sure if I know what the truth is and what are lies. I have been fed more lies in my life than truth."

"Reading the Bible, talking to God, and learning more about Him, helps you know the difference between truth and lies. God cannot lie. God is light. God is good. The enemy lies. He is darkness. He is evil."

"There are things that I have done that are bad. Really bad. God wouldn't want me."

"That is a lie the enemy pulls on everyone. He uses the same tricks repeatedly to keep us from turning to God. In truth, we all deserve permanent separation from God, but because He loves us, He shows us His mercy. Mercy is a beautiful thing; we don't get what we deserve. He took what we deserve and gave that punishment to Jesus. Then Jesus took those sins to the cross with Him because God does not want us to live permanently separated from Him. God created us. He knows how we are and loves us just the same. He watched Adam and Eve eat the fruit. When they did, they sinned and created a void between God and man. Jesus fills the void and stands in that gap between us and God. We, as humans, can never be good enough, but with Jesus' death came grace and that grace saves us."

"Wow. That is a lot."

Evie laughs. "Don't worry, you are not going to be quizzed. All you need to know is God loves you and Jesus, His son, died for you. From that information, you can decide if you want to follow Jesus. When we follow Jesus, we are a new creation. Our old life is gone. God works in us to bring us closer to His image. We're not perfect, but we can't continue to live in our sins."

Brenda is quiet for a long time. "I can't. Not right now."

"Okay. This is your choice. I can't make you do it, but I can encourage you not to wait too long. God loves you and wants to welcome you to our family. He longs to call you His daughter."

She thinks how nice it would be to be a loved daughter.

"Are you angry that I'm not ready and I wasted your time tonight?"

"Never! God doesn't waste anything. The time we spent talking is well spent. I hope you think about what I said. I'll be glad to answer any questions or just talk about this again. I want to see you standing beside me in Heaven someday."

Brenda hugs Evie at the door. "Thank you, Evie."

She smiles. "My pleasure. I love you."

Father, why does this happen? I don't mean to complain, but the ones that don't commit right away make me nervous. I know she is so close. Please keep Your hand upon her. Keep her safe and continue to soften her heart. I don't understand why she didn't just do it. I'm sorry. If anyone should be upset it is You, Father. I'm just concerned for Brenda.

Dearest Daughter, all is well. I am not disappointed. I just love her so much and wish she could grasp that. You gave her great information. She feels like she has a good reason why she did not commit tonight. It will work itself out. Rest well, sweet girl.

Evie always rests well after talking with her Father. Especially when He reassures her that all is well.

Thirty-one

Evie is startled by the ringing of her phone. "Hi Rip. Um. I don't know. When are you going? Then going to the meeting? Sure. I'll go."

Father, this is difficult for me. I want to accomplish my goal, but, well, I'm not sure about spending so much time with him. Can we please quickly get him where he needs to be with You? Thank You.

She is not hiding anything from her Father and she knows it. For some reason, she cannot come right out and tell Him she is fighting her flesh and feels she is losing.

She is brushing her hair when there is a knock on the door. "Come in!" As it leaves her lips, she knows a lecture will be forthcoming.

He smiles. "I don't have to say anything do I?"

She shakes her head. "No, but," Rip cocks his head, "I knew you were on your way. No, you don't need to say anything. Are you ready?"

“Yes. Hello Rose. We’ll call when we are on our way to get you for the meeting tonight.”

Rip goes to the door and Evie follows, pouting. Rose swats her arm. Rip opens the door for Evie. “Are you making fun of me behind my back?”

Evie giggles. “Now would I do that?”

“Yes.”

Rose peers out the window as Rip opens the car door for Evie and then drives off.

At the mountain house, Rip opens Evie’s door then reaches into the back seat and grabs a couple of grocery bags.

“So what are we checking on?”

“Honestly, my sanity,” Rip says as he puts away the groceries.

She faces him. “Huh?”

“It’s been a long week and I needed some peace. I enjoy your company and you bring peace.”

“You didn’t say that on the phone. You said you needed to check on something and wanted company.”

"Yes. I need to check on my mental health." She looks at him stone-faced which makes him laugh. "I'm picking with you. A friend drove by on the main road yesterday and thought he saw some kids sitting on my rockers out front. He thought maybe Giovanni and the kids were here. But then he realized when he got home there was no car out front and called me. He asked if he should go back. I told him I'd come up today and drive over to my neighbors to see if their grandkids were around. You okay here by yourself?"

"Yup. Question is, are *you* okay with me here by myself?" She smirks. "I'll be right here when you get back."

"Okay. Help yourself to anything. I won't be long."

The car crunches over the gravel as Evie settles into the silence. She almost falls asleep but freezes at the sound of snapping twigs getting closer.

Father, protect me.

She stands, knocking the chair over. The snapping stops.

A man comes to the porch rail. "What are you kids doing here?" Evie is speechless. "Oh." The man scrunches his face. "Sorry."

Rip comes out the back door. Evie and the man were so surprised that neither heard him drive up.

Rip chuckles. "Uh. What is happening here?"

Evie opens her mouth to tell him but all that comes out is laughter which turns into a belly laugh which starts the stranger to laugh so hard that neither can explain. When Evie tries to stop, one look at Rip, palms up waiting to hear what's funny, starts her all over again.

The stranger composes himself. "It's not as funny as all that until you think about how we must have looked. You know I called yesterday and told you I thought I saw kids playing around your house, well today I was driving by and caught a glimpse of someone on your back porch. This time I looked for a car and there was none. I parked on the street and came up the drive."

Rip nods. "Yeah. I saw that."

"I crept around the side of the house."

"Not very stealthily, I might add." Evie jabs.

"You didn't move so I figured you didn't hear me." He laughs. "When I got to the end of the house I looked around and asked, 'What are you kids doing here?'"

Rip chuckles. "Were you scared, Evie?"

"I'll be honest, for a brief moment I thought that guy found me, but then I realized, a guy found me, just a different guy."

"Evie, this is my buddy, Skip, who helps keep an eye on things, Skip, this is my friend Evie."

"You're doing a great job, Skip. Nice to meet you."

"Same. Your girl here was ready to fight though. She had those hands up."

Rip laughs and asks Skip to stay awhile after he moves his car off the main road.

Rip sits next to Evie and pats her hand. "Why didn't you go in the house when you heard someone approaching?"

She shrugs. "I didn't run, but I did pray."

He shakes his head, fist balled in front of his mouth, he taps his knuckles to his lips.

When Skip gets back, he pulls up a chair. Evie offers to make coffee or bring them a cold drink. Rip says if she is making coffee, he will take a cup otherwise water will be fine. Skip asks for a soda.

Father, not that You don't have plenty to do, but do You laugh as You watch these things unfold? You knew when I asked for protection that it was Skip. I just love You, so much!

As she drinks her coffee, she watches a large bird dip and several smaller ones follow. Looking at the mountains and out over the city below makes her grateful for the blessings in her life. From their conversation, Evie learns that Skip was on the police force with Rip. Wondering why he left the police force; she hears kids laughing in the side yard.

Skip stands up. "You want me to take care of them?" As Skip walks toward the back door, Evie notices he is limping.

"No, man. I was up there talking to Dom. It's his grandchildren you saw. I'm good with them being around my house. They're respectful. Besides, it's nice to hear their laughter."

Rip catches Skip up on what is going on around the station and out on the streets.

"I don't miss it," Skip shakes his head.

Rip grins. "I have hope for the city though. There's a large group of people who want our city back and we are doing something about it."

"Now that would be fantastic. Maybe people from the surrounding towns will move back."

As Rip shares in more detail, Evie asks if Skip needs another drink. He declines. When Evie comes back with the coffee pot, Skip is standing.

Rip stands and shakes his hand. "I'm putting steaks on the grill shortly. You sure you don't want to stick around?"

"I'm sure. I got a date later this afternoon."

"You mean you finally found someone brave enough to go out with you?"

"Haha!"

Rip comes back from seeing him out. "Great guy. I hope this girl works out. As an officer, he was superior. Everyone knew he would move up quickly. Then, one day, he and his partner were sent to an accident. Who would have thought the driver was drunk at 11am? As they approached the vehicle, the guy faked being unconscious. He waited for them to get close then tried to drive away. In the process, he drove into Skip, knocked him down, then ran over his leg. How he didn't get both legs is a mystery."

"Oh my goodness. Did he get away?"

"No. The guy then ran into their patrol car and jumped out. He couldn't walk a straight line, let alone run. Skip's partner knocked him to the ground. Initially, the reports on his leg were bad. Skip's high school sweetheart decided to leave. It was a rough time for him, but he adjusted and is so much happier now. So a new girl is a good thing."

She smiles faintly and sips her coffee. "What's the look for?"

"Do I have a look?"

"Mmhm."

"I was thinking about the physical and emotional pain Skip went through. To have a long-time love leave when you need them most. Must have been the worst time of his life. People are incredible." Rip watches the sun produce a silver lining on a passing cloud.

“Yes, they are, but there is a promise mentioned many times in the Bible. God will never leave us or turn away from us. People are fallible, God is not.”

“So you think God was there with me when Ava died?”

“Of course He was.”

“So where was He for Ava? She was a believer.”

Evie looks in her cup.

Help me Holy Spirit.

“Yes, Rip, He was there with Ava. He can’t lie. We know He was right there with her from the minute she became a believer until she took her last breath here on earth and is still with her today. He never left her.” Evie smiles tenderly at Rip. Her heart warms towards him knowing how broken and hurt he is. His love for Ava is beautiful.

“Then why? Why did He take her?”

Be raw. Be real and tell Him. Had he never known Ava, she still would have died on that day. It was ordained for her. Tell him what I tell you.

“Please forgive me if you already know any of what I say. Also, know that I mean no harm and deliver this in love. We live in a fallen world. Adam and Eve disobeyed God and, with their sin, came death. There was no death before the fall of man. The wages of sin is death. Not that Ava sinned and died because of that, but because Adam and Eve opened the door to death."

Evie takes his hand. "Rip, Ava would have died that day whether you knew her or not. God knew every day of her life; every minute was laid out before she was born. That day was determined long ago. We all have a day. That's why it's important to be right with God before that appointed time. We don't know when that day is so we shouldn't wait. God is kind and patient with us. He gives us time to turn from our sin, but people don't respect that. It's not wise to play games with our Creator."

A tear escapes Rip's eyes. "But why Ava? Why so young?"

Her heart has a deep, crushing ache that she does not understand. She can barely continue.

Help me continue, Father. Please. He needs You.

"God's ways are not my ways, so I don't know the answers. I can tell you that whether we see it now, later, or never get to see it, God works all things together for good, for those He calls and loves. He does not waste anything."

A steady stream of tears fall as Rip stares straight ahead. Evie wants so much to hug him but is fearful. She chides herself. *You don't fear men that are trying to kill you, but you fear a man who cares about you? I can't lead him on, but I did tell him upfront where I stand. Hug the man. I can't.*

Rip stands to go in. Evie stands for no reason; she cannot bear the thought of his pain and confusion about God. She hugs him and all the brokenness and pain he has held spills down his face onto Evie, and none of it bothers her at all.

Rip lets go of Evie. He looks down at her then he goes into the house. Evie, exhausted, sits. Deep down she knows she has let her heart go too far and today was the tipping point.

Father, I can't do this. Can you please send a new helper for Rip? He does not need this and yet another reason to stay angry with You. Brenda is coming around too, so it should not be difficult for someone else to finish this assignment. I have never asked this before, Father. I will never let this happen again. Please.

Dear, sweet Evie. No.

What? Wait, Father. Why, why, why, no?

You know I do what I do with purpose and a plan in mind. That is not My plan. Now, take this cup and drink from it, just as My Son did. Put your flesh down for their eternity.

Evie sobs, ashamed of her weakness and that her flesh was more important than their eternity.

I'm sorry, Father. Your will, not mine.

I love you, My precious daughter. You know you are forgiven. Be at peace, child.

She stops sobbing. Grateful for the grace her Father shows her, she is at peace.

When Rip comes back out, he asks if instead of grilling they could pick up something on the way back into the city. Evie agrees. On the way back, Evie does not feel hungry and tells him not to worry about food for her. He nods. She wonders if he is angry with her.

He opens her door. “Would you like me to call Toby to give us a ride to the church tonight?”

He runs his hand against her soft cheek and shakes his head. “No. I’ll be back in a couple of hours to get you and Rose.” Head down, she turns and starts up the steps. “Evie, thank you for the hug from one friend to another. I needed it.” She smiles softly.

When she gets in Rose is sitting on the sofa. “You’re back early.”

Evie tries to smile. “Change of plans. He’ll be back to get us for the meeting.” She goes to her room and falls asleep.

***

When Rip opens the door for Evie, she notices his eyes are redder than earlier. It is a quiet ride, even Rose says nothing. Evie and Rose find a seat. When Rip talks to Father MacKay, he nods and puts his hand on Rip’s shoulder. Rip stops by the table before coming to his seat.

He sits next to Evie. “No coffee tonight?”

She shakes her head.

Just before the meeting, the judge was told about the pastors stepping up. He calls the pastors and preachers up to the front. Seven pastors share stories of how after they prayed about what to do God opened doors no man could close. Each one gave God the glory for where they are in the journey. Two pastors say they are opening their doors this Sunday, ready or not.

Several team leads are called to the front to share. Rip shares about the progress on home repairs, how well the block parties went, and that they have one more scheduled. He puts great emphasis on the effects of the block parties on the community. They brought people together like this city has not seen in a while. Others had similar stories.

When the meeting closes, Rip's team gathers to talk briefly about the church in their area opening Sunday. Rick says he does not want to take anyone from another church, but if anyone wants to come Sunday, he would love to see them.

As Rip's team leaves, Father MacKay walks up to him. "You ready?"

“Let me drop the ladies off at home first.”

“If you have something to do, we can get a ride.” Evie pulls out her phone to call Toby.

“No. I’ll take you home then come back. It won’t take long.”

Thirty-two

Evie hears nothing from Rip for a few days. Her biggest concern is that he is angry with her or even worse, angrier with God.

Father, I know it doesn't bother You if someone is angry with You. But it concerns me. What if he never speaks to me again? Will You please put someone in his path who will succeed in leading him back to You? I cannot bear to think he may never right things with You. I know You've got this, Father.

As she steps on the bus, he calls.

"Hey, Rip."

"Hey. Can I get you and Rose for the meeting tonight?"

"It's out of your way. We can get a way there."

"I'll be out that way. I'm meeting with Father MacKay after work."

"Well, sure then. That'll work."

"Good. See you tonight."

Evie gets off the bus at an earlier stop so she can look at the vacant building again. As she approaches it, she notices the For Sale sign has been replaced with a Sold sign. Her heart sinks.

Oh, Father, I just knew that building was going to be ours. A place where the women in the city can have a chance. I know that can only mean You have something better for us. Thank You.

When she gets to the library, she is surprised by how it looks. Mark, the director, sees Evie and comes out of his office.

"Hey there, stranger. I thought maybe you finished your job and left town."

"Not yet. Been busy working though. What's going on here?"

"Your research lit a fire under my feet. I held a couple of pep rallies with my team and got them excited. They began researching and bringing things to me that could help us." He hands her a piece of paper. "Everything on that list is new except for Storytime. Isn't that exciting!"

"Yes, it is! Congratulations! It looks brighter and more welcoming in here too."

"Tricks we are learning from other libraries."

"Awesome!"

"Don't be a stranger."

She laughs. "Okay."

***

Waiting for the last few people to get to the meeting, they order their drinks and talk. While they are talking, the manager hands Rip an envelope. He whispers that a courier just brought it. Rip reads the front of the envelope. "Open in front of the team during the meeting." He sets it aside and waits for the others to get there.

They order then Rip starts the meeting. They discuss the third and final block party which will be on the grounds of the Rundell apartment complex next weekend. They talk about the church opening Sunday and anyone without a home church is encouraged to be there.

“Let’s support Rick and do what we can to help build the church. You don’t have to go to church to help cut the grass or tell others about a church opening. I’ll be there Sunday morning. Rick, your team is behind you.” Rick nods.

“I’ll be there too,” Evie adds.

“One other piece of business. This was brought by a courier. I waited for everyone to get here because it says to read in front of the team during the meeting.” When he opens the letter his brows furrow. “It’s a letter from the Law Office of Jones & Jones. This is what it says:

Dear Sir,
An anonymous donor has contacted me regarding the building formerly known as Sunny Days Assisted Living, located at the corners of Sunrise Boulevard and Rivers Drive. He is in the process of purchasing the building located at 1181 Rivers Drive, Gidesha City, and is giving it as a gift to help your team member known as Evie to fulfill her dream for said building. More information and documents will follow.
Sincerely,
Robin Jones
Attorney at Law

Evie gasps. “Is, is that real?”

Rip shakes his head and shrugs. "Not sure, but we'll find out when they open tomorrow." He looks at the paper again. "What's your dream for that building?"

"For it to be a home for the women working in the sex industry to get out and start fresh. Plus, a place for abused and homeless women to go to help them get on their feet."

The team cheers so loud that people at other tables stare and others laugh.

"Who did you share that information with?" Evie shakes her head. "It doesn't matter. It's still exciting."

Rip and Rose talk about the meeting on the way home, while so many thoughts run through Evie's mind. Who all did she mention that building to? She cannot think of another soul other than Bud. Maybe someone overheard her at the restaurant. That has to be it. Bud cannot even afford clothes that fit. Who will she get to oversee the building? Better yet, where does she even begin?

Thank You, Father! What a blessing! Please send the donor blessing after blessing. Lives will be changed for Your glory. These ladies will find hope and see that they are somebody and mean so much to You. We can help them see they have a purpose and a destiny in You. Oh! The testimonies of love and redemption that will come from this new home for women. The glory is Yours, Father. Thank You!

Rip opens the door for Rose, then Evie. Although he seems more relaxed, Rip still seems a bit reserved. "This is great news for this city. You seemed to have charmed someone. Still not going to share who the donor is?"

"I have an idea, but it is so far-fetched that I don't think I will right now. If I find out for sure, you will be the only person, other than me who will know." Evie, aware of his sadness, wishes she could ease his pain, but only Jesus can do that. She can only be a friend.

"Good night, Evie."

"Good night."

***

Evie is too busy preparing for the final block party to help at the community kitchen but asks Rose to remind Bud that they would love for him to face paint again. It is still unbelievable that someone is purchasing the building and soon they can prepare it for the women. She knows it has to be him, but how?

The how is You Father, but how could he have that kind of money? Why would he appear homeless and too poor to buy clothes that fit if he has that kind of money? Either way, Father bless him. Thank You for making this dream come true and giving me the desire of my heart.

My sweet Evie, it is easy to give you the desires of your heart, because your heart is for others. Your heart mirrors Mine. Your desires align with My will. You are more precious to Me than you can ever comprehend. I love You, My child.

She gets her phone to call Toby, but there is a knock at the door. She looks out, sees Rip's car, and opens the door.

"Hey."

"Hey. I know we are busy trying to get things together for Saturday, but I just got a call. Can you take a ride with me?"

"I was just calling Toby for a ride to get some things, but I can get them later. Where are we going?"

"The new building, which needs a name by the way. The attorney called and asked if we would like to take a look. Of course, I said yes."

When they pull into the parking lot, a woman is standing by the entrance. After introductions, she opens the door and takes them around the entire building. Evie says very little until the end of the tour.

"It's perfect."

The real estate agent nods. "I agree. There are things like several broken windows and a few doors that need repairing, but the donor said he will make all the repairs."

"Do you know who bought it?"

"I have no idea. I have only worked with the attorney. Whoever it is, they don't want any recognition."

"It is such a blessing."

"You're such a blessing. Thank you for sharing your vision with someone who could do something about it."

The woman wipes her eyes with a tissue. "My sister needs this. My family has given up on her because of her choices.

Hopefully, when this opens, she will start making the right ones."

"I hope she does too. Would you write her name down so I can pray for her?"

As she writes the girl's name and where she works, she tells Evie how one blow-up with her father, about a guy, when she was seventeen, resulted in her leaving home and moving in with him. Things did not work out and she found herself on the streets.

As the agent sobs, Evie hugs her and tells her she will pray for her sister and asks if she can pray with her. She nods and Evie takes her hands in hers.

"Gracious Father, thank You for loving us. Thank You for Your mercy and grace. You desire that no one dies and goes to Hell. We pray that You soften hearts in this city and especially in my friend's sister. Begin to work in her heart and mind to prepare her for the day she can walk away from this life she is attached to and start anew. I ask the same for her family. That You begin working on their hearts as well. Prepare them for the day she breaks free and looks for reconciliation with her family. We know You are the only One who can restore relationships and bring them back together. We know that day is coming. Your promises tell us so. Bless my new friend. Help her forgive her sister and see her through Your eyes so she can bridge the gap between her sister and the rest of the family. Have her family welcome her sister the way the Prodigal's father welcomed him. This beautiful ending will bring You all the glory, as You are worthy. You alone are the answer. Your love is the answer. In Jesus' Name, I pray, Amen."

"Thank you. I tried to help my sister, but she continued to make destructive choices. I got tired of it. I was extremely unkind to her. I'm glad I met you here today. I have some repenting and some soul searching of my own to do. Thank you for your prayers. If you have any questions about the property or want to go through it again, let me know." She hands Evie her business card and hugs her.

Rip starts the car. "You're amazing. Where do you need to go today? I can stop if you would like."

“Thank you.” She looks down at the business card in her hands. “If you have time, that would be great.”

Thirty-three

Early Saturday morning, the team meets in the open field at Rundell apartments. They set up the same food tents, stage, and dunk tank. This time, two bouncy houses were donated from the Funhowz. Another company offered a small petting zoo for the first three hours of the block party. Everything was ready by 11 am. There was lots of sun and white puffy clouds.

Evie smiles when she sees Brenda and the children. Even with everything to distract her, Janie runs to Evie. "Aunt Evie! We're going to have fun today!"

As Brenda catches up, Janie runs off. "It was all I could do to keep them in the house."

Evie laughs. "I know. Several times when I looked over at your apartment, I saw little heads peeping out."

"I told them they can run around early before the crowds get here. After that, they are with me."

"It's going to get crowded. Each block party brings more people, which is great."

Evie and Brenda stroll past a juggling clown with feet so long they wonder how he keeps from tripping. He kicks another ball to a child and motions for him to toss it to him as he juggles three other balls. Laughter and applause follow a big splash as another winner hits the bullseye at the dunk tank.

Just after noon, the crowd swells and Brenda collects her children. She dodges an errant basketball as Jimmy watches two boys compete to make the most baskets. As Jimmy tells her all the reasons he should be allowed to walk around by himself, she sees the girls at the petting zoo.

"Unless you want me to take you by the hand like a child in front of all these people, come with me to get the girls." Scowling, he crosses his arms and stomps toward her. Evie, standing within earshot near the stage, goes to the girls. Janie has a handful of feed and is giving it to a plump goat while her sisters are loving on a gray, long-eared bunny.

Brenda rolls her eyes at Evie and waits for Jimmy to catch up. "I gave you freedom when I felt it was safe. Please change your attitude before I send you back to the apartment for the rest of the day." He kicks at the ground and turns to watch the action at the dunk tank.

"Can Jimmy help me for a bit?"

"Sure, if he has a better attitude."

Jimmy turns back around wearing a forced smile. "Is this better?"

"Uh. Just be helpful to Evie, please."

"Come on, Jimmy, Let's see where we're needed."

Brenda and the girls go one way and Jimmy and Evie another. Across the crowd, Evie sees Bud at the face painting table. Jimmy follows as they dart in and out of people.

"Bud! It's so nice to see you." Bud looks a little pale.

"Nice to see you, Evie, and your friend too. I am so happy to be here today."

"I know you are. You remember my friend Jimmy."

Bud looks at him again. "Oh, yes. You asked me to paint a basketball."

"Wow! You remember me!"

"Of course I do. You are memorable." Bud smiles.

"It seems time to meet up for coffee, don't you think, Bud?"

"Oh, yes. Just tell me when and where and I will be there."

As they make plans, Jimmy does a double take at a guy with his hat pulled low.

Evie taps him on the shoulder. "Let's find Rip to see where we can help."

On the stage, he is busy checking the structure with a couple of other guys, so they go to each team leader to help where needed. They are not needed until they get to the petting zoo. The owner is busy putting up an agitated animal, and the young girl, handing out the cups of food, needs a bathroom break. Evie put Jimmy in charge of filling the cups and handing them to the children. In between children asking for food, he pets the animals. Brenda and the girls come back to the petting zoo.

Brenda smiles. "Looks like fun, Jimmy."

"I love it! I'm going to work with animals when I grow up."

Brenda looks at Evie. "It has been another great festival. Is the band playing before sunset like the last block party?"

"It's later this time. It seems they have something special planned. Rip was doing an extra check around the stage a bit ago." The young girl comes back and grins shyly at Jimmy.

"The girls are most content here so I guess this is where we will be until the music starts. Jimmy, are you going with Evie?"

Looking at the cute girl, he decides to stay and help her. Evie stops at the concession stand where they ask her to get more plates and cups from the trailer and help restock for the rush before the music starts. While searching the trailer, it shifts.

"What can I help with?" Rip asks.

"Here. If you'll carry the plates, I'll wrangle these sleeves of cups."

"You must have kept busy today. I don't think I've seen you since before noon."

Evie smiles. "I'm sorry sir, but every time I tried to ask what I could do to help, you were knee-deep in work surrounded by people."

"Yeah. This block party has been a little needier than the other two."

They restock quickly. As the sun starts to dip, the rush for concessions starts. They walk back to the stage where the band is doing a last-minute check.

"Unless you need help with something, I'm going to find Brenda and sit with her and the children."

"I can't think of anything right now. Enjoy."

Looking toward the petting zoo, she sees Janie, then Jimmy talking with the little girl and petting a pony. She and Giovanni get there at the same time. Brenda is more excited to see him than Evie. Brenda teases him by telling him he is more handsome in uniform.

Janie runs and jumps as Evie catches her. Placing her head on Evie's shoulder she yawns. Rocking Janie, she hears Brenda tell Giovanni, "I wish you could sit with us and listen to the music."

"Me too, but I volunteered to help Rip since he's short on security. I got to enjoy the other one with you, though."

"I know. I'm just being selfish." She smiles and leans into him.

"I'll be back around."

Unlike the last block party, the band starts after dark. They bring colored spotlights and a smoke machine to thrill the crowd. As the band begins, Jimmy taps Brenda on the shoulder. "I gotta go to the bathroom. I'm going to the apartment."

"Not by yourself, you're not. Evie, will you watch the girls?"

"Of course."

"I'll get a blanket for us to sit on too."

"Sounds good. We'll be right here."

The closer they get to the apartment, the darker it gets.

"Mom, it's dark over here. What happened to the big light on the apartment?"

"I don't know, the bulb must have blown."

Crunch. Brenda takes another step. Crunch. Confused, Brenda looks at the ground. "What…"

A man steps out of the shadows. "It's glass Bren, from the 'big' light."

Frozen in fear, she turns to face the owner of the voice. He has his hand over Jimmy's mouth. "Don't scream Bren. It will not be good for Jimmy if you do. Go to your apartment."

Brenda unlocks the door. As she pushes open the door, the guy shoves Jimmy inside making him fall.

"It's good to see you again baby. I've missed you." He caresses her hair. "Although, I guess I should be honest," he points them over to the couch. "I have been here, watching you, your cop boyfriend, and that friend of yours. And about Evie, I've really enjoyed harassing her. Letting her see me follow her. Sending notes. And beating up that homeless guy was a bonus I wasn't expecting." Brenda's stomach turns at the familiar sadistic laugh. "But what can you do when an opportunity like that presents itself to you? I was hoping to upset you and distract everyone by focusing on Aunt Evie since you and the kids seem fond of her." He laughs at the fear in her eyes. His hot breath on her face makes her want to vomit. "Don't have anything to say, Bren?" She shakes her head.

"Why are you doing this to us, Daddy?"

"Boy, I wasn't talking to you." He moves toward him, and Jimmy draws back.

"They will come looking for us," Brenda whispers.

Pure evil dances in his eyes. Brenda rubs her arms remembering one of the last times she looked into those evil eyes.

How could she forget? She was not feeling well and came home from work early. The older three children were not home from school, and she decided to let Janie stay at the sitter so she could rest a bit before she had to start dinner.

When she got home, her bedroom door was shut. She heard giggles and whispers coming from behind the door. She thought about leaving but just wanted to lay down. Sometimes she wishes she had left. From the living room sofa, the voices were barely audible. Unfortunately, his visitor would walk past her when she left, but Brenda did not care.

She did not hear them come out of the room until the woman gasped when she saw Brenda. Brenda watched as her ex-husband escorted the unfamiliar young blonde woman to the door. He was livid when he returned.

Screaming that she should be at work, he whipped the cover off of her and yanked her up by the arm. He pulled her toward the bedroom. The only light in the always dark bedroom came from several lit candles around the room.

She lowered her head, but he grabbed a handful of her hair and jerked her head back. All she wanted to do was sleep. He was not having it. First came the name-calling and belittling her for being weak and worthless. Then the comparison of Brenda and the woman who just left and with that always came the details.

Being sick and tired, both physically and emotionally, she asked him to stop and leave her alone. Silently, he let go of her hair and she thought his rant was over until he walked to the door and locked it. Then, as if on autopilot, he turned on the lamp by the bed and blew out the first candle. As he picked up the candle and walked toward Brenda, terror ran through her.

On his emotionless face crept a smile and evil danced in his eyes.

He grabbed and twisted her arm, then poured hot wax on the inside of her forearm. As the wax scorched her skin, she pulled back. Even with pain searing her body and adrenaline pumping through her veins, she was no match for him. She turned to run and he grabbed her hair and then another candle and burnt her other arm. All while laughing devilishly.

Her thoughts snap back to the present as she hears Jimmy's voice. She looks at him, eyes wide, and shakes her head. Too late. He had enough of Jimmy. She darts between her ex-husband and Jimmy. Staring into the pits of Hell, she says, "Please, don't hurt him."

He stops. "You were always coddling him too much Bren. I hated that. Well, now it's my turn to coddle because what happens next is just between us Bren." He shoves her out of the way. Grabbing Jimmy by the arm, he looks in the bedrooms. The smaller rooms have windows, but Brenda's does not. Shoving Jimmy into her room, he threatens that he will not see his mother again if he comes through that door. Brenda follows him to the door.

Her ex-husband knows Brenda will not run as long as he has access to Jimmy, but she knows something her ex-husband does not. She stands close to the bedroom door as her husband slowly backs her up against it.

"Bren, baby, no one walks away from me." He strokes her face. "Did you really think you could hide from me? Told you that you were stupid. I've had plenty of time to think and have the perfect ending. You know, where the punishment fits the crime. I considered taking care of you and leaving you here, but what fun would that be? Let's go. So sorry, no time to say bye to "your babies" as you so fondly call them, but good news, we'll have plenty of time to reminisce about old times on the drive."

That was all Jimmy needed to hear. Going into the master bath and quietly pulling the shower curtain open, he looks at the window. He always thought it weird, a window in the shower. Standing on tiptoes he can reach the window, but the latch is at the top. Quickly, he steps on the soap holder, hoping his arms will stretch far enough. With a fraction of an inch to spare, he flips the latch, lifts the window, and silently pops the screen out. Hitting the ground, he jumps up and runs to Evie.

"Evie!"

"Jimmy, what's wrong?"

"Mom! It's my mom!

Evie scans the crowd looking for Rip or Giovanni.

Rip's eyes meet hers. Seeing the look on her face, he runs toward them while he calls Giovanni on the radio. Not wanting to cause panic, Evie takes the children and walks away from the crowd. Rip gets there, then Giovanni. Evie calms Jimmy so they can understand him as he explains what is happening.

Rose, Alfred, and Willow are enjoying the band not far from Evie and the girls. Knowing something is not right Rose goes to Evie and takes the girls back with her. Jimmy refuses to go.

Rip calls for back-up but tells them no sirens. He looks at Giovanni. "Listen, we don't have much time. He must know someone will come looking for Brenda and Jimmy soon. I don't want to give him time to figure out we're coming. When he comes out to leave, we take him. Jimmy, does he have a weapon?"

"I don't know for sure."

"Stay here." He gives Jimmy a stern look then nods at Evie.

From where she and Jimmy are hiding out of sight, they can see the door of the apartment and watch as Rip gets in position and Giovanni runs behind the building. As they wait, more officers come and position themselves around the apartments.

Back inside the apartment, Brenda's ex-husband brings her face close to his, and whispers. "Take a good look at me. My face is the last one you are going to see. Let's go."

"Wait! What about Jimmy?"

"Not my problem. Won't be yours either." He laughs wickedly. He looks back at the bedroom door. "Stupid kid. See what all your coddling did? He's so afraid I will hurt you if he opens the door, he's not even moving. It's obvious he gets his weakness from you."

"Before we leave, this is what you're going to do. You're going to play nice. Don't get any ideas or I go back in and get Jimmy quicker than you can get help. We'll go left out the door. You better act normal and walk. Now smile."

As they come out of the door and go left, a man comes from an apartment in front of them. Brenda's ex-husband tightens his grip on her arm as a warning as he smiles at the man. The man nods as they pass. Rip whispers into his walkie and a woman Brenda has never seen before comes from the last apartment before the parking lot and walks past them. As an afterthought, the woman stops and turns around. She calls to Brenda and she and her ex-husband turn.

"Brenda, hey." His grip tightens as Brenda fake smiles at the woman.

"Hi." Her ex-husband casually looks around.

"Are you not going back to the party?" As her ex-husband looks back at the lady, Rip whispers on the radio. From around the side of the building, Giovanni quickly and quietly comes up behind Brenda's ex-husband and takes him to the ground.

As he falls, Brenda's ex-husband's gun goes off, sending a bullet into a tree near the parking lot.

Evie and Jimmy hear the shot and come around the building when they hear, "All clear."

People come out of their apartments and officers create a barrier to keep the crowds back.

Brenda's ex-husband is cuffed, and Rip takes control of him so Giovanni can go to Brenda.

As he is led down the sidewalk, Alfred pushes past the officer barricade and steps in front of Brenda's ex-husband, blocking the walkway.

Rip stops. "Alfred get back behind the officers." Evie puts up her finger.

Alfred says, "Remember me? No?" He points at Evie. "I'm the man you beat and left for dead in front of her house." The man snarls. "You remember me now. Well," Alfred steps closer to him, "I want you to know that I forgive you. I pray for you and that you find forgiveness from God." Alfred thanks Rip for stopping and steps out of the way.

As the man passes Evie, their eyes meet. As she sees the evil polluting his soul, he blows her a kiss and winks. Rip whispers something to him and the man's laugh send shivers through Evie.

Father, I have just seen the physical manifestation of evil in this world. So many are affected by this incident. Please protect the hearts and minds of Brenda and her children, especially Jimmy. Let them consider what Alfred had gone through and how he forgave. Comfort them all.

Rip places the man in the patrol car. Jimmy runs into Evie's arms, and she hugs him tight. When he steps back he is crying now that the adrenaline is subsiding.

"I did the right thing this time. I found a way out and helped my mom."

"You did, sweetheart. You were so brave."

He takes Evie's hand and leads her to Alfred. He taps Alfred on the arm and Alfred looks at Jimmy.

Jimmy swallows hard as tears form. "Mr. Alfred. Please tell me how you can forgive him. I don't think I can."

“Young man, you are brave and so smart. God is the only way I can forgive him.”

Tears flood Jimmy’s face as Alfred holds his arms open and Jimmy willingly obliges.

Rose walks over to them. “I can’t thank you enough for removing the girls from all of this. I’m grateful they didn’t see anything. I only wish Jimmy didn’t have to be a part of it.”

“Honey, I only used the wisdom God gave me.”

Giovanni approaches Evie. “Can I speak to you?” They step away. “I have to take Brenda and Jimmy to the station. You know they’ll be questioned. The apartment is the scene of a crime and will be taped off. It could be a late night. Could you take the girls overnight?”

“Of course. We’ll make it work.” Evie smiles at Brenda. Jimmy is by her side. “Please tell Brenda I love her.”

Before Rip left for the station, he asked one of his team to get the music going again. The crowd moves back toward the stage to engage with the band. Rose and Alfred take the girls to her place so Evie can see the block party to the end. Willow stays with Evie. Officers collect evidence while Giovanni takes Brenda and Jimmy to the police department, but not before getting Jimmy ice cream.

At the station, Rip checks with Giovanni before he goes back to check on the block party. "You good? Brenda and Jimmy?"

"Eh. I just hope he goes away for a long time. They're shook up."

"Yeah. I can only imagine. You need anything from me?"

"No man. Thanks."

Rip pats him on the shoulder.

While Evie waits for the party to break down, she wonders why Brenda never told her. It's possible she took the children right after the divorce and no one knew where she was. Evie jumps when Rip comes up behind them.

"I'm sorry, Evie. I didn't mean to scare you. I sent you a message that I was on my way back."

"I guess I didn't hear it over the band. Did you see Brenda? Is she okay?"

"I only spoke to Giovanni. He told me they are shook up."

Father, draw them into You. Hold them. Let Your peace flow over them and comfort them, please.

"That's understandable. Honestly, I'm just relieved it's all over."

The band winds down and people leave. Some linger, talking. Except for the incident regarding Brenda, it was another good event. Rip tells Evie she can go and he will take care of clean-up, but she chooses to stay. She and Willow pick up trash and clean the lot while Rip and the others tear down the stage.

Rip gathers team members still there. "I couldn't ask for a better bunch than you guys. All the block parties were a hit. Today's event was a little different, but it still brought people together and they had a good time. This is a great start to bringing unity to the city. We are not through yet. We have something else to work together on. If you still want to be a part, we will meet this week, on the same day, time, and place. Thanks again, everybody."

Rip gives Evie and Willow a ride to the house. He asks if Evie has a minute as he opens the car door for Willow.

He opens Evie's door. "If it's okay with you, I'd like to make the women's home our next project. It needs to be done and we have the best people to help us. I drove by today and the windows and doors have been repaired. What do you think?"

Unable to speak for the lump in her throat, and exhausted from the events of the day, she nods and cries uncontrollably. The urge to hug him makes her aware of her vulnerability.

And as much as he wants to take her in his arms and comfort her, he does not. "Good. Then that's what we'll do. I'll see you soon."

Thirty-four

Evie gasps. "Brenda, are you okay?"

Eyes bloodshot and puffy and hair wild, she grimaces. "Yes. I am fine."

"Mommy, what's wrong with your eyes?" Janie holds on to Brenda's sleeve as she picks her up, accidentally revealing her scars. Brenda quickly pulls it down, averting her eyes.

"Is Giovanni off today?" Brenda nods. "Can I ask him to take the children to the library or something for a few hours?"

"I don't know. I don't want them too far from me."

Daughter, you are right. She is fearful beyond your understanding. Her mind is racing. She is on the verge of a breakdown. Call him.

Against her wishes, Father?

Call him.

Evie calls Giovanni while Brenda sits on the sofa with Jimmy next to her, arm around her. Janie climbs in her lap. "Mommy," Janie takes Brenda's face in her little hands,

"Jesus says He loves you. He knows you're sad and it makes Him sad. He was here with you and kept you safe."

Evie's heart melts. Brenda stares at Janie's sweet little face.

Janie, My precious daughter.

Yes, Father, she is. Gracious Father, fill this apartment with joy again. Let peace reign abundantly in this place. Let the fear and pain associated with their home be removed and let life fill these walls. Comfort Brenda and Jimmy and protect the girls. Let the girls be a light in a dark spot, especially Janie. Oh, Father. Janie. She already knows. She is on her journey with You. I can only imagine the lives she will touch. Bless this family and protect them all their days. Love on them as only You can and see them through. Brenda is weary and her burdens are heavy. She will find her rest in You and when she does, she will find rest for her soul. Torment, guilt, shame, pain, and every other weight will be worked through and shaken off. She will walk in the freedom that comes from You and her burden will be light. I'm excited for that day, Father. Please let me be the one who helps her take those first steps toward freedom. Thank You for protecting my friend and her family. You are our hope. You are our answer. I love You, Father.

Brenda's babies surround her, but not understanding. When Giovanni gets there, he gestures toward the kitchen and Evie follows.

"When they said they were through with the apartment last night, I asked if she would be okay coming here or if she wanted to stay somewhere else. She wanted to be here. I told her to call me if she needed me. Being alone in here with just Jimmy must have been too much. I should have known better."

"Don't do that to yourself. Everyone is different. It's not your fault. Brenda needs sleep but is fearful. I will stay here with her."

"Okay. I'll take good care of the children."

Brenda is hugging Janie close and crying when they come back.

"Okay kiddos! Who wants to have some fun today?" Jimmy and Janie look hesitant but the other two are already at the door. Giovanni kisses Brenda's head, tells her he loves her, and nods at Jimmy. Jimmy takes Janie's hand and tells her it is okay.

Giovanni opens the door to leave when Brenda chokes out. "Keep my babies safe."

"You know I will, babe."

With her children gone, Brenda weeps and beats a nearby pillow repeating "I hate you."

Father, my heart is breaking! Can You do something?

I did. I sent you. Remember Evie, sometimes words are not necessary. Sometimes words at the wrong time do not help the situation at all.

Evie waits.

Finally, in an exhausted heap, Brenda falls over sideways on the sofa. Softly she weeps until Evie hears nothing but her breathing. She lifts Brenda's legs onto the sofa and covers her with a blanket. Then Evie walks from room to room, praying until peace and light overcome the darkness in the apartment.

Evie waits.

Three hours later, Brenda moves. When she opens her eyes, she bolts upright. "Where are my babies? Something must be wrong!"

"Not at all. You have only been asleep for three hours and Giovanni called right after you fell asleep and said he and Rip are taking the children to the cabin. They won't let anything happen to them. Are you hungry?"

"No." Brenda flattens the blanket against her legs, again and again. "Thank you for being here. I know I have not been honest with you."

"You have not lied to me."

Brenda snorts. "No, but I haven't been very open with you and I'm sorry. I'm so sorry he was harassing you to get to me."

"You don't have to be sorry. It wasn't your fault."

"Yes, it was. It was wrong of me to take the children and run."

"You did what you felt was best at the time."

Brenda shakes her head. "I don't know. I don't know anything anymore. I know I should be relieved that he is locked away, but what if he gets out on a technicality or something or he says I made him crazy because I took the children? I couldn't sleep last night for fear of him coming for us. I almost called you three different times to bring my girls home. I didn't want to be here alone, but I couldn't leave the apartment to get the girls. I was so scared."

"Brenda,"

"It's all my fault. I am weak and good for nothing."

Evie sits next to her on the sofa. "He was wrong. You were fearfully and wonderfully made by the Creator of everything. God doesn't make anything good for nothing. Everyone has a purpose."

"I don't. I know because I have been told that my whole life, since I was a child."

"It's time for you to stop believing those lies. You are loved by God. So loved, that Jesus came to this earth for you, so you could live forever in Heaven with Him."

"God doesn't love me. There's no way. I have done bad things, like take my children from their father and besides I haven't been to church, so I don't show Him love."

Using Scripture, she encourages Brenda with promises.

"God thinks so much of you and me, that He made our paths cross. He sent me here to you. I came to this city for you and to give you things that only God can provide. He wants to give us good things that He knows we need. He wants to provide for us as a father does his children when we enter in relationship with Him through Jesus."

"I believe in God and Jesus, I just, I'm not sure I believe that He believes in me."

"He knows you. Has known you since before He created the world. He believes you can be the person He created you to be."

"He cherishes me?"

"Absolutely!"

"He wants me? The mess that I am?"

"Come as you are. He will help you leave the mess behind."

"Yes. I want that."

Evie prays with Brenda and Brenda gives care of her heart to Jesus.

Weeping, Evie hugs her. "You are a new creation today! There is a party in Heaven as the angels are celebrating with us."

"It feels good. I feel good. I've never felt this good!" Brenda gushes.

"Giovanni is a strong Christian man. He will help you navigate your new life."

"What about you?"

"Well, I came to this city to give you some things that only God can provide. You just received it. My job is almost finished, but as long as I'm here, I'll be happy to help."

Giovanni calls and tells Evie he is bringing a container of fried chicken with sides shortly. She relays the message to Brenda who is thankful she does not have to cook. Brenda goes to her room while Evie makes tea. She comes back with a clean face and her hair brushed. They sit at the table drinking hot tea and talking.

"This might sound weird, but when I woke up, it felt different in here. Was that just me?"

"Nope. Not weird. I walked from room to room praying and pleading the blood of Jesus over each of you and the apartment. I prayed for peace to fill this home so evil has no place here."

"That's amazing!"

"It's the way God works. It's one of those things He promises to provide."

Busting through the door Janie comes in first talking a mile a minute and the others follow just as excited.

Evie leans close to Brenda's ear and says, "It's a good thing I unlocked that door when Giovanni called."

"They had a great time, but in case you couldn't tell, they were ready to see you." Giovanni places the chicken and a couple of two liters of soda on the table and kisses Brenda on top of her head. Rip places the sides on the table by the chicken and follows Evie into the kitchen. She asks him to fill the cups with ice.

"Giovanni told me Brenda wasn't well when he got here earlier. She seems great now." Rip sets out eight cups and gets a tray of ice from the freezer.

“She wasn’t well at all when he saw her, but we talked and prayed. It’s her story to tell, so I’ll let her tell it.” She flashes him a smile and leaves the kitchen.

At dinner, the children talk over each other about all the fun they had and what they did. After dinner, Brenda puts on a movie, and within fifteen minutes, all but Jimmy are asleep.

Evie and Rip clean up while Brenda and Giovanni put the girls to bed. Jimmy decides to go too, but before he does, he gives Brenda a long hug.

Brenda sits on the sofa with Giovanni next to her, holding her hand.

“Okay. What happened while we were gone? You’re different.” She and Evie exchange a grin. “I…am a new creation.”

“What!? Thank You, Jesus!” Laughing, he hugs her. “That’s great news!”

Brenda tells them a little bit about her past, pulls up her sleeves and shows them her scarred arms, and then shares what happened this afternoon. She shares her concern about getting in trouble for taking the children away without her ex-husband knowing where they were. Giovanni assures her they will handle whatever happens together with God in the lead.

Yawning, Evie stands. "I guess I'm going to go."

"Can I give you a ride?" Rip gets out his keys.

"Sure. That'll be great."

Rip stands in front of the passenger's door. "What is it about you, Evie?" She laughs. "You make things better."

"I can't take credit for any of it. What you see is Jesus in me."

He searches her face, then opens the car door.

Thirty-five

"Good morning, Rose. Today is the big day!"

"Oh, honey, I'm excited for you and the women who desperately need this in our city."

Evie calls Toby. She sips her coffee and rejoices that two out of her three people are right with God.

Father, I'm not sure what to do about Rip. He knows You, why is he hesitant?

Beep, beep. She places the cup in the sink and runs out the door.

"Hi, Toby! Seems like forever since I called you."

"Not that long, but too long, for sure," he laughs. "Where to, friend?"

"The Law Office of Jones & Jones."

"Everything okay?"

"Everything is great!" She explains about receiving the building from a secret donor and she is getting the keys today.

"Wow. Look at God! What He won't do, huh?"

Before she gets out, she asks him how far the law office is from the building. He tells her she could probably walk, but it's through some rough streets. He asks if he could have the privilege of taking her to her new building. She agrees and says she will call him.

The papers are ready and waiting for Evie's signature. She has the copies and the keys within the half-hour. Toby is waiting for her.

"Congratulations!"

"Thank you, Toby. God is so good! To The Strong Tower, please."

"Nice name."

"Thank you. Holy Spirit spoke it to me while I was signing."

"Should I wait for you? Or do you want to call me?"

"It's going to be a while. I'll call when I'm through."

When she arrives, she walks around the outside of the building and the parking lot covering it in prayer. She takes out the keys and prays over them as she opens the door. Once inside, she falls to her knees.

You, Father, are worthy of all praise. I honor You with a heart of thanksgiving. You love Your people and are always working for their good. You are good! Your unfailing love is forever as is Your faithfulness! Holy are You, our protector. We run to You and You save us. Thank You for the blessings that are coming to this building and this city. I love You.

Evie goes room to room to pray. In the bedrooms, she prays for every woman and child who will sleep in the room, prayers for healing, freedom, and blessings. In the shared living quarters, she prays for peace and unity among the residents. In the kitchen, she prays for provision and blessing, that they will never be without food. She prays for wisdom and that Holy Spirit leads the decision-making in the administrative offices.

Before Evie leaves, she sits weeping.

Oh, Father. My heart is overwhelmed. All over this city, I see and hear of the miracles You are doing to restore Your people and their city. Blessings, and gifts like this building will continue to bring this city back to You. Nothing can stop them now. I know You heard my prayers as I walked today,

Father, but there is one thing more and it is important; the staff. I have an idea of someone I think would be an amazing director. You already know who it is, but I need to hear from You. Only You know what this looks like and what will be best. This building is for Your glory and I pray it always is. I am in awe of Your goodness and faithfulness every day. It never ends. Thank You, Father. I love You.

Precious Evie, I love you and am so proud of you. Yes, the person you are thinking of, was born for such a time as this. You will see only the beginning, dear child, but you will get a glimpse of a person walking in true purpose and destiny. My blessings are on this building, and your director.

Oh, Father! Thank You! Please go before me and prepare the way.

***

"Thank you, Toby. I'll talk to you soon." Evie shuts the van door and takes the steps two at a time.

"Rose, are you here?"

"Yes, honey. I am in the bathroom. I'll be right out."

Evie hopes, as she reaches the kitchen, that there is coffee. As Rose comes to the kitchen Evie holds up the empty pot.

Rose holds up her hand. "I have exceeded my limit. So, you sound excited. What is it?"

Evie tells her about her trip to get the keys and then her praying throughout the building. Although she does not tell Rose who the director will be, she tells her that it was confirmed and to be praying that the person hears from God as well. Then she tells Rose that her assignment is nearly over.

"Honey, you're amazing. I'll hate to see you go, but you have been a blessing to this city, to the people you were sent here for, and to me."

"I don't know how much I've blessed you. I believe you have that backward." Evie laughs.

"Let me tell you how you have blessed me and restored my hope. While Antonio was here, he spent time in the city and noticed the small changes. Although it's not set in stone, he may move back. The company he was here to help offered him a job and they are negotiating. My son, who has not been living for God, asked me to pray and said he was praying about it. What more could a mother want?"

Evie smiles tenderly. "Her two daughters to come home too?"

"It can happen. With God, all things are possible."

Thirty-six

"Rose. Toby's here."

"Coming dear."

Evie gets in the back seat.

Toby turns to face Evie. "How's it going?"

"Fantastic! I'm so excited! Tonight, we present and discuss the building and share the general vision. This group's input will be invaluable." Evie turns somber. "Toby, my work is almost finished and I'll be leaving soon. This is the most difficult part of my job."

"You can leave knowing what you started here will affect generations to come. In good ways. I'll tell you what though if you leave without saying bye, I'll find you."

They are laughing when Rose gets in the front seat. "Oh! I missed the joke."

Evie tells Rose about Toby's threat on the way to the restaurant.

Toby lets them off at the door. Since Rip usually takes them home, Toby tells Evie, "Now don't forget…or else."

She laughs. "Okay, okay."

Eyes wide, Evie looks around the room. Rip comes to her. "Unbelievable, isn't it?"

"Who…what…where did all these people come from?"

"It's a miracle. You would think this is a small town how word gets out."

Oh, Father. I am in awe.

"We had to bring in more chairs. Are you okay?" She nods. "Well, come on. Let's not keep them waiting."

"Hey, guys. Can I get everyone's attention?" As people quietly take their seats, Evie prays for the words she needs to say.

"Thank you all for coming out tonight. I'm sure I speak for Evie too when I say we are shocked but blessed by the turnout."

Blessed? Father, did he just say blessed?

"Evie, are you ready?" Rip's hand brushes hers as he passes the mic and their eyes meet. "You got this."

She faces the crowd and laughs. "What Rip really meant when he asked if I was ready, was 'has your voice returned?'

because I was speechless when I saw all of you here. To know this ministry means this much to all of you touches my heart. I'm sure it touches the heart of God as well. I look forward to your input as we work together to get this up and running as soon as possible. I'll take questions afterward."

For an hour Evie shares from when she first walked past the building to the general idea of how it will work. Before she asks for questions, she explains she is meeting with someone tomorrow about being the director. Whispers sweep across the room.

"So, that's where we are. I'll do my best to answer your questions." Rip comes to the front and stands beside her.

She points to a woman near the front with her hand raised. "When do you think the facility will begin taking women?"

"We're not wasting any time. The previous company left some things, but we will need people to go in and take inventory and decide what is needed from there."

A man in the back stands. "Do you know how many paid staff you will need?"

"I don't. This is absolutely not my area of expertise, but the person I'm talking with tomorrow will know."

Another man stands as the other sits. "About that," Evie prepares herself. *Father, help me choose my words and to be kind if things get heated.* "In most businesses, there is a board or group that votes on things like that. Are you going to set that up before you just hire someone?"

There are pockets of whispers around the room. "I was hoping this would come up. I have consulted with the only One I feel needs to be consulted for this decision. I mean no disrespect to those of you on boards, etc., but things tend to get tied up too long. Gidesha City needs The Strong Tower now. If the director decides to have board members, then so be it."

The man, not satisfied, says, "Who did you consult with?"

"After I got the keys, I walked through the entire building, and parking lot praying. During my time at the building, I presented my choice for the director before God and asked if He agreed and He confirmed it. I'm a follower of Jesus Christ and this ministry will be built on Biblical principles and values. God, my Father, is the only One whose opinion matters to me. Did you have any other questions, sir?" He shakes his head and sulks into his seat.

Evie answers a few more questions before turning the meeting back to Rip. He announces a clean-up and inventory day Saturday and another meeting in a week. He also encourages them to jot down suggestions and share about what they are doing.

Several people approach Evie to share their enthusiasm or thank her for what she is doing for the city. The real estate agent tells Evie that whatever she can do to help, she will.

Rose and Rip talk the entire ride back home. Evie thinks about Rip saying they were blessed.

Father, it's almost time to go, but Rip hasn't found his way yet. I can't leave until he comes back to You.

Sweet child, don't worry.

But Father, I am worried about him. He needs You.

Rip pulls up in front of the house. As Rose gets out, Evie hops into the front seat.

Rip chuckles, “Well, hello there.” He puts the car in park. “The meeting went well, don’t you think?”

“Yes, but that’s not why I’m here.”

“Okay.”

“When you spoke during the meeting, it was peppered with spiritual references. Why?”

“I’ve just been doing some thinking is all.” He gets out to open her door.

“Will you let me know how your meeting goes tomorrow?”

“You’ll be the first to know.”

Thirty-seven

Brenda meets Evie with coffee as she comes in the door of Frankie's. A light radiates from her friend and Evie wonders if she has stopped smiling since the day she made her commitment to Jesus and changed her life forever.

Brenda sets the coffee down and hugs Evie. "Giovanni asked me to find a sitter for the children tomorrow night."

"Yes! I'd love to watch them."

"He's going to invite you and Rip out too, so I asked Nova."

Brenda walks back to the kitchen.

Here we go, Father. Speak for me and prepare her to receive it.

Evie waves when she sees the, hopefully, new director walk in. She stands and hugs her.

"Willow, thank you for coming to town again this weekend."

"No problem. It gives me an excuse to see Alfred, ugh, Dad again and, you, of course."

After they order breakfast, Evie speaks. "Well, it may work out that you can see us all more often. I have a job offer for you."

"You do? What would I be doing?"

"Director of a women's home."

Willow sits back in her chair, running her fingers through her hair. After several minutes of silence, she leans forward. "I don't think I can do it."

Evie already knows that she can and will be successful. "You haven't prayed about it."

"I know but even if I do pray about it, you know I'm still new to this and may misunderstand Him. Besides, I don't know how to run a facility like that. I think someone here might be a better choice."

"I don't. You are the one. God wants you as the director. Take some time to check with Him. He will tell you."

"How do you know?"

"Because He told me."

"That's not fair," Willow pouts.

"But it's a fact."

When breakfast comes Evie blesses the meal. Willow pushes her eggs around her plate and lays her fork down.

"Can you tell me more about it?"

Evie shares the same information she shared at the meeting, adding that Willow has a few financial backers, but she will need to meet with them when she becomes director. She asks questions and Evie answers the best she can.

Willow sighs and looks out the window. "I'll pray about it and let you know."

"I accept that. In the meantime, we'll pray about who else needs to be hired. We'll get you the best support team around."

Brenda leaves the check. Evie pays and then meets Willow by the door.

"Why me, Evie?"

"When we first met, I knew you would take a job here and move back. Then, when your dad was in the hospital, I saw the way you cared for him. After I heard what happened, I saw a story of grace and forgiveness. When you told me about your job, I hoped you might come here once restoration began. God has a different plan for you because I was praying throughout the building and when I asked Him about you, He told me that you, 'Were born for such a time as this.' He knows the plan for you better than anyone."

Willow grins. "Thanks for breakfast. I'll let you know."

***

Evie laughs as she passes Brenda leaving as she goes back into Frankie's that afternoon.

"Craving Frankie's?" Brenda giggles.

"No, I am meeting someone and this is where he picked."

"He? Hmmm."

Evie swats at Brenda's arm. "Nothing like that. He could be my grandpa."

"Mmhm." Brenda darts for the door. "See ya."

Bud is seated and waves to Evie. "Hi, Bud!"

He stands slowly and gives her a big hug. "Hello, sweet Evie."

The hug itself does not bother her but his bony back and thin arms do. His large clothing hides his frail frame. When the server brings their coffee, Evie encourages Bud to order food, her treat. He declines stating he is full from lunch.

"Dearest Evie, it is almost time for you to go and it is almost time for me to go too."

Confused, she puts her cup down. "Did Rose tell you that I'll leave soon? And where are you going?"

"No, Rose did not tell me. We have a mutual Friend, remember? We talk all the time. He told me you have done a wonderful job on your assignment and after wrapping up some loose ends, you will move on."

Father?

Yes, my daughter. He is Mine.

"I am guessing you just checked with Him. He told you I was His child, did He not?"

"He did."

"He is so good like that. Now that you know, you will be able to believe everything I am about to tell you. Are you okay?"

"Yes. I'm just surprised. I'm ready to listen."

"My wife was like you when we met. She traveled anywhere God sent her to help people. She may have been a little younger than you when we fell in love."

"Was she on assignment?"

He grins happily. "She was. I was starting my second year as pastor of a little country church with a small congregation. It was growing, but that was because two families had babies my first year." He winks. "My wife was raised in the city and her assignment landed her in the middle of nowhere helping a woman in my congregation."

"I get that. I feel more comfortable in the country myself."

"Well, as her assignment went on, we realized we were falling in love. We were married. After a year, God moved us to this city where we lived until she died fifteen years ago. Best pastor's wife ever, but I may be a little biased. We have one son, and he is devoted to God too."

"Wow. Beautiful."

"Have you ever been in a relationship?"

"No. I have been asked out, but I decline. I only want to serve God."

"Oh. I see. She never gave it a thought. Maybe they had an agreement." He sips his coffee. "Anyway, enough of that. I am not homeless; I am incredibly wealthy. Not by anything that I did, but by my Father's favor. I have been waiting for someone to come who saw potential in this city and begin something here. God told me to hang on because someone was coming soon. Then I met you at the community kitchen and He told me it was you."

"God placed this city on my heart in an overwhelming way as soon as I got off the bus."

"I love this city. When my wife and I got here all those years ago, it was much smaller. As it grew, our love grew for it and the people. When she died, God called me somewhere else and blessed me abundantly. I just moved back about six months ago."

"But why doesn't anyone recognize you?"

"Well, Evie," he pats her hand and leaves it there. "I came home six months ago to be closer to my son because I am dying. I am only a mere shell of the two-hundred-pound man I was when I left."

"Oh, Bud."

Holding up a finger, he continues. "You know I am ready. I will see my Father face to face and my lovely wife again. My son has all he wants of my money and things. It is time for me to give away the rest. I am giving it all to you. I know you are leaving, but I also know you hear from God, and I trust you will know what to do with it."

"Oh, Bud. I would've never known you were suffering."

He chuckles. "I guess God told you that?"

"Of course, just now. I guess He's trying to comfort me. He also told me not to fight with you about your gift to the city. You bought the building for the women's home and built the park by the library too?"

"Yes. I cannot trust the corrupt officials here. I did what I could, but things are going downhill quickly for me. All the paperwork is ready if you are willing."

"I, gee…"

"He told you not to fight me."

"That's not fair." She laughs through her tears. "I'm ready. I met with Willow, Alfred's daughter, about the director's position. God said she was created for such a time as this, so I believe she will take the position. She is praying about it."

"Very good. I trust you. I know that whatever you do with the money will be prayed about beforehand and you will be obedient to our Father."

"How long? By the doctor's standards?"

"They say six months or so, but I am ready when my Father is ready for me. I will call the lawyer's office tomorrow and let them know you will be there in the next couple of days. I would like to get this wrapped up before I go." Tears fall from Evie's eyes. "Now, now. Are those tears of joy for all the wonderful things the money will do, or tears of sadness for me?"

"I'm grateful for the money and the blessings that will come, but these are sad tears."

"I am an old man. I have lived a wonderful, blessed life. Do not cry for me. I will be in the arms of my Father. Oh, maybe they are tears of jealousy?"

Evie chuckles. "Maybe that's it. I just wish I had gotten to know you better. Heard more of your story. I am being led by my feelings when I should be living by the Spirit. Your prize waits for you. You have fought the good fight, Bud. Well done."

He wipes his eyes. "Yes."

When they finish, Evie picks up the check and Bud says he has it. She shakes her head and tells him it is the least she can do. She hugs him a little longer. Fighting back tears, she watches him pull away in an ordinary car then she turns and walks toward home.

Oh, Father.

I know, sweet Evie. I am here with you. Bud is hurting and tired. He is almost finished. I'm preparing for his homecoming, and it won't be long. Oh, what a beautiful time it will be when I can hold him again. I long for it. Now Evie, remember, his frail little body is but a shell that I placed him in to do great things on earth; and great things he did. I am so proud of Bud. He and his precious wife loved my children on earth and led many to Me. Peace My child. It'll be a celebration like nothing you can understand right now when he comes home. And the good news is, you will see him again.

Peace fills Evie as Father God continues to speak to her heart.

Rip's car is out front. When she opens the door, she finds Rip and Rose in the living room.

Rip stands quickly. "What's going on? You okay?"

She is puzzled. "Yes. Why?"

"You look like you have been crying."

"Oh. I'm okay. What's up?"

Squinting at her, he accepts her answer. "Giovanni invited us to hang out with them tomorrow night."

"You drove out this way to tell me that?" She raises her eyebrow. Rose excuses herself and gets busy in the kitchen.

"Well, no. Honestly, I had a feeling I should check on you."

"Interesting. I was going to share this with you, although probably not tonight. I need to pray about something first."

Daughter, I already know what you were going to ask Me. You will be doing the right thing. He is My child.

Wait, what, Lord? He is? I haven't...

"Evie?" Rip looks worried. "Are you okay?"

She nods. "It's just been a day."

Whispering, she tells about meeting Bud at the community kitchen and their conversations. Bud heard from God and was told to hold on because someone was coming that was trustworthy and had a desire to do something for the city. A look of recognition comes over Rip.

"That is one good man. It seems like when he left the city is when it all began to crumble. But his name's not Bud."

"I guess he uses it to remain anonymous."

She tells him that he bought the building downtown after Evie told him what she would do with it. Rip shakes his head. Then she tells him the rest of the story.

His jaw drops. "What?"

"I don't know how much, or any other details. It's all in the paperwork."

"Wow. That's. Wow."

"You know I will leave someday…soon."

"Maybe."

She cocks her head. “I will. I told you I was going to pray about something before I told you all of this, well I received my answer."

"When did you have time to pray?”

“He already knew and told me it was okay,” she pauses. “I would like you to be over the funds. Restoring Gidesha City is your passion because it’s your home. You will always do what’s best. Besides, God confirmed my thought, so…”

“That’s a huge responsibility.”

“Maybe, but you can do it with our Father’s help.”

They sit in silence. Rose comes from the kitchen. “More coffee?”

Thirty-eight

Evie rolls over and faces the wall. She prays for Bud and Rip. Then she prays for the people of this city to be on board and make necessary changes, beginning with officials. She opens her Bible and reads a few verses, but her mind wanders. It was a lot for Rip to process last night. He declined Rose's offer on a refill and left shortly after. She closes her Bible and joins Rose in the kitchen.

"Oh, honey, are you okay?" Rose hands her a cup of coffee.

"Yes. Just wrapping up some things before I leave. It's always so bittersweet." Her phone rings. "Excuse me, Rose." She goes into the living room.

Willow tells her that she will take the position. She had asked God what she was born for when she read about Esther the day before she and Evie met. When Evie told her that God said she was born for such a time, she wanted to be sure. After prayer and fasting, she knows now that it is her purpose. She gave her employer notice and will be there within the month.

Evie is elated. “One less loose end.”

***

Rip follows Giovanni to Brenda’s and waits in his car while Giovanni runs up to get her and hug the children. When he finally sees them coming, he gets out and locks his car. Giovanni opens the back door as Brenda slides into the back seat. They think Evie might be more comfortable if Brenda sits in the back with her instead of Rip. He agrees.

Evie watches for them. As she goes down the steps she notices Brenda in the back seat but says nothing as Rip opens the door for her.

On the road, Giovanni says, “It’s a little bit of a drive, but I heard of this restaurant on a lake in Samsburg. Anyone opposed?”

“Sounds great!” Brenda looks at Evie. “Well, someone had to answer.” They laugh.

Giovanni turns to Evie. “Any news on the director?”

"Yes! She called earlier, so it hasn't been announced. Willow said yes."

"That's great."

"I think so too. She gave her notice when she went in this morning. She will need to find a place here, but that shouldn't be difficult."

They talk about plans and dreams for the city, which makes the drive seem not so bad.

Giovanni opens Brenda's door. "Oh my. How lovely."

The lake is a little bigger than a large pond. Strings of white lights reflect on the water surrounding the entire lake and down the dock. The full moon hangs low over the trees on the far side of the lake and an owl serenades them as they choose a table outside.

More white string lights set the mood for the patio. A vintage metal lantern with a candle sits in the middle of the table. There are only two other couples on the patio, so it is peaceful.

Brenda smiles. "You must have been looking for something special when you came across this place."

"Only the best for you, babe."

Father, how precious are they. I don't know what the future holds for them, but I wish I did. I would love to see them together. It will be awesome to request a status check and hear they are happily married and have more children. Although she may choke me for praying for that second part.

A gentle breeze hints at the coming change in seasons. While they are eating, the server tells them they will be starting a fire in the pit if they would like to move there after their meal.

Brenda's eyes are on Giovanni. "You really outdid yourself with this place."

He holds up his hands. "I had no idea about that trick."

They decide to move to the fire pit. One of the couples from the patio is enjoying the fire and talking with another man. They sit and join the conversation when they hear the single man is an officer. The conversation jumps from him being an officer to cars to dogs to children to sports. Evie is happy to be a part of a group of strangers enjoying the night.

Before they leave the restaurant, Giovanni suggests a walk on the dock. The reflection of the moon ripples from the fountain in the center of the lake. Hand in hand, Giovanni and Brenda walk to the end of the dock as Evie and Rip follow some steps behind them.

Evie chokes up. “It’s beautiful to see them so much in love after all Brenda has been through.”

“Yes, it truly is.” Rip stops walking.

Giovanni reaches in his pocket, gets down on one knee, slides the ring on her finger, and Brenda tears softly falling, nods yes.

On the drive home, Brenda admires her ring and leans over to kiss Giovanni several times. Back at the apartment, Rip opens Evie’s door as Brenda and Giovanni decide to talk a little longer.

“Can I drop you off on my way?”

Evie smiles. “Please.”

Pulling up in front of the house, he turns to Evie. “I’ll be in charge of the money for you until you come back.”

“There is no me coming back.”

Rip looks down. "Also, I rededicated my life to Christ."

Evie gasps. "You did? When?"

"After we talked at the cabin, I met with Father MacKay a few times. The things that are happening had me thinking." He hesitates. "I took a day off and went to the cabin. I thought about what is happening in this city and realized it could only be God. What happened with Brenda reminded me how unpredictable life is, but the way it all worked out could only be God. You, the way you are. You're beautiful, but the beauty flows from the inside and could only be God." Evie nibbles at her bottom lip, fighting tears. "While I was there, I asked forgiveness and rededicated my life."

Tears pool in her eyes. "That's wonderful."

"I just wanted you to know."

"A great night just got better! Surrender it all. Give Him your pain and anger. He will heal your heart and you'll find true freedom."

"Evie, it was because of your love of Jesus and people. Watching you live what you believe made me see how a relationship with Jesus is supposed to be."

"Thank you for your kind words."

"Thank *you*."

"It's almost time for me to go. There is so much I want to watch happen, but I can't. You have a strong core of people and seemingly endless volunteers. Together you will do great things. Willow will need a strong support team, so let's be praying about that."

"How much time do you have left?"

"I don't know for sure."

"How much time between when you know it's time and when you leave?"

"Not much. I find out my next move and the time to be there. Sometimes it is immediately, sometimes a few days."

He takes her hands. "Please don't leave without saying goodbye."

The desperation in his eyes makes her look away. "I would never do that."

"How about I pick you up for church in the morning? I'd like to go to Rick's church again. It's time to find a home church."

"That sounds good."

"I'll see you in the morning."

She hurries out of the car and into the house grateful Rose is already in bed. Closing her door, she plants her face in her pillow and cries herself to sleep.

Thirty-nine

Rip opens the car door after church. "I don't think I need to look any further. This church seems like the one."

Evie slides in. "From what I've seen the few times I've been here, it's Biblically sound. Pray about it and listen to God. The more you pray and listen and learn about God, the more you will learn His voice. It will get easier."

On the ride back, he asks her if she thinks a Christian should be a police officer. They are still discussing it when they pull up at the house.

"I know if I was staying, you would get tired of hearing this, but pray about it, see what God says about you being an officer. He knows what's best for you."

"I know. I need to remember to pray about everything. Thanks for going with me this morning. I'll talk to you later."

Evie is surprised she got back from the church before Rose. She sits, sipping her coffee, and wonders why she is still here if all her people are serving God.

Sweet daughter, are you sure you are finished here? Is there not anything you wish?

Father, if my assignment is complete, I'm ready to go. Your people are in love with You and that's what's important. There is a fine team in place that can take off running restoring the city together. It will help if You reassure me that Willow will have a great group working with her.

Willow was created for this. She will succeed. The women's home will succeed. Is there nothing else, My precious child?

No Father, not a thing.

Very well. You will leave Wednesday morning. Toby will get you to the bus terminal. Evie, I love you.

Thank You, Father. I love You too.

While Evie waits for Rose to come home she calls Rip and leaves a message that she will leave Wednesday morning. Next, she calls Brenda to tell her that she is leaving. Brenda tries to keep herself together, but Evie can hear it in her voice as she invites Evie to dinner tomorrow night to say goodbye to the children. Then hurries off the phone when one of the girls asks what the furry thing in the kitchen is. Thinking of Brenda's sweet children and how much she will miss them, tears a piece of her heart.

Evie hears Rose come in. She draws a deep breath.

"Hey, honey. What's wrong? Are you okay?"

"I'm okay. I found out I will be leaving Wednesday morning. It's bittersweet. Toby will come to get me and take me to the bus terminal."

"Oh my. I will fix gravy tonight. Your last supper."

Evie laughs. "Rose, I'm leaving, not being executed."

"No, no, not like that." She giggles at her choice of words.

Evie offers to help Rose, but she will not have it.

"Sit down. Relax, honey. I want to do this for you."

Evie sits in the living room reading her Bible when the doorbell rings.

"I'll get it." Rose comes down the hall.

"Rose, I'm in here, I…"

Rose opens the door to Rip standing on the other side. Rose grins sheepishly and goes back to the kitchen.

Rip shuts the door behind him. “Hey. I picked up a shift for someone today, but I got your message. By the time I got around to responding, there was a message from Rose too.”

“No worries. I know you are busy.”

“Thank you for not leaving without saying goodbye.” He half-smiles.

“You know I couldn’t do that. You have become a very dear friend.” She looks away. “Let’s go see what Rose is doing.”

Rose has them set the table and get drinks ready as she places the macaroni and gravy on the table next to a green salad with black olives and peppers. Just before she sits, she pulls garlic bread from the oven.

Rip looks at Rose. “Would you be opposed to making meals like this for me once in a while?”

She laughs. “Not at all. Just let me know when you’re craving gravy.”

Evie reaches for the garlic bread. Rose shares how happy Alfred is with his apartment and his new life. Rip teases Rose about being a little too happy about how happy Alfred is. He asks if there is anything they need to know and raises his eyebrow. Rose giggles.

After dinner, Rose insists on cleaning the kitchen and chases them out. Defeated, Evie suggests they sit on the front steps. Evie tells Rip about the time she and Alfred sat on the steps and watched as a car flew past and heard the impending crush of metal at the bottom of the hill. Rip asks Evie for clarity on something he read in the Bible. She explains it to him but encourages him to dig deeper and ask God because He will tell him.

Rose pokes her head out the door. "Come in and get some sweets and coffee."

As Evie tries to get up, she stumbles. Rip grabs her arm and places his hand on the small of her back steadying her. She can feel his breath as he lets go of her arm but still has his hand on her back. Steadily, she steps back but struggles to take her eyes from his. Rose opens the door, then closes it quickly which distracts Evie who mumbles thank you and goes into the house.

Rose has Evie's favorite, cannoli, and coffee.

Trying to dispel the awkwardness of the moment, Evie says, "Mmm. Cannoli. My favorite." The conversation is light and Evie stays steady on her feet the rest of the evening. Evie sees Rip to the door when he leaves. She stands inside as he walks out and turns to her.

"I'd like to see you again before you leave?"

"Of course."

Forty

The house is quiet when Evie wakes. Rose must be at morning Mass.

Evie is sitting in the living room when Rose comes in.

"Oh, Evie, you're up. Guess what!"

"What is it?"

"Alfred told me this morning that Willow is moving to town. Isn't that great, and then my son will be moving back and it's all so exciting. You were asleep and even though I wanted to wake you and tell you, I decided not to and went to church so I wouldn't be tempted to wake you. I am so excited! Willow and my son are moving here!"

Evie giggles. "Oh, Rose, that is exciting! I am so happy for you."

"Honey, what is it?"

"Nothing Rose. You enjoy your good news, and we can talk later. Will you be going to the community kitchen today?"

"I think I will. Would you like to go?"

"Yes, I'd like that."

On the way to the church, Rose asks Evie why she was so somber.

"It's just tough to leave such a wonderful bunch of people. It's always difficult, but I think I may have gotten too attached this time."

"I imagine leaving is tough. Are you sure you need to go?"

"Yes, I'm sure."

Evie realizes it has been a while since she has been able to help. She sees familiar faces. Father MacKay gives her a thumbs up. Dishing out the green beans like a pro, she is sad when she looks at the end of the line and does not see Alfred or Bud.

After clean-up, Evie tells Father MacKay that her assignment is over, and she will be leaving Wednesday. She encourages him that things are set in place perfectly to get their city back on top. He thanks her for all her help and prays with her before she leaves.

Later, as she walks to Brenda's for dinner and time with the children, she thinks about how nice the block party was until Brenda's ex-husband tried to kidnap her. She thinks about how brave Jimmy was and how smart Rose was to get the girls out of there.

Reviewing all that has happened on this assignment, her thoughts turn to Rip. His kind green eyes, his country boy ruggedness smothered by professionalism, and his love for her. She shakes her head, hoping those thoughts would shake off into the wind. But they are not just in her head, but in her heart too.

She knocks and hears the all-out war on the other side of the door as Brenda tries to push through them and tells them to go sit on the sofa and not to attack her when she comes in.

After all the hugs and chatter, they settle down. Evie goes into the kitchen to help Brenda.

"It smells great in here. What's cooking?"

"Lasagna. Rose isn't the only one who can cook Italian food," she giggles. "Um. I hope you don't mind, but I may have…"

There is a knock and the children run over each other to get to the door. Evie peers out and turns to see Brenda peeking out of the kitchen. "Invited Giovanni and Rip to dinner."

Evie opens the door and while the children pile on Giovanni, Rip smirks. "I couldn't pass it up. I mean the lasagna, you know."

She laughs. "Oh, brother."

Rip walks past her and hands Brenda a bowl of salad.

"Aunt Evie, Mommy says you are going away on Wednesday," Evie bends and opens her arms to Janie. "How long will you be gone?" Her words pierce Evie's heart like nothing ever has. "Why are you crying, Aunt Evie?" Janie asks as she wipes another tear from Evie's cheek.

Evie hugs her close. "I am crying because you stole something from me."

Her mouth opens wide. "I stole something from you? What?"

Evie laughs. "You stole my heart the minute I met you."

Janie giggles and runs away.

Rip walks over to Evie and whispers, "I guess I could say the same thing of you." A funny feeling Evie never felt before grips her stomach. As she is trying to regroup, Brenda says dinner is ready. Evie points toward the kitchen and says she needs to help Brenda with the children's plates, but Giovanni beats her to it.

"Drinks," Evie calls out as she heads toward the kitchen. "I mean I will get their drinks." Evie is about done. If she does not get out of town soon, she too would end up married.

Father, please help me. I had a job to do and now it is done, and I am leaving. I am here for You and only You. My knees are weak, and my heart weaker. Strengthen me in my weakness.

Despite Evie's desire to run out the door and lock herself in Rose's house until Wednesday morning, she stays. Actually, she would not have traded anything in the world for the wonderful night with her closest friends and the children she has grown to love. Giovanni offers her a ride home and because of the late hour, she accepts. After the most painful, heart-breaking goodbyes she ever faced from the children, she walks to the car with the guys.

Giovanni says, "I am not going to lie. That was rough to watch, and I have seen rough things."

Forty-one

Evie wants to go to morning Mass with Rose one more time, but last night left her exhausted. She turns off her alarm and goes back to sleep. When she wakes, she sits with her back against the wall reading her Bible. She prays but hears nothing.

When she is through, she lays back down. Her phone rings and she debates on answering it.

"Hey Rip. Sure, I can do that. No, I'll get a ride there. Thanks. Bye."

As she slides her head under the pillow, part of her tries to convince herself to get up and shower. Always a battle of good and evil, she thinks. Good wins and she gets ready for the day.

"Good morning, Rose."

"Almost good afternoon. Are you okay, honey?"

"Yes. It was so difficult to say goodbye to those babies, and Brenda."

“And anyone else?” Evie stares at her blankly and raises an eyebrow. “Sorry.”

“Rip has called a meeting for anyone who can attend tonight.”

“I know. He called me.”

“I’ll call Toby to come and get us.”

***

When Toby drops them off at the door, Evie tells him she will see him in the morning. As she and Rose walk into the meeting room, everyone cheers. Heat flushes in her cheeks. Balloons and a sign hang from the ceiling thanking her and wishing her well. She sees Rip across the room and mouths “thank you.” Rose steps away to let others speak to her. Finally, Rip gets everyone’s attention and says that he has a few things to share before the celebration continues, but first Evie has something to say.

“Thank you for the outpouring of love. I’ll miss all of you. You are an amazing bunch. I can leave here knowing that you have only just begun, and you will get it done. I have wonderful news. Willow Parks has accepted the position of Director of The Strong Tower women's home and will begin in about two weeks. She has been working at The Veterans Assistance office. She will share her qualifications with anyone who wants to see them. Please, if you know of anyone who would be an asset to the women's home, tell them to polish up their resume. Thank you again for your love. Go, team!"

Rip adds a few things and thanks everyone for coming out on short notice. Several more people speak to Evie as the room empties.

On the drive home, Evie thanks Rip for calling the meeting and allowing her to introduce Willow as the new director. Rose invites Rip to come in. Once again, Rose finds something important to do in the other room, leaving Evie and Rip alone in the living room. He motions his head toward the door and they step outside.

"I just can't seem to say goodbye to you." Rip reaches for her hands as his kind, green eyes struggle to hold back tears.

"I know. I already know, but I still have to try. Please don't leave."

Barely able to breathe, she thinks she hears her heart crack and fall to pieces. Knowing his love for her, a fight within ensues.

Father, why? How did this happen! How can I tell him no? Help me.

"Rip, I…, I…" She searches for the right words, so she does not hurt him, but she sees it in his eyes. He understands the slow, gentle shake of her head.

He draws her into his arms. "It's okay. I understand. No words necessary." He feels her body jerk as her warm tears soak his shirt.

Rip lifts her chin. "Truly, I understand." He kisses her forehead. "I love you and always will. I have loved only two women in my life and there won't be another. I pray that one day you will come back to me and when you do, you will find me waiting."

As she watches him, pain sears her insides with each step he takes down the steps and out of her life. He waves as he pulls away.

Rose is in the living room when she hears Evie sobbing. As Rip drives away, she opens the door, brings Evie in, and holds her. Finally, Evie steps back and Rose reaches for tissues before sitting down and patting the spot next to her.

"I have been sad to leave other assignments, but none of them felt anything like this. This is a deeper, more painful heart-wrenching kind of sad. I don't know how it happened, but somewhere along the way, I fell in love with him. I'm a professional. That doesn't happen."

"Well honey, sometimes love doesn't give us an option. It sneaks in the side door and just stands there growing. Are you absolutely sure you're not supposed to stay here?"

"I'm sure. I work for my Father. It's where I am supposed to be." The chiming grandfather clock breaks the silence.

"I will miss you, Evie."

"I will miss you too."

“Save time in the morning for a nice warm breakfast so you won’t be hungry while you are traveling.”

“Thank you. That will be nice.”

Forty-two

Aromatic smells slide under her door from the kitchen as Evie packs. She tosses the last of her things in her bag as Rose taps on her door.

"Breakfast is ready."

"I'll be right out."

One more look in the closet, under the bed, and in the drawers, then she leaves her room.

Evie opens the door and sees Brenda, Giovanni, and the children, Alfred, and Bud. All her people, except Rip.

Giovanni gives her a sympathetic smile and hugs her. "He took off for the mountains for a few days. He'll be okay."

Not wanting to leave her friends on a sad note, she sets in her heart to put on a smile and enjoy the little time they have left together. Janie tugs on Evie's shirt and she picks her up.

"Who's ready for some breakfast?" Evie tickles Janie's belly.

Jimmy sits by Alfred. Brenda and Giovanni are happy. Brenda's two middle girls are watching as Rose cuts into the breakfast casserole and Janie, who is learning about knock-knock jokes cannot seem to get past the knock-knock part as she tells them to Bud. Evie's heart is full, well, almost full, but she knows in time she will be fine. Just like everyone around the table.

After breakfast, there is little time for anything else. Evie's least favorite part is goodbyes. Janie takes it the hardest and Evie holds her close.

Gracious Father, bless this child. I already know she is one of Yours and You have great things planned for her. Keep her heart pure. Lead her in the way she should go and let her never lose her way. I am going to miss this dear one. Comfort her and me during this time.

Setting Janie down, Giovanni hugs Evie and gives her an envelope with recognizable writing.

"We will miss you. Don't be a stranger, okay?" Evie already explained to Brenda that more than likely they will not get to see each other again. She seldom comes back to the same area for her job.

"Okay."

The doorbell rings, Toby is waiting at the door. She hugs Rose and thanks her again. She looks around one more time as she takes a deep breath and smiles.

"Hello, Toby. I'm all set." Toby takes Evie's suitcases and loads them in the van. Waving back at everyone, they drive off to the bus terminal.

Evie looks down at the letter on her lap and decides to wait until she is on the bus to read it. Toby pulls into a parking spot out front and opens the door for her.

Evie hugs him. "Thank you so much for everything. I will miss you."

"You're a fine lady, Ms. Evie, but you need to know there is no shame in coming back. Take care of yourself."

She is left standing alone, watching Toby leave.

On the bus, she tries to open the note three times but is afraid she's not far enough away from Gidesha City. Finally, she opens the envelope and pulls out the paper.

Dearest Evie,

I will be waiting.

All my love, forever,

Rip

Discussion Questions

1. As you read Gidesha City, did you wish Brenda would tell Evie her story earlier? The things said to Brenda by her evil father and then her evil husband were never nice. If they were both saying those things, they must be true, and so she believed them. In *John 8:44*, Jesus tells the religious leaders that they do the evil things that their father, the devil does. He goes on to tell them that the devil is a liar and the father of lies.

   As Christ-followers, we learn to disregard what others say about us and believe we are who God says we are. Even after they became close friends, she did not tell Evie. Why do you think she was hesitant to share her story?

2. *Philippians 1:6* tells us, "And I am sure that God, who began the good work within you, will continue His work until it is finally finished on that day when Christ Jesus comes back again." Alfred's burdens ruined his life. He was withdrawn, unfriendly, and could not keep a job which left him homeless. What burdens did he carry before he

came to Christ? Brenda's past held her in chains. What things held her there until she gave the care of her heart to Christ? How quickly did we see changes in them? They were not finished when they accepted Christ. As they surrendered control of their lives to Him, they allowed Him to work by healing, teaching, and guiding them. Think of burdens weighing you down. How much more could you do with the weight of those burdens lifted?

3. Initially, Evie thought by rebuilding Gidesha City, the Veteran's Assistance Office that Willow works for might consider opening a branch there. God's plan was so much better. Was there a plan that did not work out as you thought it should? *Romans 8:28* tells us "…that God causes everything to work together for the good of those who love God and are called according to His purpose for them." Can you look back at your plans and share any that turned out way better than you could imagine?

4. During the story, Evie and Rip develop feelings for each other. Bud marries his wife who was also called by God to do assignments. Do you think Evie gave his story any thought as she was preparing to leave? It was painful for Evie, but she left Rip and Gidesha City behind. In *Jeremiah 1:5*, God gave Jeremiah a message that He knew him before he was born and set him apart as appointed spokesman. Although Evie's flesh was weak, she remained faithful to her commitment. Describe a situation where your flesh wanted something so bad, but you chose to follow Holy Spirit's leading instead. Was it worth it in the end?

5. It may seem a little far-fetched for a group of citizens to take action to restore and rebuild their city, but what if that was all it took? In *Isaiah 43:19* God tells us that He is about to do a brand new thing. He will make pathways in the wilderness for His people to come home. What if He is looking for a few determined people to come together for a greater good? It can and has been done. Think revival.

What other things can you think of that would be beneficial if we were willing and united?

Salvation is for Everyone

The Bible tells us God does not want anyone to die, but to live forever with Him. It also tells us He is not just taking His time in fulfilling the promise of His return but is patiently giving everyone time to turn from sin and accept Him. Whoever calls on the Name of Jesus will be saved!

John 3:16, 2 Peter 3:9, Romans 10:13

Even though this is the most important decision you will ever make, it is not complicated. We are born into sin and trapped in this condition. With no way out, we need a Savior. If you believe in your heart and confess with your mouth that Jesus Christ is Lord, and He is the only Son of God, who was born, died, and rose again for the forgiveness of our sins and put your full trust in Him, you will be made right with God and be freed from sin. Saved. I promise you will not be disappointed.

Romans 5:12, Romans 10:9-11, Romans 3:22

If you are ready, you can pray the following:

Jesus, I confess that I am a sinner and need You to save me. I am sorry for my sins and I do not want to live in this trapped condition any longer. Forgive me. I believe You are the only way to God, and eternal life and I need You. Thank You for dying on the cross for me. I know God raised You from the dead after three days and for that I am grateful. Thank You for saving my soul and promising to always be with me. Amen

If you prayed the prayer and believe-congratulations! Heaven is celebrating you today! Be sure to share the news with someone! You are now a new person living a new life in Christ; the old you no longer exists and all the things you have done in the past have been permanently erased. You are now a child of God. I encourage you to fully surrender every area of your life to God and anchor yourself in Him by talking to Him every day about everything and reading the Bible. I suggest you begin with the **Gospel of John** in the New Testament. It gives you such a clear picture of who Jesus is. And when you see Jesus, you also see the Father. I also encourage you to connect with others who follow Jesus in a Bible-believing church. They can help you learn more about Jesus and support you as you follow Him.

Luke 15:7, Luke 15:10, 2 Corinthians 5:17, 1 Corinthians 6:19-20, Galatians 2:20, Isaiah 33:6, Psalm 62:5-6

Now that you have believed in Jesus and received His gift of salvation, you are completely free, but this is only the beginning! He has so many good things planned for you. Jesus tells us He came to give us a full life and He wants us to discover all of that now! Even though we will continue to experience trials and sorrow here on Earth, Jesus has promised to stay with us and help us through the rough places by giving us peace, joy and hope, and anything else we may need. He also promised we would overcome the difficulties and live victoriously through Him

John 10:10, John 16:33, Deuteronomy 31:6-8, 1 Thessalonians 5:11, Ecclesiastes 4:9-12

About The Author

Anne lives in Tennessee with her husband, Wesley, their four dogs, and lots of books. When time allows, they enjoy hiking and wandering around Tennessee, looking for adventures.

Anne jokes she never could figure out what she wanted to be when she grew up until in 2018, when she was introduced to NaNoWriMo and began writing a novel. Her sincerest desire is to share her one true love, Jesus, with others.

Made in the USA
Columbia, SC
14 September 2022